(865) 674-9957
WWW.WHITEPINEBOOKS.COM

★

At the doorway of the little sewing room, the odor of hot metal was very strong. The most noticeable thing in the jumbled room was the steam iron smoldering facedown on the ironing board, wisps of smoke curling upward from a lavender little nothing. I started across the room, then stopped dead.

Shimmering before me was the thin, slight body of my friend Grace, crumpled on the floor beside the desk she used as a sewing table. A pair of scissors with incongruously bright and cheerful orange handles stuck out of her chest. I knew she was dead. A small pool of blood oozed on the floor from a little dark stain on her shirt.

★

"...one of the year's better debut novels..."
—*The Criminal Record*

"Recommended."
—*The Reader's Review,* San Francisco

"A must read—delightfully entertaining."
—*Rendezvous*

"This delightful mystery...is sure to captivate readers."
—*Affaire de Coeur*

BOOK EXCHANGE CENTER
822 MERCER STREET
PRINCETON, WV 24740
(304) 487-6036

Forthcoming from Worldwide Mystery by
CHRISTINE T. JORGENSEN

YOU BET YOUR LIFE
CURL UP AND DIE

A LOVE TO DIE FOR

CHRISTINE T. JORGENSEN

WORLDWIDE.

TORONTO • NEW YORK • LONDON
AMSTERDAM • PARIS • SYDNEY • HAMBURG
STOCKHOLM • ATHENS • TOKYO • MILAN
MADRID • WARSAW • BUDAPEST • AUCKLAND

If you purchased this book without a cover you should be aware
that this book is stolen property. It was reported as "unsold and
destroyed" to the publisher, and neither the author nor the
publisher has received any payment for this "stripped book."

A LOVE TO DIE FOR

A Worldwide Mystery/March 1997

This edition is reprinted by arrangement with Walker and
Company.

ISBN 0-373-26231-0

Copyright © 1994 by Christine T. Jorgensen.
All rights reserved. No part of this book may be reproduced
or transmitted in any form or by any means, electronic or
mechanical, including photocopying, recording or by any
information storage and retrieval system, without permission
in writing from the publisher. For information, contact:
Walker and Company, 435 Hudson Street,
New York, NY 10014 U.S.A.

All characters in this book are fictitious, and any resemblance to
actual persons, living or dead, is purely coincidental.

® and TM are trademarks of Harlequin Enterprises Limited.
Trademarks indicated with ® are registered in the United States
Patent and Trademark Office, the Canadian Trade Marks Office
and in other countries.

Printed in U.S.A.

A LOVE TO DIE FOR

ONE

I GOT TIRED of being just plain Jane Smith. I also got tired of a relationship that was going nowhere and a job as an accountant, even though it paid a great salary. So I got out of all of them, in that order, and then I got bored. No love, no life, and no money makes things pretty dull.

There's a part of me that craves excitement. The sound, reasonable part says, just live life, honey, don't challenge it. But the other part cries out now and again. That part was crying out for expression the day I got up, went to the closet, and selected my purple pants, a pink-and-orange top, and a scarf for my hair...to give the impression I have wild, untamable tresses. I'm not sure it made any difference, but it was fun.

I'd noticed that the *Denver Daily Orion,* actually now a weekly, didn't have what I think of as a "stars and garters" column...astrology and advice for the lovelorn.

Loosing the wild child, as my friend Meredith calls it, I swung into the office and announced that I was there to speak with the managing editor. I hoped that I used the right title.

The receptionist reminded me of a gum-chewing Zelda. She gave me a world-weary once-over and smirked, but she called through to the bowels of the newspaper building and spoke into the telephone the very words I wanted to hear.

"Mr. Gerster, there's someone here to see you." She paused. "Course she has an appointment." She lied for reasons that were a mystery to me at the time. She rolled her eyes as she listened and chewed, popping her gum to some internal rhythm. "Beats me," she sighed, "But she's colorful." Zelda clattered the telephone receiver onto the switchhook and smirked again. "Slide on back, honey," she said, shoveling her gum to her cheek. "Down the tunnel." She pointed with a carmine thumbnail to a dim hallway. "The first and only door on the left. You'll know it."

I thanked her. Then I took a deep, resolute breath and strode, not walked, down a short dark hallway and through the first entrance on the left. The man at the desk looked up uncertainly. Then, shoving his chair back with his legs, he stood and raised his hands up to chest level, as though I had an Uzi pointed at his innards.

I know I expected to find some kind of glamorous tough guy, a handsome, virile combination of Clark Gable and Mike Hammer, cigarettes, and wry glamour that covered a passionate, woman-loving core.

Mr. Gerster was at least as old as the Rockies, had a lined, pinched face, and wore a bow tie and suspenders...of the unfashionable utilitarian kind...because he had no shape to hang his pants on. I've never found a bow-tied man to be passionate. Not that he couldn't be, I just haven't found one.

"Miss, er...ah..."

The name Smith certainly lacked the right ring. It didn't carry in clarion tones, and it didn't instantly impress.

"Stella, the Stargazer," I said, holding my chin as high as my long, rather narrow, neck would allow. My mother always referred to it as a swan's neck. She loved me, loves me still.

"Stella..." he repeated. Then he pointed to a wooden hard-back chair. "Please, ah...be seated."

I explained my plan. He listened, stonily and without blinking. When I finished, he blinked. Several times. The

in Denver is very dry. I decided he wanted to make up
r the time he hadn't blinked while he listened.

Fluffy, my pet chameleon, has only one expression...his
casional blink...so I'm quite sensitive to the expressive-
ss of blinking. Mr. Gerster was almost as expressive as
uffy.

"Let me make sure I understand," he said slowly.
ou're willing to write an advice-to-the-lovelorn column
sed loosely on astrology and your particular, ah...
nsitivity, for my paper, for the *usual fee*." He stopped
nking and was now rubbing his hands together, as though
had arthritis and was trying to rub the pain away.

"Correct. The usual fee."

"Do you have experience?"

"Of course," I lied.

"And what do you think the usual fee is?"

I had worked out what I needed to keep starvation away
om my front door. I added the rent. I added insurance. I
allowed, smiled confidently, and said, "Twenty-three
ousand a year."

His face cracked. I think he laughed.

3UT I GOT THE JOB, Meredith."

I was home now, celebrating with my best friend, Mer-
ith, and Fluffy, who was harnessed to my pink-and-
ange top. This presents a challenge for him. He gets so
sy turning colors that he forgets to blink. I recounted my
ld success for Meredith.

"...not at that salary. At a rate per column inch. And at
y rate I'm going to have to write one hell of a lot of
ches. Or I'll be losing inches...from starvation. So, all I
ve to do is get enough people writing in to convince

Gerster that it's a valuable column. Or at least a popul
one.''

"What if he doesn't like it?''

"He *has* to.'' The sudden tension in my chest told n
just how much I wanted it to be a success.

Meredith was happy for me. Underneath, of course, s
thought I was a complete idiot, but Meredith's my be
friend, so she would wait another half hour before s
pointed out that I'd soon be starving and out of rent mone

"Do you think you have that much to say?'' asked Me
edith.

"Sure. Of course. Why not?''

"You don't talk all that much.''

"I can write. And I've been doing horoscopes f
years.''

Meredith smiled and raised her glass of champagne. W
both hate it but *Pierre's* at $1.99 is the cheapest festiv
looking alcoholic drink at the corner drugstore. "I alwa
said you'd do something great,'' said Meredith. "You ha'
an aura about you that shrieks excitement.''

One of the things I love about Meredith is her ability
ascribe to me wonderful things that aren't there. There
nothing exciting about me, except my underwear, and n
body gets to see that since I broke up with Rick the Ick

"Cheers,'' I said and took a tiny sip. It was still vinegar

"Seriously, Jane—''

"Please, I'm Stella now.''

"Seriously, are you going to go by Stella all the time?

"Of course.''

"Even changing your name legally?''

"I haven't decided that yet.''

"Oh,'' she said, pondering. She sipped the champagn
"I've always been the flighty one of the two of us. It's re
strange having you be so bizarre.'' She got up from th

ouch where she'd been sitting and strolled to the front
window. The late-spring sunshine glinted in through the
window and highlighted Meredith's hair. She has wild, passionate tresses. The difference between Meredith's hair and
mine is that hers cascades to her shoulders, whereas mine
falls, straight and brown.

I live on the second floor of an older three-story apartment building in Denver's Capitol Hill. My front window
overlooks a drowsy street lined with mature silver maples
whose light chartreuse leaves shimmer in the spring breeze.
On both sides of the street cars park bumper-to-bumper
beneath the trees in front of similar three- and four-story
apartment buildings.

"I know what you're doing," Meredith said, turning
slowly toward me, her brown eyes filled with a faraway
expression. "You're planning to use your *extra sense,*
aren't you?"

"Meredith, I don't have any extra sense. I just said that
to Gerster to get a job."

"That's not true. You do. You have those spells. What'll
you do if you have those spells about the people who write
in?"

THE FIRST WEEK on my new job I mainly just got used to
the fact that I was lower on the totem pole than Zelda, the
receptionist. Actually, she ran the paper. Everybody was
lower on the totem pole than Zelda.

I decided after two days that Zelda, whose real name I
couldn't remember, had more power than anyone else there,
since she was the gate, or the barrier, to all comers and
nearly all calls. This was not the *Denver Post* or the *Rocky
Mountain News.* The *Daily Orion* was a weekly rag, pub-
lished for pennies by people who had more energy than
money. With the cheapest subscription rate in the region

short of being free, it seemed to be supported mainly by local advertisements and subscriptions from people who wanted cheerful nonnews...news they could stand to read. I loved it.

My desk was a scarred wooden antique so chewed up on the edges that I immediately vowed never to risk my meager store of stockings anywhere near it. I had a telephone nearly all to myself; I shared it with only one other person, Jason Paul.

Jason introduced himself to me as a "cub reporter." He'd graduated from some ivy-covered tower in the Midwest, followed Horace Greeley's not particularly profound advice, and gone West. That meant he came to Denver. Like a lot of people, he came without a job and ended up being happy to have this one while he decided what to do with his life. I liked him.

He reminded me of the golden retriever named Caesar we had when I was a child, a millennium ago. Caesar used to sneak out the back door and down the block to steal things from the minister of the Christian Church, then he'd drag them home and hide them under our porch. He particularly liked the minister's slippers and the minister's wife's rag rug. He ate that. He saved the slippers.

Caesar could melt your heart when he wagged his tail, grinned, and drooled on your knee. I hadn't seen Jason do any of those things, yet. But he still reminded me of Caesar. Maybe it was his eyes.

There were others in the office, but the one that really stood out was Guy. Guy Madison was tall, dark and almost good-looking...if you like them like that. Most of the time I do, but something about Guy made me notice him without really liking him. I sensed a kind of dangerousness about him, an edge that made my warning bells jingle.

On the second Friday I got the very first letter from the

blic. This was not to be confused with the first eighteen
at I got in the mail but wrote myself just to get things
ing, or the three that I got from Meredith, who had prom-
ed to write some. To celebrate, before I even opened it I
lled Meredith and invited her to come to *my office*, as I
lled my desk in the corner.

Meredith was impressed. She giggled with Jason and
ed Guy and agreed with me that there was definitely an
ge to him. For a moment I thought she was going to
mp over the desk and offer to personally polish it, but
e chance to open the very first letter from my public won
t. She contained herself.

I picked up the envelope, intending to hand it to Mere-
th with a grand flourish, and then it happened. I had one
those spells I have every once in a while.

I've had them since I was a child. I feel a cold chill,
en I get a slightly metallic taste in my mouth, then I see
ings. Well, I don't really see them, a picture just forms
fore **me**. Most of the time it's just a flash and then it's
ne. But once in a while it's longer. Today it was longer.

I felt the cold chill, tasted metal. But then the metallic
ste changed. I smelled blood. I tasted blood. The details
the newsroom faded as darkness crowded in from the
ges of my field of vision.

A body slowly materialized before me. I *knew* it was a
oman, but I couldn't see her face, and the details of her
othing were dim. She was lying down on something. I
ard a sound like water running over stones. A dark shape
as plunged into her, a third of the way down and just left
center.

I didn't know who it was, but just as I *knew* that she was
woman, I *knew* she was very dead.

I'VE NEVER TRIED to force other details from these vision
But this was different. This was murder.

I strained to see more, to see the details of the surroun
ings. But the scene instantly began to dissolve. The outlin
of the body, so awkward and dead, faded. The sound
water dimmed with a dying wail like a railroad train. T
smell and taste of blood left, and only the slight metal
taste remained, as though I had chewed a gum wrapper
was very cold.

Then I heard Meredith's voice, felt her warm hand
my arm.

"Hey, earth to Stella," she called, jokingly. "Come
or come back, whichever." She's the only one of n
friends who knows about my spells.

Jason's voice thundered in my ears, "Maybe she's g
epilepsy, you know, *petit mal* seizures or something."
could feel his arm around me. He was trying to make n
sit down. I shook him off.

"Nonsense," I said. Except for the chill and the fai
taste of metal left in my mouth, I was fine now. It w
over. Well, almost. I was disturbed by what I'd seen, bu
didn't want to think about it. I wanted to celebrate. I force
a laugh. "Come on, Meredith. Open the letter and read.

Meredith, looking at me solemnly, as though she sens
how upset I was, took the letter and picked up a pair
scissors from Jason's desk to slit the envelope.

"No," I said and snatched the scissors. Then, trying
cover up the awkwardness, I grinned and offered her a su
stitute. "I promised Mom I'd use the letter opener. A pre
ent from her. She's pleased to think I'll be able to affo
to feed myself again."

Meredith smiled uncertainly but carried on. I knew sl
recognized the letter opener. I'd had it for years.

It wasn't a very long letter. Over Meredith's shoulde

ould see the handwriting sloped to the right, and the *h*'s, 's and *t*'s were large loops. Instead of dots over the *i*'s, here were tiny circles. I'd read somewhere that little circles nstead of dots were indicative of feelings of inferiority. Meredith read aloud in her steady, husky voice.

Dear Stella the Stargazer,
I hope you won't find this letter too silly. I just had to write to you. I get so lonely and there isn't anyone I can talk to. I have a sister, but we're not close. In fact, she's part of my problem. She's a Gemini, she's pretty, she's got a good job, everything. She even took *my* boyfriend. My one boyfriend.

Well, what I want to say is that I get so lonely sometimes I don't know what to do and I just feel like I should give it all up. But that wouldn't be right, would it?

I hope I'm not boring you with this. Actually, I'm not getting any younger and I most of all would like a great love. A really great love. Like Heathcliff, or Romeo, or Lochinvar. A love to die for.

Does that sound too silly?

Your friend, *Looking for Lochinvar*

P.S. I'm a Pisces

Jason snorted at this point.

"A love to die for," Meredith murmured, holding the etter to her breast. Her romantic eyes sparkled with a tiny ilm of tears. "Oh, God, yes! *I* want a love to die for," she aid softly.

Jason looked acutely embarrassed.

"Meredith, you wrote that, didn't you?"

She looked at me, startled out of her reverie. "I didn't! wish I had. Lochinvar, what an image. Big, thrusting white horse pounding on the beach, the crashing sound of the surf, taut muscles, expanse of chest..."

"The horse, or Lochinvar?" I asked. Jason's jaw dropped.

"You can laugh, but I think it's beautiful," Meredith said. She continued to murmur the phrase "a love to die for" until I began to see her all in white, lying on a bed or a bier, a single red rose in her hand, looking for all the world like an opera heroine in the "die" aria.

"Meredith, cut it out. This job's going to demand a whole lot more of me than I thought." As they used to say, "Had I but known."

TWO

MY FAVORITE lingerie boutique, Grace and Lilly's Little Nothings lingerie shop, is a scant mile from my apartment and is one of several shops in a shoppette row along Colorado Boulevard. There are several of these rows all fronted with brick and display windows draped with goods to catch the eye and lure the shopper. Little Nothings was very good at luring me.

After the thrill of the Looking for Lochinvar letter, we had decided to celebrate by stopping by Little Nothings before going for supper. Friday nights aren't date specials for me right now, and Meredith was free, too.

We were standing in the middle of the shop. Meredith was fingering a filmy nightie, with strategic lace and little else. I was fondling a flamingo-pink teddy whose price tag was definitely larger than the garment. She held up the nightie, pretending to consider it. "Seriously, how are you going to survive? You won't earn enough at this paper to afford groceries, much less lingerie or rent."

For me, there are two *really* private things in life, sex and money. It's a principle with me. I don't tell anyone how much I have in my bank account or who I have in my bed. "Savings," I said through stiff lips, my signal that she was prying.

"Your mother said you left a job where you earned more money than you could spend."

"My mother has an exaggeration problem. I earned more than I decided to spend." Frankly, I didn't have a clue how I'd support myself on my writing income. I had savings that would last six months, maybe longer, then I'd have to do some serious job hunting. Meredith was looking hurt. I relented.

"I have enough for about six months. Until then, I'm going to have fun. I'm going to do a job that I love. I'm not going to burrow through columns of figures, or set up books for people, or talk debit, credit, or anything of the sort. I'm going to live a little." I held up a silky pink teddy against my body.

"You're going to have to give up your passion then," said my best friend, still miffed that I hadn't confided my bank account. "You're not going to be able to buy all that gorgeous stuff on what you're making."

"I know. But then I don't have anyone to see it, either, so there." I adore lingerie. Nothing makes me feel so wonderful and special as wearing a bit of satin, a little lace, a blaze of color beneath otherwise quiet and unassuming clothes.

"Of course, now that you're Stella," Meredith said, her annoyance fading, "you can wear more exciting clothes. Maybe you won't be so enthralled with undies." She gazed around the shop. "We'd better warn Grace and Lilly that they're in for a major economic slump." Meredith put the nightie back on the rack and drifted over to the lace bras.

Grace and Lilly are the two women who own the shop. We could just barely hear the low hum of their voices floating out from the back room of the shop. I'm not sure when they opened up for business, but Meredith and I have been supporting their boutique in a significant way for the last ten years, and we've been on a first-name basis with them for the last five. For two years I'd seen an aura of dark tension between the two women. Meredith said I was imagining it.

The voices rose suddenly.

"You had no right to decide that by yourself!" I recognized Grace's voice laden with the tones of hurt feelings. Meredith and I looked at each other, uncomfortable with overhearing their argument. I raised my eyebrows, signaling, "Shall we go?"

Lilly's voice, low and angry, shot forth. "Dammit, Grace, someone has to do it."

I cleared my throat loudly, and Meredith stepped to the door, opened it, and shut it with a slam.

"Hello," I called. Grace appeared, her cheeks flushed, an unconvincing smile smeared across her face. Grace is probably thirty-five to forty years old, but I always think of her as older. She's one of those gentle women who seem to peek out at life through vague, uncertain eyes. Frequently she wears glasses, I think just to hide behind. Once when she was bending over to get something I had dropped, her glasses fell off. When I picked them up, I noticed that I couldn't see any magnification in the lenses.

On her ring finger Grace wears a sterling silver signet ring. Several weeks ago, when I asked why no initial was inscribed on it, Grace just smiled and said she didn't know. She explained that her sister, Adoree, had given it to her for Christmas. She guessed Adoree had forgotten to have it done. I thought it was mean, but I didn't tell Grace, and I hoped Adoree hadn't done it on purpose. I'd never met her, but I had two images of her in my mind, both of which I think I just made up. One was of a huge, overbearing woman wagging her finger in Grace's face, the other was of a gentle, doelike creature much like Grace, who was absentminded and flaky. I wondered if I'd ever meet her and which image would be true.

Meredith was holding up a beautiful little midnight blue brassiere with tiny handsewn tucks in it. "Did you make this, Grace?" she asked with a smile. Meredith stuck all the warmth she could into her voice. I knew she was trying to bolster Grace's sagging spirits. Grace nodded.

"I can always tell your work," Meredith said. "Your things are so imaginative and exciting." Grace's face relaxed into genuine pleasure.

"Grace, Meredith's absolutely right. Your things are the best in the shop." We were both telling the truth, even if we were trying to make her feel better. Grace was our long-time favorite. And she was a real artist at making lingerie.

Lilly, on the other hand, was a businesswoman. Without her, Grace would never make it, no doubt about that. But Lilly could get on your nerves. She was brusque and impatient at times. And then, of course, in spite of their pretense at closeness, I knew the two of them were barely speaking to each other.

Grace, still smiling, shyly asked how my column was going. I'd forgotten that last weekend when we'd been in, Meredith had regaled her with the story of my new job. Grace had oohed and ahhhed, and Lilly, ever practical, had asked how I'd manage. She knew exactly how much I spent in her shop.

"Well, Grace, it's unbelievable. Letters are coming in. It's amazing the things people think of, the problems they have. I think it's going to be great." I heard my words tumble out in a torrent of discomfort, and I realized that I suddenly felt as though I'd been asked about something very private.

"I don't mean to pry," she said as if she sensed my uneasiness. "I just find it so fascinating."

"She got one letter—" I jabbed Meredith in the side. "She got an aura from it."

"Ooooh!" Grace cooed. "What was it?"

I was now extremely uncomfortable. I didn't want to talk about my auras and spells at all, and I definitely didn't want to talk about the letters casually. "Meredith gets carried away," I said glowering at Meredith, who was concentrating on a lurid display.

Meredith squeaked. "Grace, what are these? Are they really chocolate?" Grace blushed. "Yes," she murmured.

"Oh, oh! Oh!" Meredith moaned. "As soon as I find my love to die for, I'm buying a pair of these!"

I TOOK THE LETTER, or rather a copy of it, home with me so that I could write a good response. I didn't want to blow off the very first genuine letter I got. Even though I don't have that fatal romantic streak that Meredith has, I thought the letter was pretty touching. I had just ended a miserable relationship. But that didn't alter one bit the fact that in my secret heart I, too, wanted a love to die for. I think everyone does.

After I'd reread it a couple more times, I had a clearer sense of the person who wrote it. I pictured a woman in her late twenties to mid-thirties who dithered about decisions so long that someone else ended up making them for her. I also sensed she was a potentially stormy person, someone who held grudges inside, keeping mental records over the years until there was the real possibility of an explosion. This was the Pisces in her. Subservient, keeping records, never forgetting a wrong done to her, yet unable to openly confront the wrongdoer.

The challenge was to write something incredibly tactful and profound that would help me stretch her limits and break out of her self-imposed mold.

I labored over my response. I've been casting horoscopes for years now, but I was having trouble with this one. When I couldn't come up with something profound, I finally just wrote my naked thoughts. After all, I rationalized, how much impact can a stargazer have?

Dear Looking for Lochinvar,

To find the man of your dreams you must harness your energy and focus. Reach out of your Pisces self. Beware of appearing wimpy. Yours is a sign of true love, and inner peace. Pisces women are kind but have a tendency to be gullible and easily led because you trust others so easily.

You may need to simply throw yourself into a course of action and stick to it. Don't hesitate. This is a propitious time for love for you. But...it is your responsibility to seek it out. Pisces is a mutable water sign. Look for another water sign for a match. A Cancer would be a fine sign for you.

Stella the Stargazer

I decided that my naked thoughts were the best. I wished now that I'd called myself Stella of the Stars. It had a better ring to the signature. Maybe in my next life. I put the letter on the hall table.

By eleven o'clock that night I was tired, and Fluffy had become catatonic. He's about as long as my hand, but most of his length is tail and he's only about as big around as a cigar. Actually, if you put him next to one, he'll turn that color and look like a cigar with legs. I got him last summer from a traveling circus that I went to with Rick while we were still involved and before I'd begun to refer to him as the Ick. Fluffy was the only remnant of that romance left, except for a big, protective streak of distrust in men.

Tonight, Fluffy looked a bit pale, probably from too much color-adaptation work. He didn't even blink when I transferred him to the branch in his cage. I always take his little harness off when I put him back in his cage so that he won't accidentally become hung up by it. Meredith says that it's my fantasy that he sometimes moves.

After Fluffy was settled and I'd refreshed his water and promised him a fresh insect tomorrow, I set coffee for the morning. Then I relocked the front door, adjusted the window so that I could get just a tiny draft of fresh air, and checked to see that the wooden peg was jammed in place so that a burglar couldn't raise the window as I slept.

Then I reset the alarm. Even though the next day was Saturday, my shopping date with Meredith wasn't until eleven, and I always awake at 6:00 a.m. automatically without needing an alarm.

Finally, I realized that I was stalling. I didn't want to close my eyes for fear that horrific scene would appear again.

Never have I envisioned violence before, not even its aftermath. This was new. And terribly unnerving.

I wandered over to my bedroom window, which is in a bay, and peered out. Below in the tiny patch of yard between the buildings, a cat was stalking something beneath the lilac bush. A trash can lid clanged to the ground. Probably another cat looking for a midnight snack. Later tonight they'd howl in a primal chorus, staking out their respective territories and their lust mates.

And that reminded me of Rick again. Because we weren't. Lust mates, that is. Or even soul mates, anymore. If ever. My thoughts were disjointed. It was still painful to think about it.

After a first year of being passionately in lust and two more years of trying to find any other interest in common, we had a general cooling-down period. When I told Rick that I thought we had a relationship built only on sex, he'd grinned and said, "Yeah, it's great!"

At first I missed the comfort of his arm around me and the warmth of his long body next to mine in bed. Then I bought a giant, extralong down pillow, and it provided the warmth I missed. And it didn't snore or sweat.

I got into bed, wrapped myself around the pillow, and closed my eyes.

THREE

AFTER THE THRILL of getting a first *real* letter, I wanted more and more. And I was secretly scared to death that there wouldn't be any more.

Each day through the next week I went to the newspaper office full of hope and excitement. So every day when the mailman brought a new batch of letters, my heart thumped and my hands almost shook with anticipation. It was wonderful.

My answer to Looking for Lochinvar appeared in the Wednesday (and only) edition. That day I wanted to look every inch a pro, so I strolled nonchalantly through the office, announced I was going for coffee, then raced to the newspaper box on the corner. There, I bought all the copies available. It probably only took my entire salary for that week, but since I hadn't seen my first paycheck, I didn't know for sure. At that point I didn't care.

On Friday Jason brought several envelopes, dropping them with a flourish on my desk. I guess it was no secret that I looked forward to my mail.

I reached for the little pile and drew the top one toward me. Even before I opened it, I knew it was from Looking for Lochinvar. I picked up the envelope. But not a single odd happening. No scene, no scent, no rushing water. Still, I *knew* it was a Lochinvar letter.

I opened the letter.

Dear Stella,
Thank you for the reply, it was lovely. So encourag-

ing. You don't know what it means to me to have someone who can understand me as I believe you do. I've been so lonely. It's amazing how with all the people around me I can still be alone. And yet I am. And so lonely!

I've decided to take your advice and reach out. You're right, I'll never find my Lochinvar by keeping silent. Please check my horrorscope and let me know if the stars say I'll be lucky. I've enclosed an envelope.

Thank you a thousand times.

Looking for Lochinvar

But there was no envelope; she had forgotten it after all. I reread the letter several times, my gaze catching each time on the curious misspelling of the word horoscope. The rest of the message was so well composed, at least by comparison with most of the letters I received, that the error was striking. I wish I could say that I was glad that she had liked my reply. I really wanted to feel joyous, but instead I felt a gnawing sense of foreboding. I wasn't sure whether it came from the letter or from Jason, who was hovering around me as though he wanted to say something but didn't quite know how.

I suddenly wanted to get out of the office. That letter and all the rest that had come that afternoon I swept into my purse and I left.

At home, I pinned Fluffy in his harness to my shirt and went for a walk. I find that a little mild exercise, like walking, helps ease tension. So does ice cream, so with the help of a double-dip cone of chocolate chunk and almond mocha I was able to raise my spirits right up out of the cellar.

That night, after my carbo-loading at the ice cream shop, I got out the letters and spread them before me on the living

oom floor. That way, I was already down if I had a spell.
But nothing happened when I picked up the letter.

I worked over my reply several times, trying to strike
ust the right note of suave *je ne sais quoi*.

Dear Looking for Lochinvar,
I can read your stars much more clearly if you send
your precise time, place, and date of birth. But the aura
of your letter and the sense I have of you tells me that
you may already know the man you're looking for. He
may be among the ones you count in your circle.
    But always use caution. It can be hard to see beyond
the surface, and yet you must look deep into a person's
character before you entrust your love.
    Yours,
    Stella the Stargazer

I hoped to attain a mystical ring while reminding her to
be careful. A certain feeling of dread or maybe a sense of
urking disaster threatened to rise to the front. I pushed all
he rest of the letters into a heap and stacked them on the
nd table by the couch. I had plenty of time to deal with
hem later.

I was just about to call Meredith when the phone rang.
t was Rick the Ick. The black mood that I had struggled
ll night to repress rose with a vengeance.

"Hey babe!" His voice hadn't changed. I'm not sure
why I thought it would have.

"How'd you get my number?" I'd changed a lot of
hings when we broke up.

"Called the paper. Figured that was you. Stella the Stargazer. You were always interested in the odd and weird.
So what'cha doing?"

"How'd you get the paper to tell you my number?"

"You want to get together tonight?"

"No. Who told you my number?"

"Come on. Don't you want to go out?"

It was a dream come true. An opportunity to use all th[e] vile, cutting words I'd rehearsed a thousand times. An[d] now the moment was here.

This was what I'd longed for during sad nights. And her[e] I was. Empty. There wasn't a damn thing I cared enoug[h] to say to him. It was finally over. I didn't care anymore. [I] had matured.

"You're history, Rick. I don't need you anymore; I re[-] placed you with a down pillow. Have a good life, good[-] bye." I hung up.

I didn't have a thing to say to him, not even one re[-] proach.

Although to tell the truth, when I gave it a little thought[,] he had several hundred faults that I could have pointed out[.] I almost picked up the phone to tell him about them, but [I] reminded myself that I'd grown beyond that.

The next morning I awoke to the sound of the birds and [] the chirp of the telephone. Mother always calls on Saturda[y] morning, need it or not.

"Hi, Mom," I mumbled. I could almost smell bacon and [] eggs, her favorite breakfast.

"Hello, Janie dear. I had a dream that you met a won[-] derful man last night, someone who will love you and tak[e] care of you all the rest of your life."

"I'm going by Stella now, and I didn't meet anybody[,] Mom. I'm not looking." I peered at the clock. It was 6:20[.]

I rolled out of bed and dragged the telephone on its long [] cord to the kitchen, where I poured a cup of coffee.

"It isn't right to palm yourself off as an astrologist and [...]

advice-to-the-lovelorn expert when you're lovelorn ourself.''

"At least I have experience.''

"You're an absolutely beautiful girl. You could have any man in the world that you want,'' she said. My mother actually believes this…her loyalty and devotion to my sister, brother, and me are topped only by her devotion to my father. Most of the time all of us bask in it.

"Well,'' she continued. "I don't know how you're going to support yourself on the pittance you'll earn at this paper. You left a fine job earning more money than you could spend. By the way, why is it called the *Daily Orion* when it only comes out once a week?''

"It used to be a daily.''

"Well, I don't know what the world's coming to. The weekly paper says it's a daily, my daughter Jane says her name is Stella, and it's all going to lead to trouble.''

Now if I were hearing this dire forecast for the first or even the second time, I'd have been alarmed. But it's like the refrain in the chorus of a popular song, it rings in my ears endlessly, so I grazed through the refrigerator while she talked to me of pounds and ounces, reminding me gently that I had plenty of both.

By the time she cheerfully rang off I had rediscovered the comfort of emotional eating. The other thing I'd discovered was that I was flat out of all the wonderful things that satisfy my emotional yearnings. Coffee, orange juice, and the morning paper just don't fill the void. What does begin to fill this maw is a giant, freshly baked sticky bun like the ones sold at the BonBon Bakery in the shoppette just a couple blocks south of Little Nothings. And, I told myself, if I power-walked it, the mile and a half there and

the other mile and a half back, I'd use up the calories I
consume in the sticky buns.

Furthermore, I told myself, I could share one with Gra
in the back room of Little Nothings. Grace always sew
at the lingerie shop in the early morning, even on Satu
days. She'd need the energy. So I'd be doing a good dee

Fluffy loves these little outings, so he was pinned in l
harness to my shirt, and I could feel him clinging to tl
inside of the breast pocket.

Last summer I'd been powering down to the BonBon f
cinnamon rolls, for Fluffy of course, and I'd cut throug
the alley behind the shoppette where Little Nothings is l
cated, to get to the BonBon a tad quicker. I'd seen the ba
door open then and found Grace sewing away. Since the
I'd occasionally stopped by to share coffee and a roll.

I remembered when I got to the alleyway behind Litt
Nothings that this weekend was a big sale weekend at tl
shop. They were calling it the Stars and Straps Sale. I
said that I thought it would be more fitting for the Four
of July, but Grace had smiled and shrugged and Lilly ha
snorted and said that they needed to move some of tl
merchandise.

I could see Grace's car parked at the rear of the stor
and the door was propped open a crack, like she might l
hoping I'd come by. I was almost there when I felt one o
those spells coming on. The taste was in my mouth, and
suddenly seemed to have run out of oxygen. My knees wei
a little shaky. I decided that I was overdoing the powe
walking, so I slowed down and reached for the door. I
planned to call in to Grace and see if she had any parti
ularly favorite roll for me to pick up.

The door opens onto the general storage area with shelv
ing on the walls, boxes, an ironing board, and rack to hol

e hanging merchandise. Whenever I'd been there, the
om has been dark. I think Grace tries to save on the
ectricity. There's a little room on the left that Grace made
to a sewing room, and a slice of light from her bright
mps shone out. I could hear her radio playing, tuned to
VOD. It sounded like Mozart.

I pulled the door wide, stepped inside, and had my mouth
en to shout to her when I heard a furious commotion. I
sumed it was Lilly's voice, but it was so clotted with
ger it sounded very different.

"What do you think you're doing? Did you think I'd
ever find out?" There was a sound of shoe soles scraping
n the cement floor.

"I didn't think—"

"Did you think you could get away with it, and I'd never
tch on? Just how stupid do you think I am?"

There was no answer.

The rage of whoever was there was so huge it swept
verything away before it. It got so quiet I heard a bird
hirp from outside. I'd have given anything to be outside
ith him that very moment.

Uncomfortable, immobilized, I tried to call out, to let
em know I was there, put the stopper of politeness on the
rgument, but my voice was caught in my breast. At least
at's how it felt, because I couldn't seem to get any utter-
nce out of my mouth. Little worms of anxiety crawled in
y chest. Fluffy crawled on the outside, nosing his way
ut of the pocket. He's quite sensitive to tension.

"You don't understand," came a voice that I did rec-
gnize. It was Grace, pleading. "I just couldn't help it. It
ll just happened too fast. I was caught up in the moment.
 didn't plan to do it." There were tears in Grace's voice,
nd something else that I didn't quite recognize.

The hard slap resounded through the shop.

My feet finally moved. I stepped back out of the sh
into the piercing sunlight and walked away toward t
BonBon as fast as I could. Until the day I die, I will wi
I had done differently.

FOUR

DIDN'T FEEL all that well when I got to the bakery, so I got a cup of coffee and sat on the bench in the storefront until they called my number. My appetite had dwindled, but I decided to get an assortment of rolls to take back to Little Nothings and offer around. Maybe food would soothe the savage hearts I'd heard in the shop. I felt sad that two women who had been such close friends could have so bitter an argument. And I wondered what Lilly had been so furious about.

All the way back to Little Nothings I felt a sense of burden, dread maybe. I don't usually mind a little conflict, but today I didn't really relish returning and considered passing on by. Let them settle down, you have no need to stick your nose into this, I thought. But as I got closer, I began to feel shaky again. By the time I got to the back door and pulled it open, I definitely felt unwell. I slumped against the back wall in the still-darkened back room, feeling foolish and a little alarmed.

Light from Grace's sewing room slanted across the floor, and I heard a Bach fugue playing from the radio, so, I thought, maybe peace was restored.

"Hello!" I called. My voice sounded strange to my ears, like it had come from someone else's dry throat. The storeroom was cool, as though it was devoid of life. And a barely discernible metallic taint was in the air, a faint, bright scent of iron, which I suddenly associated with death.

My knees were very big-time shaky, and I slid to the floor. I didn't think to call out again. I rolled onto the floor

behind a long rack of slips and stretched out. Usually thes
spells pass quickly, so I just lay there in the dark with m
eyes closed, feeling the cool of the concrete against m
back. Immediately, I felt better. I started to get up, bu
darkness crowded in, and I knew I was going to see some
thing this time. I forced myself to remain sitting.

Before me formed the same vision I'd seen in the news
paper office the day before. A body, crumpled, with a pai
of scissors sticking out from the chest. But this time I coul
see the face.

It was Grace.

I'm not sure how long I stayed there, probably only sec
onds, maybe a minute. I *had* to get to the sewing room.
remember that I didn't feel strong, but I no longer fe
shaky. I pushed up to my feet, put my hand out to stead
myself, and knocked over a rack of slips. They fell slowly
like in a dream. All the little hangers jingled against eac
other as they fell, and the iron rods of the rack clanged an
rang as they bounced on the hard concrete floor.

From the alleyway I heard a car start. I thought abou
trying to run after it to get company to go into the sewin
room, but my feet wouldn't move. And then, I heard
drive away.

At the doorway of the little sewing room, the odor of ho
metal was very strong. The most noticeable thing in th
jumbled room was the steam iron smoldering facedown o
the ironing board, wisps of smoke curling upward from
lavender little nothing. I started to cross the room, the
stopped dead.

Shimmering before me was the thin, slight body of m
friend Grace, crumpled on the floor beside the desk sh
used as a sewing table. A pair of scissors with incongr
ously bright and cheerful orange handles stuck out of he

chest. I knew she was dead. A small pool of blood oozed on the floor from a little dark stain on her shirt.

In a state of shock I started toward her. Then I thought maybe a paramedic could do something that I couldn't. Smoke was thickening in the room.

I needed a telephone.

I remembered Lilly using one once to answer a call about a nightie some customer wanted reserved for her. I remembered because I'd been on the point of purchasing it, and of course as soon as it was beyond my reach, I wanted it a hundred times more. Grace had felt badly and made me one very like it to compensate.

I stumbled past the dressing rooms through the curtained doorway into the front of the shop to the sales counter. The front window curtains were still drawn against the morning light, and the shop had the eerie presence of the not quite real...more pronounced because of the absurdly gay decorations for the sale. Balloons dangled curly ribbons and floated over each mound of filmy garments. I almost expected confetti to drop from the ceiling.

The telephone sat beneath a beautiful handsewn camisole. I knew Grace had made it even though I couldn't see the label through the film of tears in my eyes. I could tell by the design.

The police arrived sometime later, along with an ambulance and a fire truck. I don't remember crying, but my face seemed to be wet, and the officer who led me out the back of the shop to the fire truck and oxygen mask thrust a little packet of tissues into my hand.

By some miracle the fire hadn't really started yet, and the firemen controlled the smoldering immediately. After a little oxygen I felt much better. Well enough to drop the mask when I heard a police detective say, "Okay, so where's this body?"

The man who asked was medium-sized and wearing a comfortably worn sports jacket and shirt with a teal-colored tie that didn't quite match and had cream-colored flowers all over it. He had dark hair that stood up crisply, like it was saluting, and blue eyes that probably were warm and lovely but right now were icy and suspicious. He didn't look as though he had a sense of humor.

"She's in the sewing room," I said, choking on an ache in my throat the size of a walnut.

"Well, miss, we didn't find her. Can you give us a description? What she was wearing, what she looks like?"

I looked at him. He didn't look stupid. Or like he was joking. "She's there on the floor beside her sewing table."

"What does she look like?" he asked warily. In the background I heard a large vehicle like a fire truck drive away. Two firemen in yellow slickers and boots sauntered over to the rescue truck where I was sitting and looked at me out of narrowed eyes. They seemed to be staying carefully out of reach.

"She's small, thin, with nondescript brown hair. She's wearing a…" I closed my eyes to picture her. "She's wearing a plain white cotton shirt and brown slacks." I opened my eyes. The detective was writing each word down in a hasty scrawl. I leaned toward him. "It was Grace."

"Grace?"

"Grace. And she was dead." I felt like I was made of stone, stiff and cold.

"How do you know she was dead?"

"I could tell. There was a pool of blood on the floor and the scissors…." I gulped. It was horrible to remember the scene, but far worse to tell about it. The words made it real again.

"The scissors?"

"Bright orange handles. And a little blood. Just left o

center in her chest." My eyes clouded with tears that threatened to stream down my face.

"What's her name?"

"Grace."

"Got that. I mean her last name."

"Oh…uh, it's uh, I don't know. I can't think. It'll come to me. Grace…" I felt a complete fool, and the more I tried to pull her last name to mind, the more it eluded me. It was a testimony to his flat affect that he didn't just roll his eyes and walk away. In his place, I would have.

I looked around for something that could confirm my story. It certainly sounded odd, even to me. "Maybe in her car. On the insurance card. She probably has one in the glove compartment; it'll have her name there."

"Her car? Where's her car?"

"By the Dumpster, right over there." I pointed. My mouth slowly fell open. No car was there at all. "Where did it go?" I glanced at him. He was licking his lips, probably wondering how long it would take the rubber room squad to get here and evaluate me.

"I think you'd better start at the beginning," the detective said. To his credit, he wasn't being sarcastic.

"Who are you?" he asked flatly.

"Uh, really, or more recently?"

He shifted restlessly, making a brief note on his pad. "Try both."

"My real name is Jane Austin Smith. But I write a column in the *Denver Daily Orion* under the name Stella the Stargazer."

"Stargazer? Is that one word or two?" He eyed me briefly, then started to write again. When he looked up his expression changed from stoic to incredulous.

"I don't want to alarm you, miss, but there's a…a lizard on your chest."

I glanced down. Fluffy had crawled completely out of my pocket and was looking around. I knew he was frightened because he was a vivid shade of chartreuse, his fright-and-fight color. "Oh, that's all right. This is Fluffy, my chameleon. It's okay, he's on a leash."

The detective tried not to show any surprise, and he did pretty well until his left eyelid began to jump with a tiny tic. He rubbed it with his thumb surreptitiously, but it continued to tic. "So," he said too loudly, "which of these people are you right now?"

"You don't need to get sarcastic, I'm just a little shocky, and it's hard to be cold and cerebral...like you. My name is Jane Smith. My job is writing a column in a newspaper. Who are you?"

"Detective Lee Stokowski, Homicide, Denver Police Department."

"Well, Detective Stokowski, follow me." I knew that if I could just get inside, show him the bloodstain, then things would go better. At least something would corroborate my story.

I power-walked...straight past the two firemen who had narrowed their eyes at me, past the spot where Grace's car had been, past the uniformed officer at the door, through the doorway, and into the storage area. It was not brightly lit.

The rack of slips still lay on the floor. "I didn't imagine that!" I said triumphantly pointing to the fallen slips. "Your men should find a bag of sweet rolls under there somewhere. Fresh. From the BonBon Bakery."

I slowed my step, peeked into the sewing room, and felt my heart stop. It looked like a snowstorm had blasted through. The room had been thoroughly sprayed with a powerful fire extinguisher. White powder covered everything, including the floor. The footprints of the firemen vere everywhere. If Grace had been there, they'd have tepped all over her.

Rashly, I stepped into the center of the room and knelt near where I remembered her lying. I dabbed at the powder. She *had* been there. I'd seen her, hadn't I? A sick feeling vas in the pit of my stomach. I brushed harder at the spot where I thought there might be a bloodstain. Nothing.

Stokowski leaned against the doorjamb looking like he vas deep in thought. At least he wasn't openly laughing at ne.

"Honestly," I protested. "She was lying there, on her back, her right arm flung up overhead, her left arm down bout five inches from her side, hand slightly closed." My oice had a disgusting whine to it. I swallowed hard. I ouldn't have believed me if I were him.

"Try up and over about six inches," suggested Stokowski. As soon as he mentioned it, I noticed a barely perceptible difference in the powder. I inched forward and rushed. There it was. A dark, irregular stain about three nches in diameter on the floor in front of the desk cum ewing table.

"There. On the floor. Blood." My lungs swelled with a eep breath of relief that there was some proof that Grace ad been there and had been dead. Then I noticed the dark reak of blood, Grace's blood, that stained my fingers. I prang to my feet as if I could in some way leave the horror f its meaning behind and scrubbed my fingers on the back f my shorts, where I couldn't see it. I pivoted, trying to ide my shuddering from the skeptical eyes of the detecve.

He stepped forward, knelt, and touched a finger to the ain, then lifted his finger close to his face so he could see better. "Right," he grunted. He called to the other detctives and pulled me out of the room into the doorway.

While he talked with one of the other detectives, I ex
amined what I could see of the rest of the sewing room.
wondered if there had been a struggle, if Grace had suf
fered. Or had she died in the instant, her soul slipping awa
as she fell? There was an ugly quality in the room, a
ambience that I hadn't ever felt before. I hoped I'd neve
meet it again.

The ironing board was a foam-encrusted mess. The shap
of the iron was blackened and burnt into the top of th
pressing form. At the end of the board the iron itself stoo
upright, its cord dangling to the floor. One of the fireme
must have stood it upright.

"I warned Grace that it wasn't safe to leave the dam
iron on," I muttered. Stokowski looked up sharply.

"She always had it on when she was sewing," I ex
plained. "She said it was so that she could press things int
place…it made the sewing easier and the results better."

"Did she always come here on a Saturday morning t
sew?"

"Always…so far as I know."

"Who else would know?"

"Lilly." I shrugged, considering. "Really, anyone migl
know. She always left the door open in the summer. That'
how I learned she was here."

"Who's Lilly?"

"Lilly is Grace's partner. Grace and Lilly run the shop.'
It's funny how little things stick in your mind when you'r
under stress like that. I watched him make notes on hi
little pad and was fascinated to see that his fingernails wer
chewed down to the quick so that his fingers were roun
at the ends. It made his hands look nearly square.

He looked up and frowned. "Anything missing here?"

"The long scissors."

He looked at the desktop. Behind the futuristic-lookin

ctric sewing machine was an array of scissors, at least
r pairs. His eyebrows crawled up his forehead.

'Her stilettos. The pointed ones with six-inch blades and
ght orange handles.''

He scrutinized the scissor collection, then picked up a
r of short-bladed scissors using a tissue, I guess so he
uldn't leave prints. I took it as a hopeful sign that he
ieved me about Grace. He drew his finger across the
e of the blade. "She always keep these things this
rp?''

'She likes them razor sharp, then they make a cleaner
n on the garments. She makes the most beautiful lit-
..'' My throat ached and mercifully he nodded, so I was
e to stop talking.

He replaced the scissors just as they had been.

'Anything else you think is missing?''

looked around again trying to remember what I'd seen
previous visits. All I could think was, *How can this be
pening?*

'I heard someone arguing with her this morning.''

'You heard someone?'' He was good at reflecting
ases, I thought. I took my time before I answered. I told
self he believed me, but I caught a speculative, deep
e expression in his eyes that said he still wondered if I
s a candidate for the funny farm or, worse, just making
ll up.

'The first time I came. I stopped on the way to the
ery to ask her if she wanted anything in particular. The
k door was open like it usually is in good weather. I
ne in, but I was feeling shaky, so I leaned against the
ll for a moment. Then I heard someone shout, almost
a wail, 'What do you think you're doing? Did you
nk I'd never find out? How stupid do you think I am?'
en I heard a slap and I...I left.'' This time I couldn't

just swallow the ache in my throat. I had to stop and coll‐
myself.

"You see the person?"

I shook my head. I didn't trust myself to talk just ye‐

"You recognize the voice?"

I thought carefully. "Not really. At the time, I thou‐
it was a woman's voice. You see, I just assumed that
would be Lilly, but it didn't sound a bit like her. It wa‐
bizarre voice, almost a screech. I guess it could have ev
been a man's voice if he was angry enough. And th‐
Grace said, 'I didn't plan it. It just happened.' And th‐
the slap, and I thought, I should get the hell out of here
never dreamt..."

"Was her car here when you first came?"

"Her car was here then *and* when I came back!" The
was a commotion at the back of the shop, but I could‐
see what was happening because Stokowski was in ‐
doorway.

"Is the shop in good financial shape?"

"I don't think so, I don't know...you'll have to a‐
Lilly."

"Ask me what?" Lilly's voice sliced through the lit‐
sewing room like a well-sharpened blade.

FIVE

OKOWSKI DID the same thing I did. He stared at Lilly. I
nk we stared for different reasons. Lilly is a very good-
king woman. Forty years had come and gone, never
ving even a trace of their passing on her face.

The atmosphere had gone from neutral to chilly with a
ing of dread. I wondered if Stokowski noticed. I felt
ffy dive into my pocket again. Fluffy isn't fond of Lilly,
ce Lilly regards Fluffy as a large insect. Stokowski scru-
zed Lilly, who scrutinized what was left of the sewing
m.

I couldn't tell whether Lilly knew what was going on or
. She stood in the doorway, all imposing five feet nine
hes of her, and gripped the doorjamb with one well-
nicured hand. Her other hand dangled at her side; no
mor was visible. Her makeup was, as always impeccable.
eemed to me that this porcelain exterior hid a frightened
erior. I realized guiltily that I was looking for signs that
 had just lugged a heavy weight out of the building. My
s dropped involuntarily to her shoes. She was wearing
lish slacks with low-heeled, navy pumps...both clean
 dry.

Lilly's mouth was a surprised O shape. I still couldn't
 whether it was feigned or not. Her eyelids, heavily
ished with deep turquoise eye shadow, rose and fell as
 surveyed the room.

"Why was there a fire?" she asked, still visibly totaling
 damage. She keeps a running tab of the boutique's prof-
losses, costs, and revenues right inside her perfectly

coiffed head of hair. She was sniffing the air and did seem to notice that neither of us had replied.

"Where's Grace?" She turned to Stokowski. "Who you?"

"I'm Detective Lee Stokowski, Denver Police Dep ment, ma'am. I'd like to ask you a few questions." He calm, unemotional, and understated. I noticed that he did mention that he was from homicide. I felt Fluffy digg into the corner of my pocket and wondered what knew…if he knew anything. Lizard brains are pretty ti

I realized that I was holding my breath, trying to m myself invisible so I could stay to hear the questions shrank back into the hallway that led to the front of store, where I hopefully wouldn't be noticeable.

Lilly looked blankly at Stokowski. "Sure, I guess s she said. She wasn't her usual crisp self, but I still could tell whether it was an act or not. Maybe he had the sa effect on her that he had on me. When he asked me qu tions, I felt flustered and could barely think straight. It v as if all the little sins I'd committed all my life came mind, crowding out my common sense, and I felt guilty hell and twice as scared. Now, while he scrutinized Li and asked her questions, my brain worked just fine.

"Is there a place where we can go?"

She gestured eloquently, her red-lacquered fingern showing off well in the overhead light. "We can go i the front of the shop. With the lingerie. This is all th is," she murmured. "I thought Grace would be her Then she looked at me and seemed to reregister my pr ence. "Why are you here? We're not open yet. You're most determined shopper I know."

Stokowski moved toward me before I could answer a clamped a firm hand on my forearm. "Thanks for y help. Give your name and address to the officer outside

steered me through the hall and gave me a little push
ard the rear door.

took his light frown as a warning not to say anything,
he didn't need to worry. I'd read enough mystery stories
now that I shouldn't give Lilly any clues. Besides, she
s a prime suspect in my book. Thinking of that, I realized
h a jolt that although I finally remembered Grace's last
ae, Peary, I didn't know Lilly's. We had always just
ed them Grace and Lilly.

squeezed past Lilly, who remained stock still in the
rway, and caught the scent of her favorite perfume, Poi-
. But Grace hadn't been poisoned, I reminded myself. I
gged my feet and walked real slow, hoping to hear the
inning of Stokowski's questions, but he signaled one of
other officers, and this man officiously escorted me out-
: to the alley, noted down my name and address, and
I me I could leave.

VAS NINE-THIRTY in the morning, and I was cold and no
ger hungry for rolls or anything else. I felt tired and
couraged, and most of all, sad. I was going to miss
ace.

3ack at my apartment, I made toast with strawberry jam
coffee. Even though crumbs invariably get all down
front, toast with strawberry jam is an outstanding com-
. food. When I broke up with Rick, I'd eaten nearly an
ire loaf of bread and a jar of jam, even though I was the
who broke it off.

was incredibly lethargic, as though the cocoon of shock
n this morning was wrapped around my brain, so I lay
vn for a little nap.

Meredith and I were supposed to meet at the newspaper
ce at one, I thought drowsily. I had to remember to wake
in time for that.

Fortunately, seconds before I fell asleep Fluffy scrabb[led] out of my pocket. If he hadn't stepped on my face with [his] clammy little feet, I'd have gone to sleep with him still [in] my shirt, and *that* could have been his end. My moth[er] would have had one more tiny little cross in the Memo[rial] corner of her garden with a headstone commemorati[ng] Fluffy the Chameleon, RIP.

My brother had contributed most of the tiny crosses d[ur]ing his preteen years when he practiced being first [a] preacher, than a funeral director. So RIP and some oth[er] far more creative commemorations adorned this one cor[ner] of Mother's garden. The year his minnows died from [the] August heat, the backyard was a forest of tiny wh[ite] crosses. He works for Restful Gardens now. As mother [al]ways said, he was a child with a focus. Of course, unt[il I] left accounting, I had always been a child with a focus, t[oo.] After all, I had counted the minnows and the crosses.

I unpinned Fluffy and returned him to his cage, then [lay] on my back on the couch, thinking. This "rest in peac[e"] business kept coming to mind along with the memory [of] Grace, who wasn't resting in peace, or even staying in [one] place.

How on earth had her body moved from when I left [her] in the sewing room to telephone 911? How could it h[ap]pen? And why didn't I hear anything? Or see anyone?

It had seemed like an hour but was probably only [five] to ten minutes that I'd been in there telephoning, then w[ait]ing for the police. Surely I'd have heard it if someone [had] been there. Shifting a body, even a small, thin one, is[n't] like tossing a pillow into the corner.

Someone would either have had to hoist Grace over th[eir] shoulder and carry her out, or they'd have had to drag [her] out. Now that would make some noise. I'd have heard t[hat.]

It occurred to me that the killer could have been arou[nd]

hile I was. Not just the first time, but the second. How
lse would Grace be there, and then not be there? Before I
ould follow that train of thought with any resolution, a
icture of Grace at her sewing machine crowded in.

Whoever she'd argued with must have reached over,
rabbed the scissors in a rage, and rammed them into
race's chest. What was missing? In my mental picture,
race was sitting in front of her sewing machine, turned
oward her attacker, in the same way she always turned to
e when I brought in the sweet rolls.

I leapt up from the couch and paced the floor, excited
y this new piece of noninformation...that something was
issing.

I'd looked into the sewing room, seen the smoldering
oning board, then I saw Grace on the floor of the sewing
oom in front of her sewing table, dead. She *had* been there,
thought. I'd almost stepped on her when I started toward
e ironing board.

I stopped at Fluffy's cage. "So, Watson, what's wrong
ith this picture?"

Fluffy turned his head. I took the clue.

Grace had been moved. Somehow. She wasn't very
eavy, but dead weight was very hard to manage. A man
ould carry her over his shoulder. But a woman, even a
rong woman, would have had to drag the body. The de-
ctive, Stokowski, had been scrupulous not to move things,
xcept for the scissors.

There had been no heel drag marks on the shop floor, of
ourse; the firemen had marched through numerous times
nd would have obliterated anything while covering the
oor with their foam. And outside, the paving was tar mac-
dam that wouldn't show marks of any kind.

There's a Dumpster at the end of the parking area. Next
the Dumpster there is room for one car to park. Then

there is the back door to the shop and then the parki
space for Lilly's car.

Grace *always* parked her car next to the Dumpster.
figured that was because she was at the shop so early a
so much she always took that first spot. There really wasr
much space in the back. I tried to picture how the polic
the fire engine, and the ambulance had all been able to g
in. I finally had to admit that I couldn't reliably picture t
scene at all.

I paced to the kitchen and grazed through the cupboard
vaguely hungry. It's something I do when I can't get n
thoughts straight.

If I couldn't remember what was missing in the roo
could I trust myself to remember Grace as she had bee
I stopped with the refrigerator open, the cool air blowi
on my face.

What if I hadn't seen Grace?

What if I'd seen a vision?

But what about the blood?

"MEREDITH," I SAID, shouting at her in frustration, "Y
just aren't listening to me! Grace's dead and missing! A
we've got to do something."

"Well, we've done too much already. Don't you thi
that going to Little Nothings pretending to try on thin
and sneaking out of the dressing rooms into the back of t
shop is enough? And don't you think that scaring the cle
to death when you tried to get back into the dressing roo
is enough?"

Meredith stamped her foot. It's a trite gesture, but s
only uses it when she's really furious.

She continued. "That clerk is sure to tell Lilly all abo
it when she gets back. And then where will we be? I mea
it's not like there are so many customers in that shop th

we're unknowns! If Lilly is a killer, now she knows that we know."

"At least we know for sure there are no drag marks on the floor," I said defiantly. "And the blood is still there. *And* the police have put yellow tape across the sewing room door."

"And we found that there are no tracks out to this alley."

"Or that if there were they're all obliterated. Now all we need to do is go to Grace's house."

"Wrong! My horoscope said to anticipate many difficulties today and to avoid any risky relationships. You, Jane, are a risky relationship."

"You are being a timid, negative Pisces. Only reading negatives instead of seeing challenges."

"Well, Grace is, or was, a Pisces too, and look what happened to her!"

"That's just it, Meredith, we don't know what happened to her. We're looking into it."

She went after all. She wasn't happy, but I know she cares about Grace as much as I do. She was just nervous.

I checked the phone book on the off chance she was listed and found that she'd lived fairly close to the shop in a very nice area between University Boulevard and Colorado Boulevard. It was such a good area that I was surprised. And realized there were a lot more things I didn't know about Grace...like if she'd ever been married. And where her family was.

The area, called Bonnie Brae, is a neighborhood of very nice homes with a touch of old England to them. Most were built in the thirties, forties, and fifties, with gables, two-storied with some half-timbered effects and steeply pitched roofs. Regardless of the design of the house, the trees are mature, the homes well landscaped, and an air of serenity pervades the streets. No madding crowds or overhead air-

planes. No colorful people such as in Capitol Hill, just col
orful flowers. Sidewalks are a part of the decor and ar
accepted so long as they aren't used too much.

Grace's home was a lovely, unpretentious house set back
from the street at the end of a short winding walk. On on
side of the walkway stood a mature weeping birch. A youn;
mountain ash stood on the other side. I could see the over
arching branches of a silver maple over the roof. Ther
were other homes on the street much larger and newer an
more gorgeous, but none were as just plain homey a
Grace's. I felt my eyes grow moist and hoped I wouldn'
get all teary.

"We're going to go straight up to the door and knock
just like we were expecting to find her," I said to Meredith
who sat in the passenger seat.

"I'll wait here for you," she said, not moving.

"Come up to the door, then if no one answers you ca
wait there," I pleaded.

She climbed reluctantly from the car and slammed the
door. "I don't know why I'm doing this," she said.

Nobody answered the door, but we could hear a littl
dog barking from inside. Meredith stayed on the fron
porch, knocking and waiting, while I went around to th
back. Bonnie Brae is the kind of neighborhood where fif
teen years ago you didn't need to lock your door. I wa
hoping that Grace still left a door open.

Her backyard was as lovely as the front, but different
Where the front had been mostly grass and trees, here sh
had flowers, but the irises were up, roses were leafing out
and Grace had bedding plants all ready to put into th
ground. There were zinnias, petunias, and sweet alyssun
that I could identify quickly. I wondered who would pu
them in this year.

I peeked through the dining room window and saw onl

a highly polished table, with place mats at either end. The dog, a white miniature poodle, barked furiously at me and scrabbled against the wall in a vain attempt to reach me. I made a face at him. It made him even more furious, and he barked and yapped twice as fast.

The neighbor on the other side of the driveway peered out her kitchen window. I waved at her and shouted, "Have you seen Grace today? I'm supposed to meet her!" It was a minor lie.

The neighbor shouted back, her voice barely audible through the double-glazed window, "She must have left real early this morning. I didn't even see her, just heard her car pull out."

I thanked her and strolled to the front, where Meredith still waited on the front stoop. We started for the car.

"I believe in these visions of yours more than you do. But I'd give anything for this to be wrong."

I stopped in my tracks. "You think I saw a vision in the shop?"

Meredith looked at me solemnly. "Sure. That's what you've been telling me, isn't it?" She stopped walking, too.

"No. It isn't. I *saw* Grace.... But..." I thought some more. "But it *is* the only thing that makes sense, you know. If I got there just after it all happened. Then what I saw was the image of her. Not her really. Just her aura. And if the killer already had Grace's body in her car, then all he had to do—"

"Was drive away. But you got there too soon—"

"So the killer either was in the room when I came in and hid, and while I telephoned, he—"

"She!"

"...maybe she, ran out the back and drove off." I thought it through. It didn't quite fit.

"I thought I heard a car drive by while I was still in the

storage room. But maybe I heard a car drive *away*. If that was what happened, then the killer was actually outside in Grace's car with Grace in it when I came in.''

Meredith shivered. ''Either way, you know what this means? The killer saw you.''

My skin prickled.

SIX

MEREDITH AND I were both a little spooked. Food being the primal comfort item in my life just then, we went to a little restaurant that caters to the feminine appetite and serves large meals in small courses so that you never actually have to admit to yourself how much you've eaten.

Meredith ordered a house salad with no dressing that looked barely large enough to be something I'd put into Fluffy's cage for him to use as camouflage, while I ordered an hors d'oeuvre "snack" that probably had close to two thousand calories packed onto a small plate.

"Jane—"

"Call me Stella."

"Stella, where do you think Grace is...really?"

I thought for a while. "I don't know. Do you have an idea?"

Meredith nodded. I picked at my hors d'oeuvres. I thought I knew what she was going to say.

"Jane, I mean Stella, do you think you could 'see' where she is?"

That ruined my appetite. Meredith consistently maintains that my spells are vestiges of extrasensory perception. I, on the other hand, have given them very little credence, and I've tried not to pay any attention to them at all. Until lately. Just now I was feeling shaken and uncertain about the whole thing.

Before this episode, all the spells I had had were funny little inconsequential things. Like in fifth grade when I "saw" Larry Johnson behind the hedge throwing snowballs at my sister, Joan. Or in high school when I "saw" Tyro Burnell and his buddy, Arlen Finkelmeier, painting big-nosed caricatures of our principal on the sidewalk in front of the school.

And the time in college when I'd "seen" Suzie Jean standing on the fire escape trying to get into the dorm after hours. She was very grateful and explained that she'd left a shoe in the door to keep it open, but *someone* had pulled it out. She was ever so grateful and couldn't understand how I'd known to come to the door at that hour (3:00 a.m.). I never enlightened her. I didn't understand it myself.

I also didn't tell her that I'd been the someone who'd pulled the shoe out of the door. I didn't want her to know that I was so naive at that point, I just figured someone had forgotten her shoe.

There had been many similar inconsequential happenings that I neither understood nor could produce at will, and I had always set them aside as odd coincidences. It wasn't until I had a peculiarly revealing spell while I was still at my previous job that I began to give more credence to them. Now I didn't know what to think. I only knew that I was, for lack of a better word, unnerved. And the thought of purposely pulling up such awful sights was appalling.

That finished lunch, and Meredith needed to get ready for a date. Meredith is what teens call a romance freak. She's in a state of perpetual Romance Renaissance. In her book, if it's pink, it's wonderful. If it's purple, it's passionate. If it's male, it's a possibility.

She's a good-looking, attractive woman: tall, slender, long-legged with, as I mentioned before with envy, an abundance of auburn hair...on her head where it belongs even.

Meredith has a tendency to overwhelm men with her intensity. A tendency only slightly larger than her tendency

o want to change them. It's not so much that she has an
archetype that she is seeking, as that she just likes to change
them...into someone else. When it comes to men, Meredith
has always been in the driver's seat. And she likes it that
way.

Her last lover, a buddy of Rick the Ick, always said that
Meredith just liked to redesign the male personality for the
sake of it. Obviously he wasn't the most objective of people. In fact, he's fairly bitter now, and the last I heard he
had decided to join a monastery but was having difficulty
finding one.

Meredith maintains that one day she'll meet the man
who's her match. I told her that I'm not sure what that'll
be, and I'm not sure I'll want to know about it. It could be
fearsome.

I didn't feel like going home yet, so I decided to go by
the newspaper office to see if the postman had left any more
letters. He had. Someone had sorted the mail and piled the
ones for me into a stack. My hands were almost shaking
with excitement, and several letters slipped out of my fingers and fell back onto the table on top of the stack of mail
for Guy. Then the whole pile tipped and slid to the floor.

I try not to read other people's mail. I really do. But
when you're picking up envelopes, your gaze just falls on
them and naturally absorbs information. So when I scooped
up the letters that I dropped, I couldn't help noticing that
Guy Madison had a letter from the government addressed
to Mr. Gaylord Madison. I knew from my years as an accountant that the envelope was the kind the IRS uses to
send refund checks. Why, I wondered, had he had that kind
of mail sent to the office? Then I noticed his name. Gaylord! No wonder he went by Guy.

I plucked the letters off the table and hurried back to my

desk. I decided to open them right then. That way I could
work on my column and my replies all Sunday.

The first letter I opened was written on violet stationery
edged with tiny forget-me-nots. The handwriting was medium-sized and carefully done. All the *i*'s were dotted exactly over the letters and the *t*'s were crossed halfway up.
I wondered if it was significant. It read.

Dear Stella,
I have a problem and I need your advice. My boyfriend and I are always arguing. We can't agree on
anything. He likes to play basketball and football, I
like reading and gardening.
  He likes to leave his shoes and socks in the living
room, and I say they belong under the edge of the bed.
He likes hot dogs and hamburgers and I like salads
and quiche. We fight about each of these things. I say
we should stop seeing each other, but he says I'm too
rigid and everything would be fine if I'd just "go with
the flow." Who do you think is right? I'm a Virgo
and he's an Aquarian.
  Down in the Dumps

I scrawled a note to myself across the bottom of the
letter. *Incompatible sun signs—nothing in common, ditch
him, look for a Capricorn.* I folded it up and returned it to
the envelope.

The next one I opened was written on inexpensive lined
notepaper. The handwriting was large and loopy and hard
to read.

Dear Stella,
My mother and I fight about my friends all the time.

She says my friends are not good and I say they're fine.

What should I do?

P.S. What is a sun sign? Is it a new kind of sunsuit?

Billy Jo

I didn't have anything to say to that yet, so I refolded it I put it on top of the first envelope.

When I opened the next letter, a snapshot fell out onto desk. The letter was written in a cramped hand, and all letters were spiky looking.

Dear Stella,

I'm a single, great-looking guy who's looking for a groovy, swinging gal, single or married. If you're interested in a great time, call me at 555-1932. I'll be the best you've ever had.

Big Dick—get it?

I got it, and it made me nauseated. I dropped the letter o the wastepaper basket.

"Hey! You get a bad one?"

I jumped a mile in my chair. I hadn't heard Jason come but there he was, halfway across the room and loping vard me.

I nodded and watched him with interest. In spite of his uth and awkwardness, he moved silently and covered the tance in no time. He peered into the wastebasket.

"Mind?" he asked. I shrugged. He pulled the letter out d held it up, then snorted in disgust and threw it back. 'ou get many like this?" he asked.

"No." I pulled the snapshot toward me, using the eraser d of a pencil. "Here's a picture of him." Jason leaned er my shoulder. The photo showed a thick-set man with

hair carefully combed over his forehead. His belly w
girded by a wide belt, held together with an even bigg
belt buckle. It may have been my imagination, but I thoug
the buckle said Dick. All it needed was an arrow pointi
down. I used a tissue to pick it up and dropped them bo
into the wastepaper basket. I hadn't anticipated anythi
like this. I felt dirty and in some way violated.

"You look like you could use a break," Jason sai
"Want to go to a movie?"

I looked at Jason. His never-ending energy and optimis
were welcome after everything I'd been through that da
but a movie didn't appeal. I shook my head.

"Coffee?"

I relented. I swept the opened letters along with tho
not yet read and dumped them into my oversized purse.

We walked to a little café two blocks down the stre
from the *Daily Orion,* where for a dollar you can buy bur
coffee and perch on stools that will break your tail if yo
stay there for longer than thirty minutes. On purpose,
course, to keep customers turning over. I wasn't sure I
be able to move when we left but I plowed ahead.

"Hey!" Jason called out. "Over here." He pointed to
café chair he'd dragged up to a tiny little table. "I'm n
hurting myself on those things," he said, indicating t
stools. He pulled another chair to the table. I think I e
pected him to order me a coffee and get a soda pop f
himself. I felt mildly surprised when he placed two bla
coffees on the table. I tried to analyze why I thought
him as so young. I decided it was because somewhere b
tween eight-thirty this morning when I found Grace a
now, I'd aged.

I focused on my coffee. It was suddenly very hard
think of anything to say.

"So how do you like it?"

'Like what?'' As soon as the words were out, I realized
displayed more feeling than I meant. I stretched my lips
﹥ a phony grin. He looked puzzled.

'The newspaper job,'' he said. ''What else?''

'Nothing else.''

﹞e thought for a moment, then leaned toward me, his
﹒d tilted just a little as though he were speaking to a very
﹒ll, simple child. ''Do you think you might be a little
upset?''

'Upset?!'' I flared. Then I saw the little smile lurking
﹒his eyes. He really did look like Caesar. I could have
﹒ed him on the head, then suddenly my eyes were brim-
﹒g. ''I'm sorry, Jason, I'm really not in a good mood. A
﹒nd of mine was found dead today. Well, really she
﹒n't found dead. I mean she wasn't found, but I think
﹒'s dead. No, I mean, I saw her, almost...'' I clapped my
﹒d over my mouth. I had to stop babbling.

'Heavy,'' he said.

﹒started to protest, ''Actually, Grace is quite light....'' I
﹒iced Jason's astonished expression, I couldn't help
﹒ghing a little. At least it stopped my babble. ''You're
﹒ht, I'm upset. And I'm completely insane. Absolutely
﹒d. To have taken this job.''

'But you didn't take it. You created it. And then you
﹒nanded it. I heard all about it.''

'Well, whatever.'' I ran my tongue over my front teeth,
﹒cking to see if the coffee had eaten away the enamel
﹒. It seemed to be there still. ''What is it you do?''

'Oh, a little of everything. Sell ads, write the socials,
﹒coming events, community events, high school sports,
﹒ obituaries. You wouldn't think a weekly like the *Daily*
﹒*ion* would do obituaries but if you're a subscriber to the
﹒*ion* and your family wants a memorial to you, then the
﹒*ly Orion* is there to do it. I've written so many obituaries

I hear them in my sleep. My last sports story sounded
like an obit.''

"Jason, wait a minute. How does a sports story e
sound like an obituary?''

"They shouldn't, but they do sometimes.'' He gazed
the ceiling, contemplating for a moment.

"'Hopes for a championship for Gilliam High died i
sudden-death overtime in the quarterfinals Saturday ni
against Eastridge. After a hard-fought battle, Gilliam s
cumbed to fatigue and the superior defense of the Eastri
team. Eastridge will go on to the semifinals against W
liams.'

"Compare that to, 'William Z. Zlattner died peacef
in the Everest Peaks Nursing Home Saturday night. He s
cumbed after a long battle against liver cancer. He is s
vived by his wife, Louisa, et cetera.'''

"Oh, horrible. It's a wonder they let you write a
thing.''

"I also covered the Easter parade.''

"I didn't think there was one.''

"There wasn't. That's what I wrote about.''

"There's a real nonstory.''

"That's just what Gerster said, too.'' He looked n
mentarily dejected, then he brightened. "I'm just here g
ting to know the business.''

"Oh. And when you know more about what you w
to do—'' I caught myself before I said "when you gr
up'' "—you'll move on, I suppose.''

"Yeah, something like that. How'd you know?''

I smiled knowingly.

He noticed my coffee was gone. "Want so
more?''

shook my head. "I don't think my tooth enamel will
l up."

Je paid the bill, and then we walked back toward the
ce. "So you and Guy do sort of the same thing?"

"I don't like to think of it that way," he said. His brow
owed. "Actually, Guy is the main reporter; he does
ically all the stories. What he's not interested in, he
ns out to me."

"You okay with that?"

"Yeah, sure. I mean, he's been here for several years.
ows what he's doing."

"But...you don't like him."

Je frowned and kicked at a stone on the sidewalk.
'e're just different." He wanted to change the subject.
ire you don't want to go to a movie?"

"Fantasia?"

Je looked taken aback. "Well, I hadn't been think-
..."

"It's okay, I don't really want to see it, either. I really
it to get home." I thanked him for the coffee and hur-
l to my car.

'luffy was in his cage poised on a twig. I could see he
unhappy. "Longing for a fly, aren't you?" I mur-
red. He blinked. I noticed again how much he resembled
Gerster. "Soon, Fluffy, the flies are just beginning to
ie out now." He looked skeptical.

'eeling guilty for breaking last night's promise to get
a fresh insect, I went to the kitchen and pulled a little
ce of frozen raw steak from the freezer. I sawed off a
e corner, thawed it, and molded it around the end of a
gth of black thread. I spent the next half hour dangling
a front of his disgusted little lizard face until he finally
nted and snarfed it down.

IT WAS BARELY four-thirty Sunday morning by my beds
alarm clock when I woke with a hot sheet twisted aro
my legs. Sweaty, sticky, and irritable, I sat up, pulled
the sheet until it was undone, and tried to remember w
I'd been dreaming that had seemed so important o
minutes before.

Had I been running? I didn't think so, but something
made my heart thump in the dark, some image
wouldn't quite come in out of the dark.

I turned on the lamp at the side of my bed. The curt
at the window blew gently in the early predawn breeze
the yard below, the neighbor's cat moaned and made
hair stand up in a chill. It was a sound that brought
ghosts out of the closet.

I slumped down in the bed, pulling the covers and
sheet straight over my head, then turned the edge down
under my chin so I could feel the cool fold of cotton
my neck. The long down body pillow lay in the center
the bed, and I snuggled up to it. It wasn't the same as Ri
but that was okay. A lot of things weren't the same, I
minded myself, and closed my eyes. Most of them w
for the good.

Rick was a long and meaningful chapter of my life
I had carefully and thoughtfully closed. I made fun of
and myself frequently to relieve the loss, I think. Or ma
just because I have a twisted sense of humor at times.
maybe because I don't believe in living in a land of regr
There is no returning on most things, and I believe you
have to live with it.

Cut your losses.

Rick was definitely a loss. But even now, as I lay in
cool safety of my own room—one that he has never e
laid eyes on because I changed my residence, my job,

ne, and the locks on my front door, my bedroom door,
l my heart all at the same time—I missed him. Just a
e bit.

And I still wasn't entirely sure just what in particular set
ff.

'd wanted the relationship to work out, or work into,
ichever. So I'd made adjustments, compromises. All of
ich you have to do to some extent. But in the end I had
npromised myself away. And that didn't leave much for
:k to love and almost nothing for me.

turned over, leaving the soft side of the pillow, curling
) a comfortable solitary figure. Sometimes in the early-
rning misties as I think of them, I can get entirely too
occupied with the more ethereal things I'm facing. This
e I found myself drifting gently in a semidream state
) a memory lane that was bittersweet. I didn't like it; it
s leading to more introspection than I was prepared to
ke then. I turned over.

The cold truth of it was that I'd broken off my relation-
p with Rick because he'd been seeing another woman
he same time and I'd known it and had begun to accept
is the price for having a relationship. I'd lost that much
my own self-respect. And if I'd lost it for myself, then
eventually lose it for everyone else around me. That's
way it goes.

For several—no, for four months—I'd suspected that he
s seeing another woman. When I confronted him, he
mitted it, casually. "Hey, no big deal. I just was in-
;ued, but I'm really in love with you. I'll give her up."
ly he didn't, and I knew it, but—and this is my private
miliation—I looked the other way for a while. I just
In't wanted to believe that I'd invested that much time

and energy in a relationship that was so...so person
worthless.

It's hard to admit to yourself that you can make suc
misjudgment in anyone, much less someone to wh
you've given yourself...in any way.

That was when I realized that the little visions were i
They aren't usually visions, as I've said before. The
like a sudden, overwhelming, *I just know this to be t*.
I've tried for years to put a name or a good descriptio
them, but without any real satisfying success. Most of
time it's a silent whisper in my head, a sudden convic
that I know something. Or it can be just that I look
someone and *know* what they're thinking. It's really
being inside their mind for a moment in time. I've ne
been able to stay there, to know the twists and turns
someone's logic or their history; it's just a thought, a to
of thoughts, and then it's gone.

I don't know for sure whether I tune in on some ti
warp in the future or whether I see someone's plan for
future.

I pulled the pillow closer. It's always at this point th
start to get the chills, feel scared and tired, and wish
Rick were still here. He was so down to earth and so
actually stolid and stupid, that he gave me balance.

"Hey, babe, come over here. Don't give me that cr
what you need is a good lay."

Like a hole in the head.

When I'd begun to think in terms of a real hole in
head—and it was his head that I wanted to put the h
in—I broke it all off.

Meredith thought I was holding all my grief in beca
I didn't cry, but that wasn't true. I didn't cry because th
wasn't any reason to. Birth is a time for rejoicing. An

rebirth. I didn't need to waste my tears on a relationship
at didn't mean anything to Rick. So that was one reason
decided to make a major change. I told the world I just
eded to have a change.

The other thing in my life that held meaning at that time
d been my job. I'd become an accountant because that
as a naturally easy thing for me to do, and because it
dered the universe in a neat package of credit and debit.
I worked really hard, I could make all the figures add
. Now that's a neat trick.

Anyone who can manage their world in a way that makes
nse in black-or-white terms of dollars in and dollars out
ould be on their way to comfort. Only it doesn't work
at way. The structure of accounting, the idea of arranging
e cosmos in tidy terms that one can manipulate, formu-
e, control, and predict, is wonderful. And it's an illusion,
anyone who has lived in this world for longer than ten
conds ought to know.

But as I said. The illusion was powerful. The security of
predictable, controllable world is a powerful trap. It was
accident that I left accounting when I did. I had grad-
lly become aware that someone in the firm was syphon-
g off company profits a cent or two a transaction, from
r clients and our employers.

I'm actually a thorough person, not necessarily brilliant
all, but careful. I like it when the columns match. When
checked several of my transactions one week after they
ere completed, I found that there were differences of a
w cents. This sounds very minor, but in a big house, it
ds up to a lot of money. It's not a new kind of theft. Just
t mentioned much because, of course, solid financial in-
tutions don't want to spread panic, but it is a problem
at they've been alert to for some time. I just never ex-

pected real theft to be that close to home. I was the scap
goat of this scam.

I had a *sense* that something was terribly wrong.
checked my savings account and found some discrepanci
in the accruing of the interest. Not enough to be suspicio
under ordinary circumstances, but added up it was plen
And it looked like I had done it.

The thief underestimated me. This was the first time
discovered that what I had was a genuine ability to sn
my way into trouble. I was good at it. I got into a bunc
of trouble. I'm not sure I'd have been able to get out
that trouble if I hadn't relied on this "sense" that I had
what was happening.

Security was alerted. The culprit was thwarted. I
wasn't actually identified because the theft couldn't
traced. But I *knew* who did it. I couldn't prove it, still can
But I stopped him. And then I left the job. I just decid
that the world didn't really fit into columns, it still was
predictable, and it was time for a change. A big one.

So out with the old job, out with the old boyfriend, a
just to be complete, I moved to a new apartment.

Sunday morning was cold and dark, with early clou
covering the eastern sky. They would burn off before noc
A fly bounced against the windowpane, and I remember
my promise to Fluffy. Within minutes I'd snatched the f
unsuspecting insect off the windowpane and shaken him
disorient him and dropped him into Fluffy's cage. Fluf
blinked his thanks.

I shuddered. I remembered what my dream had been. I
dreamt that I was wading in a stream at the bottom of
small, narrow ravine. When I looked down at the bubbli
water, I discovered that the stream was blood red.

SEVEN

SUNDAY MORNING had come very early, and I was tired, but once I'd remembered that gruesome dream, I didn't want to risk any more sleep. I tried to distract myself first with rockabilly music, and then with Beethoven, but it was nearly impossible to shake off the weight of the blood red image. I think that's why I lost my appetite for strawberry jam on my toast that morning.

Even the thick Sunday papers weren't enough of a distraction. As I read, I wondered where Grace's body was. And I remembered her house, her yappy little dog, and the gardens waiting to be planted.

I called Meredith as soon as it was eight o'clock, but she wasn't up to more than a muffled curse and a feeble promise to call back. "He's wonderful," she mumbled and dropped the receiver back on the hook.

Fluffy was snoozing after his fly, and I knew calling Mother would only provoke an invitation to accompany her to church, which I'd refuse, and then she would *tsk* for the safety and future of my soul.

Finally, I remembered the unread letters from yesterday and spread them out on the kitchen table. They lay before me like a kind of Norwegian Sunday-morning smorgasbord...a table full of the most unexpected, unusual, and exciting things. I started with the one on top.

Reading them was an entertainment all its own. The vast majority of them were from people wanting to know what kind of man would be the best lover and/or mate. A smaller,

but still significant, number were from people interested
making money…like the one I read about midway throug

Dear Stella,
I've just inherited ten thousand dollars and I want to
invest it so that it will grow and become a fortune as
soon as possible. I'm a Leo, birth date July 31, 1960,
3:30 a.m. I need to know when would be the best time
to invest according to the stars and what I should invest in. Please don't publish this in your column, it
could make things awkward in my family.
   Thanks, Brenda P.O. Box 130 Arvada, CO 80220-
2013

I wondered if it was a sibling or her husband from who
she was hiding her inheritance and set that one in the pi
of those who wanted a brief horoscope reading of son
sort.
A few letters have a certain twang to them, a certa
something that sets them apart and makes them just diffe
ent enough that they stand out…either because I get a sp
cial sense from them or they clearly say something th
stands out.
Two stood out in this batch. The first was this one:

Stella,
I know what people like you do. You sneak inside
people's minds and try to read there [sic] thoughts.
People like you make me sick. You better not try to
get inside mine, because I'll know it. There's no moral
swamp in my brain for you to hide in and I'll catch
you. So get out of my head.

It's really hard for me to think of what to say to people
ke this, so I put the letter in a pile of its own.

The second one was this one:

Dear Stella,

I couldn't wait for your reply. I just had to write again.
The most wonderful thing has happened. The man I've
loved for all these years, the one I thought was out of
reach, has confessed to me that he loves me. He loves
me!!! Stella you cannot imagine what happiness I feel.
How much and how long I have wanted to hear him
say those simple words, to hold me in his arms, to feel
his breath on my neck, his voice in my ears. My cup
runneth over.

    With love in my heart,
    Looking for Lochinvar (and I found him)

I felt a cold, clammy sweat break out on my face, neck,
d arms. There was something so unearthly about this let-
r, like the other one from Looking for Lochinvar. She
uld not have known what my second reply to her would
. It hadn't come out in the paper, yet she had found her
ve among her circle of friends. Could I really see the
ture? I didn't know whether to be happy or scared. I
ttled for both.

The insistent ringing of my telephone broke through my
veat. The receiver was cold and a little slippery against
y palm, and there was the slightest quaver in my voice
hen I said hello.

It was Meredith, and her voice was warm, welcome, and
mforting. Frankly, looking back at it, I think an ax mur-
rer's voice would have sounded warm and welcoming at
at moment because I was really having a spell. But as I
id, fortunately, it was Meredith. She'd had a wonderful

time the night before with her new date, and she talked o
and on about his merits, mental, and his assets, physical-
as opposed to monetary, in which Meredith has never bee
particularly interested.

"We're going out again tonight. Oh, you can't imagin
how nice he is. He's such a gentleman. He said he wante
to take it slow, just a kiss for the first night. He doesn
want to rush it."

She described this paragon as "Mr. Wonderful," th
man she's been searching for, "kind, sensitive, strong, d
cisive, charming, dashing." Dashing, she actually used th
word *dashing*.

"Meredith," I said. I felt compelled to inject at least
little realism into this saccharine swamp. "There must b
a hitch. Why isn't he married already, if he's so wonde
ful."

"He says he's been waiting for the right woman."

"So how many has he tried out?"

"Oh, for crying out loud!"

"'Crying out loud'? 'Crying out loud'! First you're u
ing the word dashing, now you're saying 'crying out loud'
What's happened to you? Where are your old, familiar e
pressions? Are you dating someone from the thirties?"

"I'm trying to clean up my act."

Or, I thought as I rang off somewhat later, *changing* h
act. I tried to picture Meredith as a proper old-fashion
girl on a bicycle-built-for-two, but it just wouldn't com
From previous experience with Meredith's heartthrobs,
figured this one was definitely more serious than her othe
especially if she was actually going all out after just on
date. Maybe she had found Mr. Wonderful. I certain
hoped so for her sake, since that was her current goal
life.

And that brought me back to my current goal in li

hich was to write such a wonderful column that it would
t syndicated and earn me enough money to maintain my-
lf.

To that end, I flung myself back in the chair at the
tchen table and worked on the letters. The letters fell into
veral natural categories: those who wanted a brief horo-
ope reading or interpretation, those who wanted to pour
t their lonely hearts, those who wanted advice (a sur-
isingly small number), and those that were weird.

I've been casting horoscopes for several years now, but
n fairly slow and methodical, so it takes me longer than
lot of people.

The first horoscope was the letter from Brenda, who
anted to know when the best time to invest would be.

Time slips by when I'm absorbed in something. It was
ening, and the light in the kitchen had begun to fail when
next noticed. At that point I had finished most of the
ters...except the Lochinvar one, which I had put aside.

I reread my response to Brenda:

Your sign, Leo, is a fire sign, and yours is a regal,
dramatic, even bold, aspect. At your birth Mars was
in Taurus, which forecasts that you will do well financially, either through your own efforts or even through
inheritance! People with this planet position tend to do
well handling and investing money, but they also tend
to become depressed or bad tempered with losses.

Saturn in Capricorn influences people to be ambi-
tious, determined, and hard-working. Negatively, they
may become suspicious, fearful, melancholy, and dis-
satisfied with their progress.

Jupiter in Sagittarius at your birth indicates a sharp
mind, expansive outlook, and a craving for excitement,
change, and/or travel. The position of Mercury at your

birth bestowed excellent managerial skills and ability, so that you possess the ability to run your own business. The synthesis of all your birth signs indicates that *where* you put your money is more important than *when*. I recommend that you contact a reputable financial adviser and discuss the possibility of investment in your own business, such as a travel agency, or another enterprise that will combine your talent for management, hard work, and personal gain.

I decided that I'd been pretty long-winded, but since was going in a letter and not in the column, I left it. Th letters that were not going in the column I responded personally. It occurred to me that it would be wise to kee a file of the letters and a copy of my reply in each case. wouldn't take long to make files tomorrow, and it wou give me something to do…a sort of legitimate way to crea the illusion of action.

It was now seven o'clock and I realized that the hole my stomach was due to lack of food. Grazing through th refrigerator was distinctly unappetizing. The only thing th looked vaguely edible was some leftover hamburger a chili bean mixture that I had fixed for taco salad a few da ago. It had been delicious then; right now it looked ju like dog food.

As soon as I thought of dog food, I thought of that yapp little dog at Grace's. I wondered if he'd been fed, watere and let out. Of course, Adoree—her sister—would ha done something for him, wouldn't she?

I closed the refrigerator door and thought about it. Al could think about was how hungry I felt and that the po little guy would be feeling just as hungry and twice lonely if he hadn't been fed.

I figured the neighbor would have a key and would kn

her someone had come by. Grace definitely impressed
as the sort to leave a key with her neighbor. I had also
n some more thought to where I might find a key hid-

Denver, late spring—early May to be exact—is a time
a the days are long and twilight hangs on long after
un has slipped behind the wall of mountains. Grace's
nborhood basked in an amber-colored Sunday-evening
, the sort of quiet that says that everyone is either in
family room munching popcorn and watching "Mur-
She Wrote" or in their car on I-70 still coming in from
y in the mountains. All the houses but one had at least
rosily glowing window. Grace's home was dark.

pulled my car to a stop directly in front of the house
walked to the front door. The doorbell sounded even
loudly this time, probably because of the greater sur-
ding quiet. The dog barked just as ferociously, or at
nearly so. I thought I detected the faintest note of thirst
starvation in his little *yapyapyapyapyap!*

ere was no answer other than the dog's bark. A sliver
ght leaked out of the neighbor's window. I could feel
urious eyes on my shoulders.

mbled over. At my second knock the front door swung
, and I gazed into curious eyes. I smiled.

can't help you one bit," she said. The unmistakable
of Scotch whisky drifted my way.

eld up a hand, like a Hollywood movie Indian.

Grace's dog. Has anyone been around to feed him?"

No one's been here since yesterday, not since her sister
by. Ackshually, not since you came by. Not that
e seen." She was weaving just a little.

'm afraid she's depending on me to feed it." What's
le lie in a good cause?

My husband thought he saw someone in the yard last

night late, but by the time he called the police to c
check, no one was there.'' She peered at me with perple
slightly watery eyes. She had a way of ending her s
ments with a lift of her voice that made me think she
checking to see if it was all right to say what she'd sa
wanted to reassure her it was okay to breathe.

"So Grace didn't arrange with you to feed him?''

"Oh, no. No. No, Grace wouldn't do that. I'm a
gic…to the dog.'' *At the very least,* I thought.

"So, you wouldn't have a key to her house, by
chance, would you?'' I brushed at an imaginary hair o
leg of my jeans. This truth-stretching was making me
comfortable.

"She didn't give you one? I'd have thought she w
if she wanted you to feed Saunci.''

"That's the problem, we didn't really get to straig
that all out. I'm just worried that the dog will die wit
food and water.'' I put on a pitiful face. "I just cou
bear it if Saunci died.'' I stared at her with my best g
inducing look.

"Oh, well. That's true. There's nothing worse than a
dying in the house. I mean, to come home to a
dog…well, it would be…awkward…at least…maybe
She mercifully quit talking, came to a decision, and
on her heel. "I'll be right back,'' she flung over her s\
der.

When she returned, she handed me a key with a
strand of orange yarn attached to it. "It fits the back do
she said nervously. "I'd be glad to go over there, but
understand, I'm allergic.''

I nodded sympathetically. "That's okay.''

I peeked in the window of the back door as I turne
key in the lock. I couldn't see her, but I heard her. Sa

d on her little hind legs, pawing the door, snarling, and
ing. I knew her little eyes were beady and hostile.

turned the knob and pushed the door open a mere inch.
teeth gleamed at me. Pointy, sharp little teeth. For the
time I realized that she wasn't just funning with me.
little animal was prepared to bite. A lot.

Maybe, I thought, I should return tomorrow when star-
on and thirst would make her lethargic. She snarled
erically. I pulled the door shut again. I looked over my
ulder. The neighbor's head was silhouetted in her
hen window, watching. I waved at her with reassuring
chalance and wondered what I'd do next.

My gaze caught on the garden spade; little clods of earth
g to the blade. I reached to touch them. They were dry
crumbled away from my fingertips. Then I noticed the
of old-fashioned rubber gardening boots.

was surprised to find that Grace's feet were as big as
e when I pulled on the boots.

his time I turned the knob, pushed open the door with
fidence, and thrust my right foot inside. Pointy teeth
ped hard on the ankle of the rubber boot. Snarls issued
between her jaws. I stepped inside and dragged the
, now latched to my right rubber boot. My triumphant
faded to a throat lump as I watched her pathetically
g to protect Grace and the house.

h Lord, I thought. This was no time to cry.

tried to say something soothing to the dog, but only a
y grunt came forth, so I dragged my foot with the
ling, head-shaking animal locked onto it into the
hen. In the meat drawer I discovered a white butcher's
r package, inside of which were two scrumptious filet
nons. The only other item in the drawer was a scrappy-
ing piece of red snapper...not my favorite fish. I hated
acrifice filet mignon, so I offered Saunci the fish. She

renewed her bite on my ankle. One of her teeth pierce‑
side of the boot.

"Here!" I thrust one of the filet mignons toward
nose. She hesitated momentarily, then clamped her s
little teeth on the steak and, still snarling, took it to her
in the corner. I found a bowl and filled it with water
offered it to her. She snarled in appreciation.

I edged away from her and into the dining room.
table was set for two, with cloth napkins. Cloth meant ‑
pany in my book. The sterling silver flatware, Lenox ‑
plates, and champagne flutes meant company and a
bration. New candles in the candle holders hinted at
mantic evening.

The living room was tidy, tasteful, and had wilting ‑
ers in a vase, roses.

I wandered back to the hallway to her bedroom. T‑
were two bedrooms. One had been converted to a se‑
room and was filled with half-finished pieces of lin‑
and bits of lace and satin ribbon. An old electric se‑
machine stood on a table against the far wall. Wh‑
switched on the light, I noticed there was no dust or
machine and it was threaded with an elegant peach-co‑
thread.

Her bedroom was at the back of the house. Simple
most austere, it contained an antique armoire and a m‑
ing double bedstead with an exquisite hand-stitched
as a bedspread. I checked the pillows beneath the ‑
Fresh, ironed pillowcases, embroidered with glossy v‑
thread.

In her closet a peach-colored gauze-and-lace confe‑
shimmered from the front hanger. Before I realized
was happening, my fingers were stroking the delicate
ice. This thing would make a fishwife look appetizin‑
didn't take any special powers to figure this out. We‑

egligee and a lover's smile on her lips, Grace would
goddess.

rned, leaned against the bedroom wall, and slid gently
e floor. My knees felt wobbly and my stomach
ed. The words in the last letter from Looking for
invar echoed in my head, and a clammy sweat broke
n my forehead.

EIGHT

GRACE WAS LOOKING for Lochinvar. Her intense intere
my astrology, my column, the quick flash of friendship
had developed in the last two years into a warm, recip
relationship...I should have been able to see through
letters. If I had just been more alert and thoughtful. I
have warned her...maybe prevented this awful thing. It
my column, my advice that had spurred her on. I tho
my heart would break.

Saunci gobbled the steak and lapped the water like
was starved. Then she padded around after me and fi
began to wag her tail. I'm not sure why it mattered t
that the dog liked me, but it did.

It also mattered to me that we find Grace. I knew
wasn't just off on a pleasure trip somewhere. Some
was dreadfully wrong. I was convinced that I'd seen h
my spell and I'd seen her in the shop when she was act
killed.

For me, the proof was Saunci being left without
and water or a caretaker, one more indication that C
had planned to be home.

I seemed to be the only one worried about her. A
was very worried. An internal clock was ticking; w
didn't know for certain was whether it was already too

I looked for anything that would tell me about her
friends, about people she might have confided in, abou
man she was seeing.

I found Grace's personal address book next to the
phone and paged through it. In her careful hand she

ted Adoree's phone number and address. I wondered if
called her sister so infrequently that she needed to look
the number, or if she put it in just to have an entry in
otherwise sparse book. I found Lilly's name in the
l-N section, but no last name, just an address and phone
ber. The name Mandy was penciled in with a phone
ber beside it and the word *temp*. If I remembered right,
ndy was temporary help in the shop. I noted these down
a scrap of paper from my purse.

When I paged through a second time, I found Grace had
d my first name and phone number in the *I-J-K* section.
ciled after that was "Stella" and the newspaper's PO
number.

wondered if Detective Stokowski would want to know
her house looked empty and abandoned...if it would
e any difference in his investigation. Maybe it would
ire him to work harder and faster. I picked up the
ne, dialed police headquarters, and asked for Stokowski.
voice on a message informed me that he was not at his
but I could leave a message. I did.

aunci pawed the back door, then brought me her leash
hint, so we went outside for a stroll. This time at the
I noticed a dried puddle where she'd gone in desper-
n. Sympathy flooded through me, and I reached to pat
pitiful head. She bit me. There was a damn good reason
the neighbor wouldn't take care of her.

aunci sniffed every square inch of yard, savoring all her
gy odors and past leavings. The evening breeze re-
ded me of water running over stones and the dream I'd
, but I couldn't think of a single streambed I was fa-
ar with. Saunci finally did her business, scratched the
s, and trotted over wagging her tail. I bent to pat her.
bit me again. Only a nip this time.

he bounced away from me, dashed around the yard, and

finally stopped at a flower bed. She yipped and stuck
nose in the dirt. She sniffed and snorted. Sneezed dirt. T
began to paw frantically in the heaped-up dirt.

A chill rose on my arms. I did not want this dog to
anything. And I had an idea of what she might find.

I scooped her up and raced inside. The door had ba
banged shut when I grabbed the telephone and punche
the numbers for the police department. A bored nasal v
answered. Saunci whined and wriggled in my grasp.

"I've got to talk to Detective Stokowski. Or some
who can help me. Please, hurry." I dropped the dog,
yipped and snarled. "I know it's Sunday evening. But
an emergency."

I'd like to think that all the commotion convinced
operator I really needed help. I'd like to think that beca
otherwise there's no redeeming value at all to the third
I got from Saunci. This one bled and I had to wipe i
my jeans to keep it from dripping on the carpet.

A squad car pulled up in about three minutes. This ne
borhood had a lot going for it.

I put Saunci in the bathroom before I opened the
to the officers. They listened very sympathetically. I
decided before the officers arrived that it would be har
explain that I knew Grace was dead when we couldn't
her body at all, so I repeatedly referred to it as Stokows
case and begged them to call him.

These two officers were like a well-married couple: T
could communicate unspoken paragraphs in one mean
ful glance. The tall one went to the squad car and s
time with his radio. The other stayed with me. I offe
but he declined to have Saunci demonstrate the diggin

Conversation was stilted to say the least, and it see
like hours before the tall one returned. His expression
impossible to read. They must teach flat affect in p

chool. They discussed something and ended up telling me
hat we would be waiting; Detective Stokowski decided to
:in us.

Throughout this time Saunci had scratched without ceas-
ng on the bathroom door. Her toenails had to be worn to
he nubs. This time I didn't ask, I just let her out of the
athroom, and as she bolted forth, I stepped on her trailing
each so that she couldn't attack the officers. I needn't have
vorried.

Saunci skidded to a stop in front of them, snarling and
napping. She couldn't decide which one to go for, so she
tood her ground at a safe distance and held them at bay.
t would have been funny if Grace had been there and if
ny hand hadn't hurt so much.

The tall officer asked me to go over my story again. He'd
egun to realize that there were holes in my explanations.
When for the third time I tried to explain the need for me
o get into Grace's house to feed the dog, Stokowski
howed up. At least *he* wanted to see the dog dig.

It turned out to be a long night.

After a brief interlude while Saunci checked her favorite
pots, she dug fervently until she had a hole about a foot
leep and wide. Then she wrestled a glove out of the
ground.

Unfortunately she didn't want to give it up.

Stokowski finally prized it free from her iron jaws, put
t into a plastic Ziploc bag, and stuffed it into his jacket
ocket. We waited for a while to see if Saunci would dig
n another place, but she lost interest altogether and stood
n the back step by the door, whining pitifully.

Stokowski had asked questions to which I not only had
o answers, I hadn't even thought of the questions. Such
hings as, what was Grace's financial state, did she have

children, had she been married before, where did she go o
vacation, did she have a vacation home?

"Let me get this straight. You and Grace are friends, bu
you have trouble remembering her last name when I as
you. Nevertheless, you and she are buddies, and she aske
you to take care of her dog."

"She didn't ask me to do it, I just knew that if she wasn'
back someone would need to. And no one had. The neigh
bor says the dog's too mean. She bites her."

"It looks like she bites you." He eyed my jeans wher
I'd wiped the blood from my hand.

"He's not very good at relationships."

It got a little sticky.

He let me go because I have a basically honest face. O
maybe because there was no body, and therefore n
crime...yet. Or maybe he just believed me because
showed him the dog bite. Anyway, I had plenty of time t
think while I waited in the emergency room at Denver Gen
eral Hospital for a tetanus shot.

It would have gone more smoothly there if I hadn't aske
the night clerk if I could run down to the morgue while
was waiting to see if there were any unidentified femal
bodies that I might know. At that point I heard her whispe
to the head nurse that a social work consult would be
good idea. At first I was insulted, then I kind of wishe
they'd called for one. I needed someone to talk to, an
social workers are generally good listeners.

I had begun to think I'd die of rampant old age befor
they finally called my name, rolled up my sleeve, an
jabbed me with the needle.

I tried to call Meredith while I was still at Denver Gen
eral but she must have been out. That raised a new anxiet
in my growing pool of things to worry about. It seemed t
me that she'd gone completely overboard for this new in

erest, something that she usually didn't do. If anything, Meredith was usually pretty detached and levelheaded about men, able to distance herself and see the relationship pretty objectively. This time, she seemed too totally taken with this man. I hadn't even remembered to ask his name.

All told it was a very depressing evening. However, I had learned Adoree's address and phone number, and the name of her husband. Nathanial Foster.

The next morning, Monday, the key to Grace's house was burning a guilty hole in my pocket. I'd been through that house as thoroughly as I knew how, but I still had the feeling that I'd missed something.

When I gave Fluffy his wax worm, I told him about Saunci and how I'd left her at Grace's. Frankly, nothing short of a million dollars would have persuaded me to bring the beast home, but I wondered if she'd lapped up all the water from her dish. She was too short to drink from the toilet, and anyway the toilet seat cover had been down. I left a note to Grace on the door of the fridge asking her to call me as soon as she got home, but I knew I wouldn't hear from her. Guilt was eating at me. I should have been able to warn her.

Jason didn't have enough to do that morning, so he hung around my desk. Actually, he just sat at his own desk, which was next to mine, but it felt as if he was intruding on my space. When I glanced at him from beneath my eyelashes, I found he was staring at me. When he smiled, it was as if he was covering up something. At some point I realized I was getting paranoid, but just because I was paranoid didn't mean it wasn't real.

I became restless with a sense of foreboding. Waiting for the other shoe to fall is how my mother would have put it. I couldn't decide whether I should wait in case the police called or go out and try to find her. I compromised. I

walked around the newspaper office on zillions of unnec
essary trips.

During one of my many strolls I passed Guy's desk and
noticed that the stack of mail that had been waiting for him
on Saturday was gone. In its place was a short stack of pink
message slips.

I really didn't mean to read his slips.

I didn't even bump his desk, but someone must have
walked by very fast, and the wind from their passing must
have blown that stack around. I was afraid that if I didn't
tidy it up, he might miss a message or two. I didn't exactly
read them, but I did notice that his wife had left a message
at eight-thirty that morning. I could taste disgust. I remembered that IRS envelope. Two to one he'd had it sent to
the newspaper office so he could hide the money from her.

Then I looked a little closer. His wife hadn't left a message. Zelda had. She'd written "Wife called..." I wondered why his wife would call but not leave a message,
especially so early. If he wasn't home at eight-thirty in the
morning and he wasn't here, then where was he?

I didn't have enough to do. And I couldn't seem to concentrate on anything useful.

Somewhere around ten o'clock Guy drifted into the office with a shadow on his chin and bags beneath his eyes.
He looked as if he'd been up all night, and I asked Jason
if Guy had a big story. The *Denver Daily Orion* doesn't
have big stories, of course. Jason shrugged and said it had
been quiet.

"What's his wife's name?"

"Why are you whispering?"

"Where do they live?"

He shrugged as though he didn't know, but his right
eyebrow went up like he was apologizing. I figured he

new but didn't want to tell me. As a course of basic information, Jason was a dud.

"What on earth would you do if either of them showed
up missing and the police asked you for that very information?" He frowned and looked at me as though I'd asked
him something peculiar. But I was thinking about all the
questions Stokowski had asked me about Grace, and how
I didn't know much at all about her. I wished I had called
the morgue and asked about unidentified female persons.

Jason gave up. He looked at me with bewildered eyes.
"I think I'll go write those obituaries Mr. Gerster assigned
to me."

"The *Daily Orion* really does obituaries? I thought you
were joking."

"If the person is a *known*, local, a longtime subscriber—"

"And you need an excuse to leave? Are you going to
the morgue?" The words were out before I could stop
them.

"Why would I go there? Nobody there talks."

"Right. I know that."

A HUNDRED YEARS went by before lunchtime came, and
then when I finally went to Fanny's TakeOut my appetite
disappeared before I could decide what to order.

Grace's key was in my wallet and right next to it was
the scrap of paper with the addresses I'd copied down from
Grace's address book. So I took a drive in my car.

Little Nothings was closed, but it always was on Mon-
days, so that was no surprise. I wondered how Lilly was
holding up and if she'd thought of anything that would help
us locate Grace.

Actually, I wondered if she would show signs of extreme
guilt, like lack of sleep, red eyes, nervousness, manic de-

pression. All the things you think of when you remembe *Crime and Punishment.* Since I had her address fro Grace's book, I decided that it would be worthwhile goir to see her.

She lived in a modest, one-story brick bungalow bui sometime in the thirties, of the sort that populates much o Denver. The lawns in this area are all trimmed, but n with the precision I'd seen in Grace's neighborhood. In th area all the wives worked, and needed to. Lilly's car stoc in the driveway. I pulled to a stop in front of her house.

There were little signs of neglect about the house. Th steps to the porch were warped, and the front door scree was bent and ragged. Any self-respecting housefly woul be inside in a minute. The drapes were still pulled acros the front window, giving the house a sleepy, depresse look.

It took Lilly a while to answer my knock on the doo and when she finally pulled open the door, I could see flicker of surprise cross her face. Her eyes were pink an slightly swollen as though she'd wept recently. Just lookin at her, I felt grief well up inside me, too. At the same tim a small voice inside me reminded me that Lilly might hav a very good motive for killing Grace. The shop.

She waited for me to speak.

"I just stopped by to see if you've heard anything from Grace."

She shook her head, hesitated, then pushed the stor door open. She was wearing jeans and a worn red-flanne shirt with a red-and-white bandanna tied at her throat. Eve at home in her grubbies, she was a coordinated woman wit a wrinkle-hiding scarf.

I followed her into a pleasant living room with a bric fireplace along the far wall. The walls were painted a fai blush color that was almost white but warmer, and a beau

ful beige-and-blue Oriental rug was on the floor. It looked
st like I'd thought her living room would look: tasteful,
fined, and practical.

She led the way to her kitchen, done in coordinated tones
blush and blue. Breakfast dishes were still in the sink. I
dn't see a dishwasher. It was tasteful and well done, but
didn't see evidence of wealth, or even extra cash.

Several snapshots were on the refrigerator, held on by
agnets. I squinted at them. Before I could stop, I sucked
a breath of surprise. Standing between two handsome
enaged boys was Guy Madison.

"These your boys?"

"The one on the right is Jarrod, he's seventeen. The one
n the left is Allan, fourteen." She looked at the pictures
ith me, as though she were seeing them in a new light.
It always surprises me how old they've become."

"And the man in the middle, your husband?" I did my
vel best to sound ordinary and casual. Lilly looked at me
ut of the corner of her eye.

"So they say."

"I..." I stopped before I blurted out anything more.

"I assumed you knew, since you work at the paper."

I shook my head. "Just didn't connect the two of you."

She poured two cups of coffee and pushed a cup toward
ae as she sagged onto a chair. She propped her elbows on
ae table, the sleeves of her shirt falling away from her
rms. A large bruise, green and several days old, was on
er left forearm. I was about to comment on it when she
ised her head and spoke.

"This is all just too much. I can't imagine where Grace
. She's been so, so different lately." Her voice drifted off,
d she took a thoughtful sip of her coffee. I thought she'd
ald her mouth, but she didn't seem to care about the heat.
he rim of my cup was so hot it seared my lower lip. I

puffed across the surface of the coffee and nodded sym
pathetically.

"What do you mean...different?"

She shook her head slowly, her gaze focused on som
small point above the back door.

"Did she mention anything to you about a love inter
est?"

"I don't know what to think," she said, looking at m
as if I might hold the answers.

"Has she ever gone off before? I mean, is this typical?

"Never."

"Do you know of anywhere she could go? Like a secon
house, a condo in the mountains?"

Lilly shook her head, momentarily lost in thought. "Yo
know," she said, thrusting her face close to mine. Tiny fin
wrinkles deepened at the edges of her eyes, little lines tha
underscored the intensity in her voice. "I'd kill any woma
who tried to take Guy away from me."

NINE

TRIED TO display worldly sangfroid, but my coffee cup
rattered in my saucer. I shoved both of my hands deep
into my lap to hide their cowardly tremor and suddenly
understood the meaning of the phrase "an awkward moment." There really wasn't anything else to say. I couldn't
possibly reassure her that Guy was on the straight and narrow, because it had been my clear impression that he was
out hunting. Meredith had noticed it last Friday in the office.

In a desperate search for a healing word I noticed Lilly's
fingernails, so different from just two days ago when they
were lacquered brilliant red. Today they were ragged and
stained with a tinge of earth. Or coffee. It was just possible,
I reminded myself, that she had sat all morning with her
hands in a cold cup of coffee to get that certain disgusting
brownish stain.

"Planning a garden this year?" I remembered now that
she had brought in extra zucchini last summer. In my mind,
"extra" and "zucchini" are redundant, but I understand
there are people who pay cash money for them in the grocery stores.

Lilly was startled by the change in topic but rose to the
challenge. She pushed back her chair abruptly and went to
the back door. I followed. Lilly had started to climb the
ladder of suspicious behavior.

Her backyard showed signs of recent work. My gaze
rushed to the sides of the yard. Along each side fence was
a flower bed with freshly turned earth. Both beds were

about a coffin length each, I calculated. Enough for tw
bodies. I wondered if she had the strength to haul a bo
out of a car into one of these makeshift graves. In the mi
dle of the night, a desperate woman like the one who ha
just told me she'd kill anyone who tried to take her G
might be able to do it. What Guy had that would inspi
such devotion was a mystery to me. On the other han
Guy easily had the muscle. I wondered if he'd cover up f
Lilly.

Murmuring some platitude, I made an escape. Lil
seemed relieved to see me out, and I was relieved to g
into the warming sunshine. That house had a creeping ch
that was hard to fend off. Even outside in the backyar
there had been a depressing pall.

An alleyway ran behind her house, and I decided to dri
through at a hopefully non-attention-getting speed for a
other look. I wasn't fond of Lilly, and it was fairly easy
think of her digging a grave. It was a lot harder to imagi
her killing someone and lugging them into her backyar
That might account for the bruising I'd seen on her arr
And the bandanna may have been to cover damnin
scratches. I craned my neck to see into her backyard. Th
bushes that overgrew the back fence effectively hid the ya
from view. At night, I thought, with no moon, late, whe
everyone was asleep...

The neighbor's Doberman pinscher bounded up to th
fence, woofing wildly. My hand jerked the steering whe
to the side, and the car swerved toward a brick garage.
hauled on the wheel and straightened it out before I h
anything, but a mist of sweat broke out on my forehea
Every one of the dog's teeth was huge and white and shar
and his bark was loud enough to rattle my bones. Mayb
it wouldn't be so easy to bury anyone in the yard at nigh
Unless the dog slept inside.

As I turned into the street from the alley and drove
through the intersection, I saw a car that looked vaguely
familiar pull into the street half a block behind me. The
visor was down in the front window, even though we were
proceeding north away from the sun. It was very suspicious.
I decided to try a diversionary tactic. I stopped at Sammy's
Subway for a snack and a chance to gather my wits. The
car drove on by.

In the air-conditioned cool of the sandwich shop I ordered a bite to eat and took a seat at a table by the window.
The car I had seen earlier cruised by, going south this time,
and turned the corner. Then it reappeared going the other
way. The visor screened the driver's face, but he was wearing a jacket that looked like a gray blur.

My sandwich arrived.

I was halfway through it with tomato falling through my
fingers and mustard smeared across my face when Jason
sauntered in, wearing a gray tweed jacket. Even in a haze
from the food craze it occurred to me that it was too much
to be a coincidence.

Jason slouched over to the table and sank into the chair
opposite me. My "appestat" flashed warning lights inside
my head, and I lowered the remains of my sandwich to my
plate. It no longer held appeal. Jason smiled loosely. To
my very jaundiced eye his lips had taken on a killer's cruel
twist.

"Hi!" he said.

This was no time to be hasty and choke. I chewed slowly
and swallowed carefully. "So how were the obituaries?"

Jason's gaze dropped guiltily to the tabletop while he
played with a spoon, tapping it restlessly against the For-
mica surface. The waitress at the counter looked at us and
raised an eyebrow. I shook my head. She shrugged and
turned away.

"I, uh, need to talk to you."

"So, talk."

"There weren't any obituaries."

"Really!"

"Yeah, I lied." He had that earnest golden retriever lo
again and I could feel myself melting. A few more minu
and he could tell me he ate canaries for breakfast and t
the wings off butterflies and I'd have said, "How lovely
He had the appeal of a lost child in a snowstorm, and I w
ready virtually to hold out my hand to him when he turn
his head and looked uncomfortably out the window.

Beneath his right jawbone was a long raking scra
across his neck. It looked like a fingernail scratch...the ki
a woman gives in the midst of a desperate fight. I felt
muscle strings in my back and neck clench, and it got ha
to push the breath in and out of my lungs regularly.

"Jason," I said. My voice was louder than I had
tended, and his gaze darted back to me, startled.

"Jason, what happened to your neck?"

His hand went immediately to the scratch. "Oh," he sa
and laughed. "Playing volleyball. Bad, huh?"

"Volleyball?"

"In Wash Park. Yesterday. Rough game."

"Washington Park?"

He nodded, staring at the uneaten portion of my san
wich. "You going to eat that?" he asked. I shoved it
him.

"You play with a regular group?"

He shook his head, his mouth full of my sub. A thin li
of mustard rode his upper lip. He swallowed. "Naw. J
joined in with a group that was short a player. I don't ha
a regular."

Washington Park is a large, very popular park in sout

ral Denver. Weekends, there are endless games of vol-
all as long as there is light to play by. A perfect alibi.
e finished the last crust of sandwich, wiped off the
tard, and settled back in his seat.

'Guy told me about your friend being missing,'' he said.
rry about that. I, uh, noticed that you were a little ner-
s.'' He waited for me to respond, but I didn't say any-
g. ''I guess that's why you were talking about the
gue like that.''

'How did Guy know about it?''

'Lilly told him.''

'What did he say?''

'That you were in the shop on Saturday and thought
saw Grace. You called the police.''

he scratch moved up and down on his throat when he
llowed and when he spoke. The surface was scabbed
r and dark red, so it might have been just a day old. Or
ight have been two days old. I made a mental note to
a doctor as soon as I could to ask about dating scabs
scratches...and bruises.

'I thought you didn't know Guy very well.''

'Well, uh, I know him a little.''

'I thought you didn't know his wife's name.''

'Oh, well. It just slipped my mind. You know how that

did. But I didn't admit it.

'He said you think Grace is...that something happened
er.''

'I think she's been murdered.'' I hadn't meant to say
; the words just fell out, strange and cold. And I felt
the world had turned dark and sour in an instant. Say-
it made it so much more real. Jason's mouth opened in
rise. He didn't say anything, he simply stared at me
n a peculiar, intense look in his eyes. I didn't know

whether to bolt from the door and run away or to [?]
planted in my chair where a waitress could call the p[?]
if Jason turned into a snarling, murderous villain [?]
reached across the table to strangle me.

He didn't seem like the killing type, though. I mean[?]
killers ask for your leftover sandwiches and wear mus[?]
on their upper lips?

After an almost interminable silence I stood up and [?]
the check to the counter and paid for the sandwich.

I headed out of Sammy's Subway, with Jason follow[?]
close behind. The back of my neck was a little creepy, [?]
otherwise I had pretty well convinced myself that Jason [?]
no more dangerous than Caesar and the only harm wo[?]
be if he drooled on me or slimed my silk blouse.

"Where're you going now?" he asked.

"Where did you think I was going when you follo[?]
me?"

At least he looked sheepish. "I thought you might be [?]
a story."

"I do astrological lovelorn columns."

"So can I go with you?"

"Only if you get rid of the mustard on your lip." I sw[?]
he wagged his tail.

ADOREE FOSTER and her husband, Nathanial, lived i[?]
very nice part of town, the Creekside Country Club a[?]
Creekside is an older, gracious country club that has b[?]
there long enough to have a history that includes a dis[?]
past of vast exclusivity, of the sort that excluded folk[?]
they had too many freckles. Currently, it is the home [?]
comfortably established golf course and tennis courts [?]
a dining room that is fabled for the business deals c[?]
cluded there.

Across from it is the Creekside residential area. Th[?]

streets are shaded by overarching maples and elms, and
ough most of the elms have a sparse look now because
he ravages of Dutch elm disease, they still have the class
ook well trimmed in the midst of their death throes. It
he epitome of gracious urban living. My grandmother's
k iron flamingos never stood on these lawns.

Adoree and Nathanial lived in a genteel home that spread
r the lawn with an air of belonging that comes from
wing you have enough money to buy it all. Cash.

parked in front of their home, turned off the engine,
started to get out of the car.

"What are you going to say?" Jason asked.

looked at him, struck for the first time with the full
kwardness of the situation.

He cleared his throat. "I mean, you can't just go up there
say, 'Hello, do you think your sister is dead?' can
?"

ndignantly I got out of the car and marched up the walk.
the time we reached the front door and rang the bell, I
w I was in up to my armpits. Possibly over my head.

A maid wearing a white apron with a ruffle around the
ge opened the door and looked passively at us.

"Ms. Stella Star and Mr. Jason Paul, friends of Miss
ace to see Mrs. Foster." I made my neck as long as an
rich so that I could look down my nose just so. It more
less worked. The maid said "One moment, please" and
sed the door firmly.

The maid reappeared and ushered us into the home and
wn a hall corridor to an airy observatory. My grand-
ther would have called it a "side porch...with plants."
parked us on a tiny bamboo couch and left us to fight
a giant fern, saying that Mrs. Foster would be there in
moment.

Seconds later Adoree swirled into the room in a cloud

of perfume with every hair in place, eyelids cool, mak
fresh, and the whites of her eyes white and clear. She w
a simple leisure outfit that shrieked Needless Markups
trailed from her bejeweled fingers a tragic handkerchief
she dabbed at her still-clear eyes. Her presentation of
was outstanding. I wanted to applaud. I had pictured so
thing very different, but this was worth the trip.

Adoree smiled poignantly and lowered herself ont
portion of a chair seat. She had the kind of ankles that w
born knowing how to cross elegantly and slim knees
made it look natural. I thought of Grace and wondere
they had grown up in the same house. Could they ever h
played games together? Had they shared a bath as ba
on a hot summer night? Hard to imagine.

I glanced at Jason to see if he was still conscious.
was. He was staring at a large plant about two feet av
from him. I followed his gaze and found myself star
straight into the eyes of a large pink-and-orange pa
perched on the upper branch of an ancient philodend
The parrot scratched his wing with his beak and closed
eyes.

"That's Nathanial's special pet," Adoree explained
voice that was surprisingly musical. Again, not what I
imagined.

"I came about Grace, Adoree," I said. I felt my w
not knowing what would be the best approach. "I kr
you must be terribly worried about her."

Adoree looked at me blankly. "I'm not particularly w
ried. Grace lives a very independent life, she has her in
ests, her friends, she does things when she wants and h
she wants and seldom tells me about it." Adoree too
deep breath. "I worry some, but Grace is a strong wom
I'm counting on her to call me up any minute and :
'Addie—she calls me Addie—Addie, I'm back.'" Adc

bbed her eyes. "I'm not the least worried." Her sigh
dvertised a stunning bust line.

"Did she tell you she was going somewhere?"

"Well, sort of. Maybe. She said something about some-
ne special." Adoree leaned forward, artfully arranging
erself toward Jason. From the corner of my eye I could
e that he appreciated her effort.

"Do you remember what it was?"

Adoree smiled sadly. "No."

"Does she have a mountain home or place she goes to?"
She tilted her head carefully. "Now you're Grace's
iends, is that right? I would have thought she'd tell you.
ne's a very private person. I'm not sure she'd want me to
ll. I'll just wait until I hear from her." Adoree's steely
enter was showing through in spots now.

I smiled in what I hoped was a disarming way, tilting
y head the same way she did, turning my hands palms
p in my lap...the old I'm-a-real-sweetheart body lan-
uage. "Grace had been telling me about her friend, the
an she was interested in, you know, really interested in.
'hat was his name? I'm blocking on it." It didn't work.
doree's eyes narrowed just enough to let me know I'd
isstepped, not to mention misspoken. She was very silent,
ill smiling but studying me like I'd broken out in a new
d interesting rashy disease.

"I don't remember from where you said you knew
race." Her distinctly proper grammar was a hint. The
mosphere had changed. I wasn't sure what it had changed
to, but it was sharply different and uncomfortable. My
onscience stabbed me where I lived, in my stomach. Jason
ifted on the couch as though he sensed the change and
aned forward toward Adoree.

"We're worried about Grace," he said, beaming his vel-

vety brown gaze at her. "As close as the two of you a
we're sure you must have some idea of where to find her

Even the Washington Monument would have bent a l
tle, and Adoree absolutely softened beneath his ga:
"Well, she did say something last week, but I can't
member what. Something about going away for a while
think things out. I think she was having trouble with I
partner in the shop."

"She didn't say where?" I asked. Adoree glanced at n
then turned back to Jason. "I just can't seem to rememb
It's a bad habit of mine." She was as languid as a sna
at that moment, and Jason was clearly in danger of bei
swallowed whole. I tugged at his jacket sleeve. "Perha
we should go," I murmured. He considered it for a m
ment, then smiled into Adoree's face.

"You've got a beautiful home here."

"Would you like to see it?"

"Another time." I swear he smirked.

Adoree glided from her perch on the chair, and Jas
slithered after her. I followed.

We were at the door mouthing niceties when a tall sle
der man with prematurely graying hair strode up the ha
way toward us. Adoree turned abruptly toward him, an
sensed yet another change in the atmosphere. This was
exhausting household to process.

"Why, Nate, you're home early," she said. He look
up and registered mild surprise. He rubbed his face with
slender hand as though he was only now focusing on
"Headache. Thought I'd get in a round of golf. Might ta
the tension away." He was trying for joviality, and his li
curved in a semblance of a smile, but his voice was tigh
controlled and emotionless, as though he were coveri
something. One of Adoree's eyebrows twitched. She did
buy this any more than I did.

"We're friends of Grace," I piped up. I figured Adoree
had no intention of introducing us. Nathanial was distinctly
more interested now than before. "Have you heard from
her?" he asked.

I shook my head. "You don't know where she might
have gone, then?"

He shook his head. "No. I mean, she's her own person,
she could go anywhere, but, it's not like her," he trailed
off absently. Adoree roused and pulled open the door, her
hand resting on Jason's forearm. "It's very kind of the two
of you to come by," she said. I found myself propelled
outside. She was good at getting people out the door.

TEN

WHEN JASON AND I got back to the office, Detective St[okowski] was slumped in a chair in front of Zelda, who w[as] chatting warmly about her troubles with plastic fingernai[ls] that fly off. She told me later between gum chews that [he] was divorced, had no children, was in his late thirties, a[nd] had been on the force for seventeen years. He liked a[n]chovy pizza, the color red, and classical guitar music. Sh[e] has great technique. It occurred to me that, instead of Jaso[n] I should have taken her with me to the Fosters.

Using Adoree's trick of the trailing hand on the forear[m] I got Jason's attention and whispered into his ear, "Get a[ll] the information you can on Nathanial and Adoree Foste[r.] Everything. Down to the kind of laundry detergent the[y] use."

"What about Guy and Lilly?"

"Them, too."

He grinned. "Right, chief!"

Stokowski stood and replaced a tattered *People* magazi[ne] he hadn't had the chance to read. I tried to read his fac[e] but it was a blank tablet...no clues about what he wante[d.] But as I also learned later, he was sucked dry by the Zel[da] information-gathering machine. As she says, you learn a l[ot] sitting at the front desk.

Stokowski followed me to my desk, pulled the chair fro[m] Guy's desk over, and straddled it. He folded his arms o[n] top of the chair back, and his jacket pulled tight across h[is] back, riding up around his neck. It made him look like h[e] had no neck.

Jason was at his desk, phone to his ear, scribbling on a
llow legal pad. Stokowski surveyed the room, his eyes
omentarily falling on the scratch on Jason's neck. He filed
all away like an automaton. I had no doubt that he'd
edge it all back up as soon as he needed it.

"This is the most private room you got?"

"There's a rest room down the hall."

"Let's go for a ride." He stood and walked to the en-
way of the room. It was irritating to be taken for granted;
en I realized that I wasn't being taken for granted. It
sn't exactly a social invitation. I rolled my eyes at Jason,
no looked very impressed, then very busy.

Outside, Stokowski strolled to a medium-sized generic
ite car with no official markings on it. It didn't need any
ficial markings. A spotlight mounted on the left front by
e window, an extra aerial—it looked exactly like a police
r.

"Great car," I said. He squinted at me and turned the
y in the ignition. We rode in silence for a while at a
:ady thirty-five miles an hour.

"Have you found Grace yet?" I asked. He shook his
ad.

"I wanted to talk about that." He turned onto Speer
ulevard. "I need you to tell me again about that morn-
. What you heard."

"I was going to the bakery..." I droned on, barely pay-
g attention to him. Cars whizzed past us. We were west-
und on Speer Boulevard viaduct just over the tracks
en his radio crackled and interrupted. He picked up the
:eiver.

I've never been able to easily understand what the voices
those radios are saying. I don't know how many times
ve tried to understand the taxi radios, but they never make
nse to me. But that day I got it. It may have been because

he tensed. It may have been the words Coal Creek. Or the
way the words were spoken, but I knew what it was.

"Ride along?" he asked. I nodded.

They'd found Grace.

IT WAS A very long ride.

We went west past Golden, then north along the Foothill
Highway, then turned west again and wound into the foot-
hills. Somewhere along the way the sun went under a cloud
and out of my life. Water over stones. A body. I'd seen it
before. I'd heard the sounds in my spell, and I'd seen the
gully in my dream.

"You all right over there?"

"Sure."

We drove along a narrow two-lane tarmac road as it
curled up the canyon. There was a breeze in the aspen trees
and the tall pines that stood guard over the rock face of the
canyon looked darkly green.

I knew when we were close because orange cones were
set in the road warning of an obstruction. I glimpsed the
flashing yellow lights of a wrecker parked at the side of
the soft shoulder. Men in plain navy jackets were standing
along the edge of the road, and a uniformed officer with a
gun in a belt holster was climbing down the steep side of
the canyon.

A stream ran along the canyon floor. Cold and splashing
over slick, water-rounded rocks. I felt chilled. But a mere
jacket wouldn't have warmed me up.

We parked inside the coned-off area, still back a ways
from the main cluster of cars. Stokowski looked at me, his
brow raised in silent question. I nodded.

I remember the handle of his car was hard to find and
then stiff to open once I'd located it. My eyes didn't seem
to see very well. There were rocks at the side of the road

though there had been a rockfall recently and someone
d cleared the road by throwing them to the side.

I stumbled over one of them. I could see, but I couldn't
m to coordinate my feet very well.

"Do you remember what she was wearing?" Stokow-
's voice seemed to come through a curtain; it was distant
d husky.

"White blouse, brown trousers, red blood."

"Take it easy. Sit over there. This'll be a while yet."

A warm, rough hand on my elbow pushed me forward.
e rock on which I sat was warm, hard, and had a sharp
ge that I plumped onto at first. The pain cut through some
the fog, and I seemed to become more aware after that.
I sat there for I don't know how long. I do know that
okowski was shaking me by the arm.

"Do you do that very often?" he asked.

"What?"

"That. Stare like that. You didn't hear me. Didn't see
. I had to shake you."

"How long was I staring?"

"Dunno. Maybe a minute. Maybe less. Didn't you hear
?"

I hadn't. I hadn't been aware, hadn't seen anything, and
dn't even realized it was happening. Could that have hap-
ned Saturday morning? I started to shake.

"You having a seizure?"

"No. Just cold." My teeth began to chatter. If this had
ppened Saturday, I could have seen Grace, gone into one
these things. From shock? I looked at Stokowski. I was
red.

He stood over me. I knew if I bent my neck so I could
him I'd feel dizzy. I stared at the ground. An ant, drag-
g a huge crumb, was trying to pull it over a pebble. He
n't know to go around.

"I think I didn't see the real Grace there that mornin I think I saw her aura."

Stokowski knelt down next to me. He looked solemn into my eyes. "This is weird stuff."

"It's happened before."

"You know what it looks like down here, don't you'

"Yes."

The expression in his eyes turned hard and flat. A maybe just a little sad underneath.

"I didn't do it."

THE RIDE BACK to town was even worse than the ride had been. There was no friendly silence. No warmth knew he was suspicious, and when I went over it all in mind, I was suspicious. It was awful. I considered tellin him more, but decided it would only make matters mu worse for me than they already were.

I tried to think what I should do next. Should I find lawyer? If I insisted on calling one...if I could think of to call...wouldn't that look even more guilty?

He hadn't read me my Miranda rights, so maybe I w okay. No, I remembered, they only have to do that wh they're charging you. If they're just talking to you, if you just talking to them, they don't have to tell you a thing started to shake again.

The only lawyer I could think of was a specialist in wa rights. A hot topic in Colorado, but useless for this proble There was a real hotshot or two who hit the papers w every really big crime, but that was big dollars. Dollar didn't have.

"I'd like to pick up my car at the newspaper office."

"We need to talk first."

NONE OF THIS seemed very real. I'd never been inside big gray cement building that is police headquarters in c

Denver. Stokowski drove into the underground parking
t off Cherokee Street, and we took the elevator up to the
d floor where he led me to a small bare room with one-
y mirrors and a table. City ordinance banned smoking,
it smelled stale, like sweat and fear. I didn't want to be
re.

'Coffee?''

refused. Proserpina when she was abducted by Pluto
I been condemned to Hell six months of each year for
ing a mere pomegranate seed. God only knew what a
ole cup of coffee would do. ''I think I'd like to leave.''

'Sure. You can leave anytime. Just help me with a few
estions first.''

sat gingerly on the hard straight-backed chair. The For-
a tabletop looked like it wouldn't hold up to the De-
tment of Health, so I rested my hands in my lap. And
d to keep from twisting them.

'Now,'' Stokowski said, pulling out a small pad and
. ''I need you to just explain once again, about Saturday
rning.''

His head was tilted to one side and his eyelids were half-
sed, as if he were hiding his thoughts from me. I won-
ed if he really suspected me or if this was just to scare
It didn't seem very official somehow.

'I decided to get something from the BonBon Bakery.
ut Fluffy into his harness, pinned him to my shirt, and
out. I thought I'd see if Grace wanted one. Sometimes
have rolls together on Saturday morning. She's there
ving, I stop in to ask her what she wants, I go get it
ile she makes coffee, and when I get back we have rolls
I coffee together.

'Last Saturday I got to the door, didn't feel too good,
I went inside and was just catching my breath in the
k—''

"The door was open?"

"Door was open. Ajar. Like she expected me." I too[c] deep breath. "I was just going to call out to her whe[n] heard arguing. I didn't know what to do. I waited ju[st] moment, then decided that I could just go ahead and [get] some rolls and come back. So I left."

"Cars?"

"Only Grace's. None other."

"Did you look in the car?"

"No."

"Go on."

"I went to the BonBon, sat in the bakery for maybe [ten] minutes. I still didn't feel good. Then I got sticky buns [and] took them back to the shop."

"Cars?"

"Only Grace's. The door was still ajar. I went in, [felt] really sickly, and ended up dizzy. I laid down on the fl[oor.] When I got up, I knocked over a rack of lingerie. I cal[led] out to Grace. There was no answer. I went to the doorw[ay] of the sewing room, and she was on the floor. I started [to] cross the floor...then I stopped and decided I should [call] nine-one-one."

"So you didn't touch her?"

"No."

"How did you know something was wrong?"

"How many people you know lie on the floor and p[lay] dead for a friend early Saturday morning?"

"And then?"

"And then I went to the front of the store where I [re]membered there was a phone and I called nine-one-one[.]"

"Did you do any of that staring?"

"How would I know?"

"Have you ever done anything you don't remember[?]"

"What on earth do you mean? Of course I've do[ne]

ngs I can't remember, hasn't everyone? Haven't you?
t that doesn't mean I did things, bad things, in a trance,
1 don't remember them. Come on.'' I snorted and acted
lignant and hoped I wouldn't embarrass myself by throw-
, up out of sheer terror.

''Maybe you got all spacey and stabbed your friend.
ybe that's why you knew she was dead.''

'Not true.'' I grew cold and felt the blood drain from
· face.

''You got to know Grace just from shopping in there?''

''Yes. From buying the lingerie she makes.''

''That's a lot of fancy underwear.''

He was right. I'd bought a lot of lingerie there. I stared
:k at him until he dropped his gaze to his pad and made
:w notes. He had tiny creases at the corners of his eyes.
)o you smile at small children and puppies, or only when
1're skewering old ladies?'' He didn't appreciate my at-
1pt at humor.

''So she makes this underwear for you specially?'' His
ce had a nasty edge to it. A tone I hadn't heard before.
10ught I knew where this questioning was going.

''Occasionally. Once when I wanted a special thing and
was already sold, she made me one.''

He made a series of miniscule notes on his pad. ''You
ve a boyfriend?''

''Not at present.'' I could feel myself getting more tense.
w the questioning was feeling much more official.

''So, did you get to know Grace's partner, too?''

''Lilly. Yes, but not well. She's not as approachable.''

''Not like Grace.''

''Right. Not like Grace.''

''Does Grace have a boyfriend?''

''I think so. I don't know for sure.''

"You think so, but you don't know for sure. Would
care?"

"Why would I? I think it'd be nice for her to have on
I shrugged. He suspected me, all right.

"You wouldn't have been jealous, would you?"

"Jealous of what?"

"Jealous that Grace got herself a new friend."

I stared into his beady little eyes. "You're sick."

ELEVEN

ECIDED I needed to get the hell out of there, no holds
red. If he wanted to sit there and make innuendos, he
ld do it with a lawyer present. If he was just idly asking
stions, then he could stop. I rose from the chair, put my
ds palms down on the sticky tabletop, and said, "I'm
ving. If you plan to charge me, tell me. Otherwise, I'm
ta here, buddy."

"Fine." He leaned back in his chair, examining my face,
ulders, arms, and then my hands, as if he were measur-
my strength. I couldn't tell what his expression meant.
should have left before then. But I had stayed because
wanted Stokowski to believe me, to exonerate me. He
ldn't have, of course. Even I had begun to doubt myself,
that was worse than Stokowski doubting me. I refused
offer of a ride. Nothing in central Denver is too far to
k to when the alternative is riding with a police detec-
: you almost liked before he accused you of being a
er. If nothing else, it confirmed my belief that I couldn't
t anyone anymore.

All the while I walked, I thought about Grace and how
tally her life had been cut off. The scissors were still in
body when they found her. I'd learned that much. And
t they figured it would take a fairly strong, but not overly
ge, person to do the killing and to move the body. Who-
r had done it had driven to the edge of the road, pulled
from the car, then pulled and dragged her into the floor
he canyon. They hadn't found her car yet.

Mine was parked at the curb just down the street fr
the newspaper office. I started to get in, just wanting
drive away from all of this mess straight into the sur
but I decided to check my mail again. I still had a job
least for a little while. I wondered what Mr. Gerster wo
say when he learned his new astrological lovelorn col
nist was a prime suspect in a murder case.

Everyone had gone home except for Guy, who was
ting at his desk, phone to ear, grinning lasciviously into
distance. As soon as he saw me, he finished his call, to
too low for me to listen in to, and cradled the receiver
stack of mail was on my desk. I scooped it up and drop
it into my overlarge bag. Beneath the mail I found a n

"Phone me, asap. J."

I sat at my desk, not sure whether I should call fr
there or go home. Guy pulled a dopp kit from his desk
headed for the lavatory. Big money said he'd be back re
ing of some sickening cologne and ready for a hot ni
Big money also said that it wouldn't be with Lilly.

Men didn't appeal much to me at this moment, s
didn't call Jason. I called Meredith instead. Chances w
that she'd be between work and home, so I tried work f
then home. She picked up the receiver on the second r

"H'llo."

I was so glad to hear her answer. "D'you want a piz
Brownies? Anything? I need to talk to someone bad."

There was a telling silence, then she spoke, all apolog

"Oh, Jane, I'm so sorry. I've got a date. I'm going
with this guy, you won't believe how wonderful. It's
you always see in the movies…flowers, perfume, so lov
You can't imagine. I've never had such a lover. This is

"Meredith, are you sure you can't spare an evening
To tell the truth I was a little—no, a lot—put out. "We
been friends since we were kids. Can't you take a nigh

ur life to see me when I need it? Meredith, it's impor-
t.''

''I know. Look. Let's meet tomorrow. We can go to the
alth club, work out, get rid of tension, then we'll get a
te to eat and just talk. How about that? That'll be great.
d I'll tell you all about him.''

''What's his name?''

''Tell you tomorrow. I've got to go.''

''How long have you known him?''

''A week. A lifetime. Wait'll you hear.'' She hung up.
I listened to the dial tone for consolation, but it didn't
lp. Guy rolled back in. I swear he was accompanied by
swarm of flies. Whatever Lilly saw in him was a mystery
me. The slimeball. He winked at me.
I took my cynical self out of the building, wishing I
uld go through Guy's desk and private papers. Just for
e satisfaction of putting his tail in the ringer, I'd like to
d out who he was chasing. Or from the looks of his
tisfied anticipation, who he'd caught. I had no doubt that
lly could be difficult to be around, but he was carrion.
I wondered if he came on to every woman he met. He
ent time dripping over Zelda's well-rounded shoulders,
t she seemed so streetwise, surely she wouldn't have
len for him. She did laugh at his jokes, though.
Grace would have hated him, I was sure. She was so
ntle, so genteel...so naive, so vulnerable. I stopped with
y car keys in my hand. What if he had really pursued
r? The thought was revolting. I shoved the key in the
ck and twisted it.
The car was still hot from the afternoon sun. A fly
zzed out, and I automatically tried to catch him for
uffy. He escaped, very narrowly. It was still light out,
d I drove slowly, thinking about the scenario of Guy

chasing Grace. As totally unacceptable as it was, I co▪ see possibilities.

Saunci would need water again, and food. I turned ▪ward Grace's home. Her key was still in my purse, s▪ knew the neighbor wouldn't be feeding her.

When I turned into Grace's street, I saw police cars ▪ front of the house. I scrunched down low in the seat a▪ cruised on by without stopping. I hoped they'd take go▪ care of Saunci.

Even Fluffy looked pale when I finally got home. A ▪ fly was in the window, and it took me several distracti▪ minutes to catch it and shake it up for Fluffy. To show ▪ gratitude, Fluffy did a mini color display for me, turni▪ first vivid green, then khaki, then brown, and at last, gr▪ again. I applauded. It was the best thing that had happer▪ to me that day.

I could barely sort out my grief over Grace from ▪ growing fear of Stokowski and his nasty insinuations. T▪ most troubling was the thought that even for a mom▪ anyone would think I'd killed Grace. I wandered into ▪ bedroom and pulled open the dresser drawer where I'd ▪ the last thing I'd bought from Grace, the gorgeous ted▪ I spread it out on the bed and stroked its soft material. H▪ would I ever be able to wear it, and for what? It wo▪ have to be some very special event, something that wo▪ commemorate the last day I saw her and talked to h▪ Tears leaked out of my eyes, dampening my cheeks. Th▪ was a pit of sorrow in my heart.

If I called Mother and told her all the troubles, she'd ▪ totally flustered and alarmed, and that would only comp▪ cate things, so I threw myself on the couch and talked ▪ Fluffy. He's an expert listener. The best one in my li▪ that's for sure. By nine o'clock I remembered Jason's n▪ and fished it out and rang him. He answered immediate▪

"I saw the news," he said. "I thought I saw you in the
ws as well."

"You did."

"Is it a great story, or what?"

"What did you want me to call for?"

"You can be sociable. I like it."

"Look, Jason. If you have something to talk about, say
Otherwise, I'm hanging up." It was a poor choice of
ords. He didn't notice it, but I gasped and immediately
ctured myself at the end of a too long, too tight rope. I
llapsed on the couch.

"You there? I said, Nathanial J. Foster is a lawyer."

"Jason, half the people in Denver are lawyers. The other
lf are employing them." I stopped before I said "to keep
emselves out of jail."

"Well." He was crestfallen, but I didn't care. It seemed
unimportant. "Word has it that Nate's not a happy man
d that he's thinking of making a change."

Why didn't Gerster fire this guy? An entire afternoon
d he had nothing newsworthy. "What are we talking
out here, Jason?"

"About leaving the firm, maybe changing careers."

"And so..."

"And so, our Adoree isn't happy about it at all."

"Did you get that news firsthand?"

"I'll do that tomorrow."

"Be careful."

Jason didn't get the sarcasm. He assured me he'd take
re of himself.

DIDN'T HAVE anything else to do and Fluffy was snoozing,
I sat on the floor with my favorite Brahms tape playing
d dumped the letters I'd picked up at the office on the
oor in front of me. I spread them out in a fan shape,

touching each one individually. There were no scenes,
chills, no metallic tastes…they were just letters.

I had just opened the second one and was trying to re
the very difficult handwriting when the phone rang.
picked up the receiver and put it to my ear. "Hello."

I could hear breathing on the other end of the line. Th
the receiver clicked and the line went dead. I hung it
cursing wrong numbers.

The second letter was written with a lavender ballpo
pen and was blotched in several places. The writer h
printed the word "tears" and drawn arrows to the blotch

Dear Stella,
I'm so unhappy I could die. My boyfriend and I had
an argument the other night about free love. He says
it's important for each of us to be free to love other
people and that anything else is a form of prison. I
think there's something wrong with this. What do you
think?

Lovelost. P.S. Please send this to me at my sister's
house

Unfortunately, Lovelost didn't give me her sister's a
dress. I put the letter back in its envelope and pencil
"waiting for address" across the front and set it to the si

The handwriting on the next envelope looked familiar
slit open the top and shook out the letter.

Stella, Babe,
I didn't here from you. Hope you got the picture. I'm
still waiting. Rite soon.

Big Dick, get it?
Believe me—its real!!!!!

Instead of throwing this one away as I had the first one
om this jerk, I put it in a file marked Scuzballs. It seemed
tting.

The third one brought tears back to my eyes.

Dear Stella,
Please tell me what to do. My daughter who I love
dearly has decided to change her name and her profession and she doesn't call me much anymore. I miss
her terribly. Please help me to know what to say to
her.
    With all my love,
    Mother.

I picked up the phone and pressed in the numbers. "Hi,
lom…"
She listened, she sputtered, she supported. I needed it as
uch as she needed to tell me how innocent I was. Maybe
ot so smart, she said, since I have gotten into all this
ouble, but innocent. She volunteered to convince the en-
re Denver Police Department but settled for just reassuring
le. She also promised to get the name of a good criminal
ttorney.

TWELVE

By ELEVEN O'CLOCK I had organized the letters into pile labeled them, and replied to most of those that would n appear in the paper. I went through my nighttime lockin up ritual and threw myself into bed. The problem was, wasn't sleepy. A glass of warm milk didn't help. Watchi Fluffy sleep didn't help. The difference between Fluf awake and Fluffy asleep is that his eyes stay closed long when he sleeps.

Whenever I started to fall asleep, I saw Grace's form the floor of the sewing room, or I saw prison bars. Neith of these images was sleep-inducing.

The scene on Saturday morning in the shop continual returned to me. The voice of anger, the slap, my fleeing t scene. If I'd called out, had interrupted then, I could hav stopped the killing. Or been killed, too. Either way wouldn't be lying here trying to convince myself that Lil was innocent and I was in the clear when neither was t least bit true.

I sat up in bed. Lilly's alibi for the time...I'd sat the in her kitchen all overwhelmed and hadn't even asked h what she was doing that morning. I smacked myself. I just assumed that because she had two hulking sons and husband, she had an ironclad alibi. But I didn't know tha

I flew out of bed, pulled on my stretchy black jeans, black turtleneck shirt, and a pair of black sneakers. I looke like a cat burglar. It was very satisfying. Now, I though if only I knew what to do.

The phone rang, interrupting a particularly blan

ught. I grabbed the receiver and put it to my ear. For
second time that night I heard light breathing. I breathed
k and hung up.

In the car I drove steadily, thinking. Lilly and Grace had
en unhappy with each other for a couple of years, and
en Meredith and I were there on Friday, they had been
iously arguing. The shop and its finances were a sore
int, but not enough to drive anyone to murder. But what
on top of that, Lilly was jealous of Grace?

Grace could be a very attractive woman, and she was
en to love, maybe vulnerable. Maybe Guy would be at-
ctive to her. If he'd pursued her, flattered her... I turned
ith on Downing and drove past Washington Park without
re than a vague sense of wanting to see if Guy was at
me.

It occurred to me that the breather might easily be a
lous Lilly.

I turned into their street and drove slowly past their
use. A soft light glowed behind the front drapes; the
chen light at the back of the house shone brightly onto
driveway. The street was dark and felt narrow from the
s parked along the curbs, although none were parked in
nt of Lilly's house. I parked in the next block and
lked back, trying to look as though I belonged there. It
s hard.

I slowed my step before I got to Lilly's and scrutinized
windows in the homes I passed. I imagined that behind
ery darkened window stood a potential witness. I could
most hear them testifying. "She sneaked down the side-
lk in the middle of the night, all in black. I knew she
s up to no good."

This was a working neighborhood full of people who go
sleep early and rise with the dawn. Any other time I've

walked streets late at night, it has been pitch dark; toni[g]
it felt as though the sky was lit up.

At Lilly's house curtains covered the windows, but li[g]
shone through them, bathing her place in a kind of se[r]
glow. At the driveway I hesitated, then ducked up the dr[i]
next to a parked car. Through the driver's window, whi[ch]
was down, I saw a sweatshirt and school papers on [the]
passenger seat and two desiccated apple cores on the da[sh.]
It must be the oldest boy's car.

I sneaked back to the garage and peeked in throug[h]
dusty window. Lilly's car was inside. So Guy wasn't hor[ne]
or at least his car wasn't. I moved along to the back of [the]
house. The common layout for most of the bungalows [had]
the bedrooms on the side away from the garage and at [the]
back of the house. From what I'd seen this morning [I]
guessed that the two bedrooms were on the other side a[nd]
the boys either shared a room or they had bedrooms in [the]
basement. I was careful not to walk close in front of [the]
basement window wells.

The back window in the rear bedroom was open an in[ch.]
Inside were two single beds with slumbering forms. D[ark]
outlines on the walls looked like posters. Snores rumb[led]
gently from inside. With the Doberman in mind, I st[ole]
back to the driveway side of the house and crept forwa[rd.]

Beneath the kitchen window I halted and listened. No[th]ing.

I was moving into the deepest shadows when I heard [the]
back door open. I froze.

The shadow of a form shone out onto the drivew[ay.]
"Guy? You there?"

I tried not to breathe, flattening myself against the s[ide]
of the house. Lilly cursed to herself, then the door shut a[nd]
locked.

I didn't move a hair. The light brightened from the liv[ing]

om; she'd moved the drapes and was looking out. So Guy
ısn't home. And she was looking for him.

I got back to my car some time later, puffing with fright,
d decided that I'd park across the street and wait. I was
rious about when Guy would get home. I maneuvered
e car until it fit into a space just up from Lilly and Guy's
use, and then I settled down.

The car clock said it was 2:25 when a car drove up and
lled into the drive beside the teen-mobile. The engine
ed quietly, and Guy stepped from the car, carefully lock-
g it before he went in the front door. I was surprised to
e that he just opened the front door without even having
unlock it. Lilly was more trusting than I'd have been.

The lights in the living room went on bright. Shadows
oved inside. The kitchen light flickered. There was a
ash. Then shouting. Then the shadow forms came back
front of the drapes. They were fighting. The taller one
sed a fist and struck, again and again.

I was out of the car and running. My foot barely touched
e curb. I streaked up the walk to the porch steps.

"Stop it!" I hadn't thought before I yelled, and I didn't
ink before I yanked open the front door and burst into
e room. Guy was standing with his fist raised over Lilly,
the couch, her arms raised over her head to fend off the
ows. He turned toward me, furious. He clubbed Lilly one
st time and then stepped toward me, his face ugly. Lips
rled in a cruel rage.

"What the hell are you doing in my house?" Behind
m Lilly half rose from the couch, one arm still held before
r like a shield. He sensed her movement, turned, shoved
r roughly back to the couch, then looked at me. "Get the
ll out of my house, before I call the cops."

"Go ahead. Call the cops. You can't beat her like that."

"This is my house. I can do anything I want." He

stepped close, his fist balled again. "You're the intrude
can beat you to a pulp defending my property." He inch
closer, eyes narrowed, watching, estimating.

"Lilly call the police." I was begging.

She cowered on the couch, not moving. An ugly r
patch spread over a portion of her cheek. Guy stepped
front of her, bigger than I'd remembered and menacing.

"She knows better. Now get out of here, before you g
the same."

"Lilly, don't just sit there, call the police." Horrified
watched her shake her head, infinitesimally.

"No," she whispered.

Guy smiled. "See? Now, get out!"

An hour later I was sitting in my car across the str
from the now-darkened house. My hands and knees we
still shaking. I'd barely calmed down enough to thi
straight, and their boys had slept through the whole thi
not a peep. Or else they'd learned to stay out of it. W
a mess.

The fact that Guy was a batterer could explain the bruis
I'd seen on Lilly, but she was still the prime suspect in
book. She probably wasn't going to confess to me or
police, either.

If she believed that Grace was having an affair with G
she could conceivably have become impossibly jealo
gone to the shop on Saturday morning to confront her, a
then in an even greater fury, she could have grabbed t
scissors and stabbed her. In a rage, Lilly might be stro
enough to kill Grace and to drag her out of the shop ir
the car. On the other hand, there's nothing heavier th
dead weight, and it would be a tough job to carry Gra
from the sewing room to the car. I couldn't do it.

I was sure the killer had seen me when I came pow
walking up the alley, toting my sticky buns. Conceivab

he knew that I didn't know who he was, then I was safe.
ut the minute he began to think that I might be able to
lentify him, then I would be in imminent danger.

If Lilly was the killer, then right now she would be won-
ering if I could identify her. Even if she wasn't the killer,
ooner or later she'd begin to ask herself why I was outside
er house at two-thirty in the morning.

If Lilly was the killer, then how would I prove it?

I just couldn't make my mind work any further. I started
ie car engine, pulled away from the curb, and drove down
ie street. I found myself watching in the rearview mirror
) see if any other cars pulled out and followed, but none
id.

At home again, still shaky, I stole through my own apart-
ient in the dark, looking for intruders. I figured it was safer
ian if I turned on the lights. Later, after I found no one
iere, I locked the door and propped a chair against the
oorknob, like I'd seen them do in the movies.

'UESDAY MORNING came all too early, and it had to be a
etter day. I called in to the office and told Zelda I'd be
/orking at home.

"Who doesn't?" she asked.

I realized I still couldn't remember her real name. I
ressed in the numbers for the phone on Jason's and my
esk. No one answered.

I drank more coffee and reworked my column. I wished
had a daily one. Not only would it earn more money, like
iaybe enough to live on, but I really enjoyed the work.
And this was work I could do from a jail cell. At this rate,
lways a handy thing.

There wasn't really all that much for me to do, since I'd
one the letters last night and there's only so much tidying
ou can do in a one-person apartment. Fluffy doesn't make

much of a mess. So by ten in the morning I was total
bored when the telephone rang. I lifted it expecting to hea
the light breathing. It was Detective Stokowski. Would
mind if he came by?

"What do you want?"

"Just to talk to you."

"I'll meet you downstairs. We'll go for coffee."

He sounded surprised, but he agreed. He evidently hadn
expected me to know that I-just-want-to-see-you trick t
get into the apartment and search it. Not that I felt at a
paranoid. I waited for him on the front steps of the apar
ment building. I wasn't even going to let him inside th
outside door if I could help it. I'd decided that a skirt an
blouse of pink, turquoise, and gold swirls with an etherea
scarf over my totally exhausted hair would create an aur
of innocence. I've never seen a murderer that looked lik
a dumpy fairy godmother.

Stokowski was wearing a beige corduroy jacket with
yellow shirt. His tie was the same teal with flowers tha
he'd had on Saturday morning. He looked a little wor
down.

"Been busy putting the thumbscrews to people?"

He winced perceptibly. "Where are we going for cor
fee?"

"Thought we'd walk down to Thirteenth to the Hole i
the Wall bakery."

"Not the BonBon?"

"Not since Saturday. Brings back memories."

"Why don't we walk down to the BonBon, like yo
walked on Saturday. Maybe you'll remember somethin
you forgot to tell me."

"Like I saw a bearded intruder wearing a blond wi
carrying Grace from the shop to a waiting semitruc
trailer?"

"Something like that."

We started off. I didn't really like the idea of going back the alley or the BonBon, but I couldn't see how I could protest too much.

It was a beautiful morning, just like it had been Saturday. I pointed out the iris in the front yard of the building in the next block, dodged through the alley of the following block, and trekked to the block after and the mouth of that alley.

I thought he'd be out of breath by the time we had come that far, because I can walk very fast and he looks as though he's a little soft in the middle, but I was the one with the fast breathing. He wasn't puffing at all. He was in better shape than I thought.

"This is it." I pointed to the trash piled next to the Dumpster behind the first shop in the row. "Even that's the same; trash haulers come tomorrow."

"Sure it's the same?"

"Absolutely. There's even—" I stopped. Something was different. "There's…" Then I saw it. "That chair. That's Grace's chair." Grace's black desk chair was sitting behind a roll of filthy carpeting that had been thrown out at the side of the Dumpster.

"Sure?"

"Yeah, I'm sure. But I thought her chair was in the shop. It was there last Saturday afternoon." Why would it be out here?

He nodded and made a note on his little pad. "Saturday afternoon?"

I scuffed the toe of my sneaker and kicked a pebble into the center of the alley. "I happened to be there looking at lingerie and I remember it in the storeroom, against the back wall."

He made another flurry of notes, then we continued down

the alley, my steps growing noticeably slower. Stokows
looked at me, but I refused to return his glance. I could te
that I'd gone a little white, my face had gone cold, a
there was a slight taste of old metal in my mouth.

At the Dumpster behind Little Nothings I stopped. T
door to the shop was open just like it had been the d
Grace was killed. I swallowed. I knew it was a setup.
had to be.

"On Saturday morning, I walked in there. I felt wor
than I do now, and I had to lean against the wall to ke
from feeling even more dizzy."

He took my elbow and steered me to the door. "Just c
what you did then."

I stepped inside the door, blinked in the darkness, a
slumped back against the wall.

"What happened next?"

I repeated again what I'd heard, almost reliving it, the
I slipped back out the door and we walked up to t
BonBon.

We sat outside for the amount of time I thought I
waited on Saturday, then he bought sticky buns and v
walked back to Little Nothings. It only took twenty minut
to get from the shop to the bakery and back. Twen
minutes can be a long time.

Back at Little Nothings I repeated what had happene
on Saturday, including lying on the floor and knocking ove
the hanging rack. The hangers made the same janglir
noise as they fell. I felt shaky and ill. Stokowski was watc
ing me closely, but I couldn't see the expression in his eye

"Right now is when I heard the car drive down the alle
Then I walked to the sewing room and looked in. The irc
was smoldering on the board and..." My breath wa
sucked out of my body. Grace was lying on the floor, sci

s stuck in her breast, blood pooling a little on the con-
te. I took a step in, then stopped.

"Oh, help!" I shouted and turned. "She's here—" I
mbled and caught myself before I pitched forward into
front of the shop. Stokowski stood watching me warily.
Then I suddenly knew. "The chair. She was sitting in
chair. It wasn't in there that morning. It was at the back
the shop, and now it's in the alley because that's how
got out of the shop. The killer wheeled her out of the
p."

Stokowski's eyes were narrowed with suspicion.

"You killed her."

ASN'T SURE that he was going to let me go. I also wasn't
e whether he would have taken me to headquarters or
the psychiatric hospital a couple of miles away. I *was*
e that I had a major problem on my hands, not the least
which was that I saw things that weren't there. Now I
s left with the fact that I'd seen her on Saturday and she
In't been there then either.

The few accounts of this sort of thing that I knew about
re from television on what I think of as nonnews spec-
le stories, and the persons involved were always so ne-
ious that I'd totally discounted the possibility of such a
ng happening. But I wasn't nefarious, and I had seen
nething that definitely wasn't there. A chimera. A shade.
atever, it wasn't there, except in my mind. Stokowski
In't seen it. He thought I was a lunatic.

"If you can see her, why don't you ask her who killed
?"

"She's dead."

"Well, try to see when she was killed."

"You don't understand... I don't do this on purpose, and

I've never seen anything like this before. I don't know w
to do.''

He rubbed his skeptical face. "Maybe you should hi
lawyer.''

THIRTEEN

DIDN'T TAKE me to headquarters. That was the good
ws. The bad news is that he said he'd be seeing me. I
nt to the newspaper office. The least I could do was get
things in order. I handed in my column, picked up more
ters, and sat at my desk, petting the scarred top, hoping
be free to see more of it in the coming days.

I didn't want to run into Guy, but I wasn't going to back
wn or let him determine what I did on my job. After all,
easoned, I wasn't the one who was a batterer. Nosy,
ybe, but mean, no. Jason came in while I was on the
one on hold waiting to talk to Meredith and confirm our
ght at the gym. He waved, grinned, and slid into his chair.
When Meredith came on the line, she was a little breath-
s and excused herself, saying that she'd just been car-
ng boxes of vases up from the basement.

"I'm so glad you called, Jane, I mean Stella. I hate to
this, but I can't meet you tonight. Something's come
."

"Something's come up? Isn't that the man's line? Can't
let you go for a night?"

"Stella. Come on. I'm sorry. It's just that, well, Jay is
set on this night. It's really important to him, and I just
te to disappoint him."

"You'd rather disappoint me? Break your, *your*, promise
me? What's happened to you?" His name was Jay. I
ribbled it on the pad I keep ready for fast-breaking news
ries and drew arrows into it. Jay had just altered my best
end's psyche, and I resented it.

"I'm sorry, Stella. Honestly, I thought you'd understa
you of all people."

"Why me of all people?"

"Because you know me and you know how import
this is."

"Meredith, this is more important. It's about Gra
and...and I can't talk about it on the phone. I'll come
your shop, pick you up, and we—you and I—will go to
gym and/or a restaurant and spend the night talking to e
other. Meredith, this is real important."

"All right, done! I promise."

"What did you say Jay's last name was?" All I he
was the dial tone.

Jason leaned over his desk toward me. "You look ki
tired. Bad night?"

I smiled with my lips sealed. He might not be ove
fond of Guy, but he had to work with him, so it would
better not to share all. "How's it going with the informat
gathering?"

"Great. You know, I saw you on the news clips, Chan
Four last night. How'd you get the cops to let you r
along? I knew I should stick with you. It all happens wh
you are."

"It's easier to get rides if they think you're involved

He had to work on it for a while, but when he put it
together, he whistled. "That's gotta be tough."
frowned. "How involved?"

"Enough."

"Oh."

"So, how're you doing getting the information?"

"Oh, great."

"Then tell me, for God's sake."

"Right." He fished his pad out of his pocket and flipp
down through the top pages. "Here. Nathanial Foster,

ney with Stattler, Bean, and Jones. High up. Has a good
come, specializes in water law and wills. He married
oree Peary seven years ago. He for the first time, she
the second. He's a local, as is Adoree. Nothing out-
nding. They belong to the Creekside Country Club; in
dition to golf, he also plays tennis and racquetball, has a
uple of regular partners. He wins and loses, good, not
tstanding, seems to be well liked." He looked up.

"That's swell."

"There's more. Adoree, and Grace, came from old
ney. Mama and Papa Peary both died a while back and
t them an estate estimated at a couple mill. Grace bought
ouse, Adoree bought a husband. Not Nathanial, but the
lier one. It was short-lived; she bought a divorce there-
er."

"You should be doing the socials."

"More. Neither has children. Adoree is less popular than
thanial, and she's been known to drink a bit too much
d to cause trouble by snuggling with other women's hus-
nds." He looked at me expectantly. I tried to smile.

"And," he said, rising from his chair to sling a hip onto
desktop, "the *pièce de résistance,* their maid said they
ht frequently, he sleeps in a separate room and some-
es stays out all night, and she threatened to kill him."

"Financially?"

"Fine. Not a shred of trouble."

"Shred? *Shred* is a girl's word, Jason. Where'd you get
ur information?"

"You're upset again, aren't you?"

I put my head in my hands. "Jason, yes. I'm upset. My
end was murdered. I was there just before it happened,
d the police think I did it. I needed you to get good
ormation on these people. My only hope is if one of
m did it and I can show it. Otherwise Fluffy and I are

going to spend time at the taxpayers' expense." I rai
my head to gaze woefully at him. "Jason, I need dirt. R
dirt."

"There isn't any."

"Don't tell me that! There must be. You just didn't f
it. If Nathanial stays out all night, he has to be stay
somewhere. With someone."

"Anna—she's the maid—said he stayed at a hotel."

"Hah! You're too nice. No one will tell you anythi
because you're too nice."

"I can see you're feeling bad. I didn't want to tell y
right off, 'cause I thought it'd only make you feel wor
but they found your friend's car. It was in the second pa
ing lot of the King Soopers on Corona and Ninth Aven
Wiped clean as new."

It was a twenty-four-hour grocery store, one of the bu
est in the city, and a car there wouldn't be noticed for da
It was probably a wonder they found it this soon. All t
left me nowhere. I didn't have even one single idea ab
where to start.

Jason patted me awkwardly on the shoulder as if t
would somehow make things better.

"You want to go to lunch?"

I swear I saw him cock his head and prick up his ea
I'm positive I heard him thump his golden retriever tail
the floor. Caesar used to do that when he wanted to go
the Dairy Queen. Then when we'd get there, he'd sit
and beg until we gave him a nickel cone. I reminded mys
that Jason was the only person, except for my mother, w
hadn't rejected me or threatened me in the last twenty-f
hours.

"Sure, that would be great." I picked up my bag, slu
it over my shoulder, and said, "I'll meet you in the lob
I want to talk to Zelda."

'Who's Zelda?''

waved to him, "Give me five."

Zelda was filing a very well preserved set of fingernails,
of which looked to be plastic. I pulled a chair up to her
k, slid into it, and made myself as earnest as I could.
netimes it feels difficult when I'm wearing my swirly
fit, like I was that day.

Zelda looked at me, assessed my outfit, and went back
er nails. "That's a real colorful outfit you're wearing."

grinned. "I call it my happy outfit."

"Looks like a...fairy godmother or something." She
s trying her best to be tactful. And I was trying to figure
how I could ask her what her name was without alien-
g her. I already had a sufficient supply of hostiles.

"May I ask you a personal question?"

"You can. I may not answer it." She held out the fourth
v on the left hand for inspection.

"Why haven't they given you a name plaque?"

he looked at me as though I'd revealed a third eye in
middle of my forehead. "I don't need one. Everybody
ws me." She opened her top drawer and dropped the
in among, a battery of lipsticks, nail polish bottles, and
es of eye shadow. "You like the job?" she asked.

"Love it. You know, I never got a full tour of the place,
know, like orientation."

"Don't really need it here. We're small. Everybody
ws everybody. Do you really do horoscopes?"

"Sure." I recognized the gleam in her eye. "I'll trade
. One horoscope for the scoop on this place and espe-
ly Guy."

he shifted uncomfortably in her chair when I mentioned
y. I waited, hoping that she'd explain.

"I'll give you Guy for free. Guy and trouble are syn-
mous. Keep yourself, your sister, your friend, your

mother, your grandmother, everyone you know away fr
him. His wife is also trouble and he's married to her
spite of anything he says. And he'll say a lot. He's fun
a flirt, but that's it. Has he been hitting on you?''

I shook my head. ''He's not really my type. I was
curious.''

''Sure. Now, the horoscope.''

''Okay, you write down your full name, full birth
and exact time if you know it, and the place of your bi
It'll take me a while. I'll do it tonight and bring it in
morrow.''

She frowned and looked speculatively at me. ''My ac
age?''

''I have to have the day, month, and year you were b
to do the horoscope. If I use the wrong date, you won't
the right horoscope, it could be completely wrong.''

She chewed the inside of her cheek until I expec
blood to trickle from the corner of her mouth.

''You aren't gonna tell anyone, right?''

''You write down the day, month, year, and time of y
birth, your *full name,* and the location where you were b
Then put down your age. I'll keep your birth date tot
confidential. If anyone pries, I'll tell them the age you w
down.''

''You're on.'' She grinned. ''My name is Sally Ann

There was a reason why she ran the place. She was da
smart. ''I saw you as Zelda,'' I confessed.

''Zelda.'' She thought it over. ''I like that name. It
So, call me Zelda.''

''You want to go for lunch with Jason and me?''

She was practically out the door before Jason even m
it to the lobby.

We had a great time. It was the best thing that happe
to me since before Grace was killed. Zelda had a grasp

'fice gossip that was awe-inspiring, although not terribly
eful but the good spirits were reward enough. I figured
the coming years I could look back on this lunch from
y prison cell and take a great deal of remembered plea-
re.

Later that afternoon I got Zelda alone and went to work
a what she knew about Guy's activities. She got specific
out his tendency to flirt and to have office affairs with
y woman at the paper. The note of bitterness in her voice
nfirmed that she had once been one of the office affairs.

"That wife of his, Lilly, is a piece of work. He's just an
shole, but she can get damn mean." Zelda leaned forward
d lowered her voice. "She threatened to kill me once,
ow that?" Zelda fluffed her hair. "Not that I think he's
orth it. But she's got a case on him. One of those terrible
ssions. She beat a girl up once...one of the temporary
cretaries here one summer. I saw her afterwards. Had to
ke that poor thing to the hospital. Almost messed her up
r good."

"I'm surprised there wasn't a lawsuit."

"There was. It took a bundle to quiet that one." Zelda
aned forward again. "Lilly's got bushels of money.
ou'd only never know it, but she does. That's why he stays.
e'd only leave for bigger money."

It occurred to me that Grace might have been bigger
oney.

"Have you read about the woman they found in the foot-
lls yesterday?"

"Yeah. Grizzly. You know, I've seen that woman be-
re. At the shop. There's some great skimpies in that place.
lly and her ran that shop. In fact, I saw Guy with her not
o long ago. If you ask me, Lilly did it. 'Cause of that
rtball. What a waste. And he's not that great in the sack,
ther."

"Did he ever get rough that you know of?"

"In the sack, like kinky?"

"No. Like abusive."

"Oh, I don't know."

It was about the only thing she didn't know. When v
finished, I'd learned Mr. Gerster's shoe size, his wife
name and age, that he had three children, two girls marri
with children living in Chicago and Houston and a son wh
was killed in an auto accident three years ago that near
killed Gerster and his wife for grieving over it. Mrs. Gerst
crocheted interminably and made little lap afghans that sh
gave to all the employees at Christmas.

The only thing she could tell me about Jason was th
he was fairly new at the paper and had come with litt
experience and so far was not making a news name f
himself, although he was nice enough. Zelda's pet theo
was that Gerster had hired him only because he was st
grieving for his son and subconsciously had hoped to r
place him. I felt like I'd been in a gossip monsoon ar
couldn't remember much else, but I was glad she liked m

"Sure I like you. Anyone who'd stroll in here and ta
her way into a job wearing a weird outfit like you did
all right. I figured you'd bring some excitement into th
place. And you did."

"I did?"

She grinned lasciviously. "That cop yesterday. Didr
you just love his tight thighs?" And then she gave me wh
she called his vital statistics: his age, marital status, ran
and estimated income.

When I finally got back to my desk, it was close to fo
o'clock, and my head felt like it was stuffed with cotto
balls. Guy wasn't in, for which I continued to be gratef
and there were pink message slips on his desk that I qui
openly read. Most of them said "phone home."

ALL AFTERNOON I'd been sort of waiting to see if Detective Stokowski and his tight thighs would come for me with manacles. When the clock stood at four-thirty, there was a definite sense of anticlimax. I found I'd begun to build his case against me for him instead of my case for innocence. The other thing I'd remembered was the blood from my dog bite on the pair of jeans I'd worn to Grace's house on Sunday night. Suppose he decided he had to have the jeans and got a search warrant for them?

They were still wadded up in the bottom of the laundry bag. If he searched my apartment, he'd not only find them, he'd see what a mess my closet was. And then I thought, what if the cops planted something on me? What if someone else did? It went on like that. I was exhausted. I dialed mother and asked her if she'd found the names of some reliable lawyers, just in case. She had, and she spelled them out for me. I decided to keep them on my person instead of in my purse, just in case. I toyed with writing them on my body in ballpoint, but it was too, too paranoid.

I was really bothered by the fact that no one else was taking this as seriously as I was, but then, no one else would be behind bars. It seemed imperative that I take a staunch, logical approach to this and investigate it myself. Even though everything I'd done so far had only made me look more guilty in the beady eyes of the law.

One thing was apparent: If I was where I was expected to be, then Detective Stokowski could find me and arrest me whenever it suited him. On the other hand, if I was just pleasantly erratic, he might not find me and that might delay things.

I'd already handed in my column for the week. I had my latest letters, so I left a note for Zelda saying that I'd be in touch. She'd be annoyed about her horoscope, but I could fix it to her. Before I left I remembered what she'd said

about my clothes. They were definitely distinctive. But
had a closet full of boring, nondescript suits in which
could disappear.

Convinced that Stokowski might be lurking behind
bush or in the lobby of the building, I cruised the street i
front of my building and then the alley behind it, scrutiniz
ing the greenery for his distinctive teal tie and his car.
found neither. Still leery, I parked two blocks away an
strolled down the alleys and into the back door of my build
ing. Our mailboxes are at the back of the lobby, so I coul
lift my mail without being seen by anyone sitting in from
I left all the bills and took only the envelopes that promise
I was the next winner of the grand prize. That way I'd hav
something to do on my fabulous weekend.

I walked up the stairs and scanned the corridor before
entered the hallway. It was clear. The lock on my door ha
never before impressed me as being noisy, but tonight
sounded like a thousand chains rattling. I closed the doc
behind me and leaned against it, barely able to control m
breathing.

The hairs on the top of my head rose up. I couldn't te
what was different. But I knew someone had been there.

FOURTEEN

COULDN'T TELL if someone was there. It was still light
tside, so I could see everything in the room. It looked
changed, but I knew something was terribly different.
ith a thumping heart, I backed into the kitchen and took
e phone off the hook. At the dial tone I punched in the
mbers for the manager.

"This is Jane, in apartment three-B. I need your help
w. It's an emergency. But don't call the police." How
nic. I finally need the police, but if I call them in, they'll
est me.

The manager has never been particularly personable, or
en helpful, but he got there in record time, and I was
ankful. I opened the door as soon as he spoke. He held
short length of pipe in his right hand, and for a brief
rrible moment I broke out into a cold sweat and won-
red if this was a setup. If it was, then I was a dead
oman. So I smiled and pointed into the living room. "I
nk someone's been here. I'm afraid to go into the bed-
om."

He flexed his biceps and marched to my bedroom. I tip-
d behind his broad back. No one was there. But someone
d been. Shocked and a little embarrassed, he stared at
e bed.

On the bedspread was the little teddy Grace had made,
e one I'd bought a week ago last Friday to celebrate my
st real letter. It was cut into ribbons, slashed, and then
ranged back together on the bed. I was more frightened

than if there'd been a threatening note. Of course, this w
a threatening note.

"Better call the police, Miss Smith." He started for
phone.

"No! I'll file it all later. Trust me." I tried to be co
"But if anyone comes looking for me, anyone, even if th
pretend to be the police, don't let them in until you che
with me first, okay?"

He nodded solemnly. "Why would they pretend to
police?"

"There are some very tricky people out there. They
do anything. So, don't let them in. Especially, if one
them is wearing a teal-colored tie with flowers."

"Teal?"

"Yeah, blue-green." While he was standing there
lifted Fluffy out of his cage and began to slip his harne
on him. Then I noticed that my desk files were out of ord

"Oh. Blue-green." He squinted at Fluffy. "That's a r
weird-colored lizard. Does he bite?"

"No, his teeth are too tiny. Thanks. I appreciate yc
help." I tried to usher him out of my living room. I
looked like he was settled in for a long chat, as though
didn't have a whole lot to do.

"That's okay. I'll be all right."

"I'll just check around once more." He looked unc
the bed, then behind the shower curtain in the bathroc
and once more at the shredded teddy.

"Thank you again." I wanted to check those rearrang
files, and it seemed to me that I didn't have much time.

"You sure you don't want me to call the police
you?" He had a large wrinkle of concern between his ey
brows.

"No. Definitely not. That won't work. Trust me. Tha

u very much. Don't tell anyone about this, promise?"
: finally promised and left.

He was barely out the door when I grabbed the piles of
anila files. They weren't just out of order. Looking for
chinvar's file was missing. A great big wave of fear
lled over my head, leaving my forehead damp and cold.
I threw a few things into an overnighter but left my suit-
ses in nearly plain view at the bottom of my closet. I set
imer on the light and the radio in the living room, then
anged into one of my remarkably nondescript suits left
m my former job and pulled on a pair of blah walking
es. Fluffy I pinned to my sweater and let him cling
neath the jacket. When I emerged from the apartment,
own mother would have had trouble finding me in an
pty room, I was that plain.

I carried the overnighter and Fluffy's travel cage down
stairs to the first floor. No one was visible through the
ck in the door to the lobby. As I pulled the door tight
t, I heard the entrance buzzer ring in the manager's
artment. It's right next to the stairs, and the walls obvi-
sly weren't as thick as they could have been. The man-
r shouted through the intercom. "I think she's there."

I raced down to the back door, inched it open, and peered
. It looked clear. A plain businesswoman toting an over-
hter and a lizard cage would stand out. I darted to the
sh bins, set Fluffy and the suitcase down behind a box,
d hustled to my car parked in the next block. Then, still
ing to be very casual, I drove back to the alley, opened
door, snatched them up, and threw them into the pas-
ger seat. I drove sedately, but fast, to the street, then
ned and drove in front of my apartment building, just to
ck. A plain white unmarked police car was parked in
loading zone.

That was when the shakes set in. I was a hunted person.

The shredded teddy and the killer were behind me, and t
police were in front of me. It was like a net was closing
on me.

I've always wondered what I'd do in a moment of she
terror. At nights I've pictured situations with several d
ferent scenarios where I always behave with strength, us
ally quite heroically. I've always known that reality
different from fantasy, but I'd never pictured this reality.
was humiliating.

I was shaking, sweaty, and absolutely scared. Worst
all, I was hungry. For some people the reaction to fear
fight, others it's flight. For me, I discovered, it's feast.

I drove to the nearest grocery store and parked. I need
to collect my wits and think. In the glove compartment w
one of those coupon books that children sell to raise mon
for band uniforms and trips to Washington, D.C. I flipp
through it and found several twofers in local motel/hote
My first thought was to go as far away as I could, headi
south. Then I changed my mind and decided on a mo
hotel off Colorado Boulevard, not far from the area.

In the grocery store I cashed a sizable check; for
that's fifty dollars. I picked up juice, a few basics like Or
cookies and popcorn, and instant coffee. They don't ca
mealy worms...and I knew better than to ask, for fe
they'd remember and describe me to the next policem
who strolled their way.

At the motor hotel I registered under Jane A. Smith b
cause I wanted to use a charge card. My room was one
the less expensive ones with a view that even Fluffy did
like. I left the curtain closed. Tomorrow I would have
find food for Fluffy, but tonight I was too tired to do mo

I didn't think I'd ever fall asleep. All I could think
was the Looking for Lochinvar letters, the shredded ted
and Grace. Grace had found her love to die for.

Finally I slept, heavily, not even turning over, until three in the morning, when I awoke with the name Guy in my mind. Guy could have done it. Guy was mean, vicious, and he hit women. He was strong enough to carry Grace out of the shop with ease and he looked exhausted. Didn't most murderers get a haunted look in their eyes? I could still see the shadow of the awful rising and falling of his fist in the window that night. I think I had expected to find Lilly dead.

If Guy was the killer, then he must have been Grace's lover; otherwise, he had no motive. And he still had no motive unless Grace was threatening him in some way. The key lay in the relationship between Guy and Lilly and Lilly's bank account. So, I figured, all I had to do was to find out if Guy was Grace's lover and if Lilly really had pots of money.

That seemed simple enough at 3:00 a.m., so I fell back asleep. When I finally woke at six-thirty, the reality of just how difficult that would be seeped into my consciousness along with a revolting cup of lukewarm coffee made from instant coffee crystals and tap water. There are ways to get the information, but they take time and I didn't have much of that. I would put in a call to a connection or two from my old job and start some inquiries, but there had to be other, faster, routes.

I got a newspaper from the lobby and spent time searching for news of Grace, such as how the investigation was proceeding and when her burial would be. The police, however, were being very closemouthed about it, and there was no news of her burial. I decided I would call on the family that afternoon to console the grieving sister and brother-in-law. If I wore my disguise of nondescript clothes from my former job and life, no one I'd met recently would recognize me. Lilly would be the only major problem, of course. There were several things I needed to do before then.

All the time I was thinking this through and plannin
how to investigate this mess, I had this combined sense
urgency and lethargy. It was like I wanted to hurry up an
wait. The only explanation was that it didn't seem con
pletely real. There was a dreamlike quality that didn't ev
fully leave. I also decided that I needed to rent a differe
car. Like the hotel registration, it would be traceable, b
that would take time, and time was in my favor.

The friend from my former job agreed to check out Li
ly's financial health in detail but warned me that it woul
take a while. Next, I called the credit companies I had co
tacts at and learned that Guy and Lilly had had a mode
ately good rating until recently, but in the last six month
there had been a flurry of late payments and a nearly de
faulted car loan in Guy's name. Little Nothings also had
several-month history of late payments. The financial stre
Grace and Lilly were under had begun to show on th
books. That would have created a very tense Lilly. Grac
would have turned her worry into intense sewing, but Lil
would have shrieked.

Grace, personally, had a great rating. Just for fun
checked on the Fosters. They had a sterling rating.

Midmorning, dressed as the invisible woman, I left m
car parked at the airport in long-term parking, took m
coupon book, and rented a small vehicle from an agenc
with a mileage credit with my frequent flyer card. That,
itself, is a joke, since I'm not a frequent flyer and my a
miles have been beneath five thousand for the last thr
years.

From the rental agency I called the paper, and Zel
confirmed that Guy was in and at his desk. Then I calle
Little Nothings, holding my breath while the phone ran
On the third ring someone, not Lilly, answered. In my be
business voice I asked to speak to Lilly. When I was to

hushed tones that she wasn't available but would be in eleven, I let loose.

"Oh, how sad. Oh, dear. I so wanted to find out when services will be for poor dear Grace. It's so, so sad. I ow her sister, Adoree, must be having some kind of memorial or 'at home,' I just hate to call her over the phone, u wouldn't know when it is, would you?"

She did, the dear. And she told me.

"Did you know Grace well, dear?"

She didn't, she was new.

"Well, I know, uh...uh...the one before you was ever fond of Grace. I'm just blocking on her name, you know, lly maybe?"

"You must mean Mandy Deckers. She was here for ars."

"That's the one. I just couldn't place it. You wouldn't ve her number, would you?"

"No, and her name isn't in the Rolodex, either."

"Would Lilly?"

"I think she and Lilly had a parting of the ways." From tone of her voice I had an idea about the nature of the rting of the ways.

"Well, you've been a darling. Please tell Lilly how much ympathize with her at this sad, sad time. Thank you, bye w." I could hear her asking for my name as I hung up. at one call was worth a million.

Mandy Deckers was in the phone book, big, bright, and autiful. But she wasn't at home. At least she wasn't an-ering the phone.

I jumped in the car and drove to Lilly's. I wanted to get ide and look for that file. I was positive I'd find it, maybe der her mattress. I had a hunch that she'd leave the house locked. Or almost unlocked. Her car was in the drive, t I figured she'd leave any time.

Just before eleven o'clock Lilly came out of the hou[se], locked the back door, got in her car, and drove off. [At] eleven fifteen, shaking at the knees, I sauntered up the wa[lk] onto the porch, and turned the knob on the front door. [It] was locked.

This was a family with teenagers. It stood to reason the[re] would be a key hidden at the back door. I found it next [to] the door in one of those fake rocks you can buy throu[gh] the catalogs.

Inside, I went straight to the desk in the corner of t[he] living room, then to their bedroom closet, beneath the m[at]tress, the bedside cabinets, and finally through the baseme[nt] storage area. Time flies when you're having fun. It was n[ow] quarter to twelve. At any minute one of the boys mig[ht] come home for lunch, and it would be very hard to expla[in] why I was there. So I locked up and replaced the key. [All] that for nothing.

Once back in my car, though, I felt an incredible ser[ies] of power. I'd turned the corner. I changed from victim [to] aggressor. Last night I'd been a quaking, timid, hunt[ed] woman, slinking away from the enemies. But now, I w[as] a fearless, proactive, hunted woman. This was a defin[ite] milestone in my development. Not one, however, that [I'd] run to tell my mother about.

My stomach rumbled, so I drove to a pet store, boug[ht] wax worms for Fluffy, then went back to the motor hot[el.]

Fluffy wolfed his worm while I munched on Oreos a[nd] corn curls and reviewed what was accomplished so far. T[he] lead on Mandy Deckers was the best of the lot. I'd learn[ed] the time of the at-home at Adoree's this afternoon and ev[e]ning. And then there was my illegal entry with nothing [to] show for it, except my personal growth as a detective.

It was a kind of natural high. Now I was more ang[ry] than frightened about my shredded teddy.

Mandy Deckers still wasn't answering her phone, even ar both Fluffy and I had finished lunch, so I spruced wn, donned a pair of glasses, and set out for Adoree and thanial Foster's.

As I drove through the Creekside area, I realized that of the reasons the streets appear so broad and gracious that there are no parked cars on the street. Every home a multicar garage, so unless a party is going on, the eets are clear. This afternoon the cars lined the curbs, the street actually felt inhabited, almost crowded. A creet black crepe bow was hung on the door, so guests uld have no question about the location, or the mood.

The maid greeted me with no recognition at the door and inted the way into the large living room, but I still felt ry vulnerable and no longer quite so invisible.

At the far end of the room, Adoree was enthroned in a gh-backed chair that set off her well-groomed head, and noticed that she had found a black outfit that made her ok absolutely stunning. I suspected she'd never have rn black if it hadn't flattered her. She was talking sorwfully with two elderly women. Several other people of rious ages wandered around with little cups of tea; reshments were being served. I drifted along behind a styl-pair of women discussing golf scores and hairdressers d tried to listen in on their conversation, hoping they ght have been friends of Grace and would drop some rthwhile clue. All I learned was that Zeno is *the* hairsser of the day.

In a corner of the dining room I found Nathanial talking a vaguely familiar, gentle-faced woman of indeterminate e. Nathanial looked drawn and tired, and there was more a stoop to his shoulders than before. I hovered on the nge of their conversation until I could join in with a

sympathetic smile. He looked at me without even a bl[i]
of recognition.

I murmured something I hoped would sound sympathe[tic]
and neutral. The woman turned to me, her saddened ey[es]
scrutinized my face, and then she said four words t[hat]
struck terror in my heart. "Don't I know you?"

"Maybe from the shop?" I squinted my eyes as thou[gh]
I was terribly nearsighted, even with glasses.

"Of course," she said, smiling. "I worked there [for]
years. I forget how many people I've met over time. W[hat]
you, are you a regular?" She fingered the double strand [of]
pearls at her neck.

"I was a great fan of Grace's. Are you Mandy Dec[k-]
ers?"

I heard her say yes but nothing else because Nathan[iel]
shifted his weight awkwardly. I wasn't sure what h[ad]
caused him to look so bleak, whether he'd placed me, [or]
whether he was reacting to what we'd said. He was stari[ng]
over my shoulder. I followed his gaze. It was my turn [to]
shudder. Guy, the next to last person I wanted to meet, w[as]
strolling toward the buffet. Nathanial excused himself a[nd]
left for the kitchen.

"Let's get some fresh air," I said. I gripped Mandy['s]
elbow and steered her out of the room through the obse[r-]
vatory and outside into the gardens. We walked togeth[er]
for a while, pretending great interest in the daffodils. T[he]
perfume from the hyacinths was cloying and reminded [me]
of Adoree. I steered us toward beds of mounded earth, li[ke]
graves newly filled after burial.

"You were very fond of Grace, weren't you?"

She nodded, her gaze unfocused, her eyes moist.

"Did you know that Grace had fallen in love?"

"She called me the other night. She said then that s[he]

.'' I waited, hoping Mandy would expand on it, but she
a't.

'Did she tell you who that was?''

he stopped before a bed of daffodils fully blown. "She
I she didn't want anyone to know yet.''

'But you know who it was.''

he was silent. Her broad brow was drawn in a frown,
she steadily avoided my gaze.

'Can you tell me who it was?''

'It wouldn't do any good now. I don't think she'd want
to say. I *know* she wouldn't. She was that kind of per-
. Private like.'' She glared at me, her jaw set in stubborn
sal. ''I don't think it's anyone's business.''

'Someone killed her. I'm trying to find out who.'' I
ched her struggle with that and then added, ''Before
thing else happens.''

'What else would happen? And who are you? You with
police?'' She rubbed her palms against her dress un-
sciously, as though they were damp and she was trying
lry them.

'Let's just say I'm known to the police. Now, I know
she and Lilly were having difficulties.''

'No surprise, that. Lilly can be very difficult.''

'More so than her husband?''

he examined me more closely than I liked, her eyes
denly curious but not friendly. ''I do recognize you.
I used to come in the shop all the time. You bought
re of Grace's things than anyone I remember. Grace al-
/s liked you.''

'Was Guy the man Grace was in love with?''

she started to walk again, toward the front of the house,
aking rapidly, almost mumbling her words. ''Guy
uldn't do it, unless his precious marriage was threatened.
likes a fling, but then he's back to Lilly.''

"Why is that?" I had to hustle to keep up with her ̶
She was almost jogging, trying to run away from me.

"Her money. She's due to inherit. They don't have m̶
now, but she will. As soon as her grandmother dies. ̶
that'll be any day."

"Would Lilly kill to keep Guy?"

Mandy stopped so suddenly I nearly ran into her, ̶
stared at me like she wasn't really seeing me at all but ̶
thinking about something new and startling to her. Fin ̶
she roused. "I can't imagine her killing Grace. Grace ̶
about the only friend she had left."

I tried to get her to talk some more, but she stalked ac ̶
the lawn and down the sidewalk to her car.

I returned to the house and reentered cautiously. I ̶
solidly in the observatory when I felt a hand on my ar ̶
Guy.

FIFTEEN

Y SMILED, a very smarmy twist of his lips, as though he
some secret that I didn't know about. My stomach did
our dance, and I wondered if his secret was that he had
ed Grace. I moved away from him as though he were
tagious. My arm, where he touched it, seemed to grow
nb.

'Well, how's Miss DoGood? Coming to offer condo-
ces to the heartbroken?" He carefully kept his voice low
ough for me to hear but too soft to carry beyond. I'd
ught that seeing Guy would be scary, but now, with him
ht there, I only wondered what on earth Lilly saw in
n.

'Do you always pick on women?"

His eyes grew mean. "Curiosity killed the cat. Better be
eful or you could get hurt, too."

'Did you hurt Grace the way you hurt Lilly? Did you
e your temper when she said she'd tell Lilly? Or was it
t she was leaving you and you couldn't stand it?" I
pared to duck if he swung at me.

He rolled back on his heels, hands jammed in his trouser
ckets jingling change. He smiled like a snake. "A little
lodramatic now, aren't you?"

'Detective Stokowski didn't think so."

He rolled forward, pretending nonchalance. "Bitch!" he
d under his breath.

It was my turn to smile like a snake.

I left him, crossed the hallway, and entered the large
ing room, which I suspected they referred to as the

"drawing" room. Or perhaps they just called it the Gr
Hall.

Adoree had moved to a corner-sitting arrangement,
intimate seating of two chairs at right angles. She lea
forward, talking to a man whose back and broad should
were toward me because his face was inches from her
tistically heaving bosom. Adoree had no need of my c
dolences. I moved on to the library, wondering if Nathan
cared about such ardent consolation.

The answer to my question lay on Nathanial's face.
was seated at his desk, pouring over the photo album,
face ravaged by grief. I was caught by the raw emotio
saw. He looked up, and I stammered some excuse for
truding on him.

"No, don't worry," he said. "Just looking at some
the old family photos." He shoved the album across
desktop toward me. I glanced down. In the top photo t
fair-haired little girls about four and six years old w
laughing on the lawn while a sedate young mother watch
over them.

"Grace and Adoree?" He nodded.

At the bottom of the page were portrait photos of Gr
and Adoree. I guessed they were high school graduati
pictures.

"Grace looks so lovely and soft and blond. And Ado
was stunning!" I realized my voice sounded surprised. N
thanial's mouth relaxed into a half-grin. "Yes, she v
stunning. Blinding, even."

It sounded to me as though Nathanial wasn't quite
blinded by her good looks now as he had once been. Juc
ing by what I'd seen, Adoree was "a piece of work,"
mother would say.

"Grace was a very special person."

He looked at me more closely. A frown crossed his bro

ren't you the young woman who came the other day
m the paper? You look like her.'' He started to rise.
he police were asking questions about you. You thought
 saw her dead at the shop, didn't you?''

I wasn't sure what he was planning to do. I took a step
kward. "Yes. I came here Monday trying to find her.''

"You're Stella.''

"Yes,'' I said, stepping back two more steps.

He clenched his fist, his jaw moving. "What are you
ing to do?''

'Trying to find out who killed her.''

'You can get killed trying to do that.'' Two angry spots
his cheeks moved as his jaw flexed.

I fled. The last I saw he had been seated at his desk again,
and over his forehead, looking at the album. So far as I
uld see, Grace was the only reasonable member of her
nily.

When I retreated into the living room, I found Adoree
d her consolation prize had disappeared. Frankly, it was
elief. I was no longer the least bit compassionate, and I
s certain that it would stretch my civility to have to say
e things to a woman for whom I had a growing dislike.
The maid, Anna, entered the room, discreetly searching
 discarded teacups and sandwich plates. I was about to
roach her when Adoree called for her. She turned, obliv-
s to me, and whisked away.

 WATCH SAID it was now three-thirty, and I had nearly
 hour before I was to meet Meredith. I left the not-so-
rm at-home, stopped at a corner newspaper box, and
ught a copy of the *Denver Daily Orion.*

Every time I see my column in print I get a chill. And
s was still new to me, after all. I'd read and reread my
py until I could see it word for word if I closed my eyes,

even in the sunlight. But when I opened the paper and
the column in the top corner of the second page, I
ecstatic. I read those same words hungrily, absorbing th
as though I'd never seen them before. They were all th
Even the periods were there. I bought three more cop
Now I had a total of four, one for each hand and foot.

At four-fifteen I drove to Meredith's candle and flo
shop and parked in front. I'd been looking forward to
for days, but now that it was here, I didn't know why I
a sudden inexplicable heaviness of heart. Maybe it was
cause we were going to exercise first.

Inside the shop the scent was more heady than usual
reminded me of funerals. Meredith was waiting on a c
tomer who was ordering wedding flowers. Orders like
are important to a small shop, so I settled down in a wic
chair, picked up a magazine, and listened in.

When they finally concluded the arrangements and
tled up and the customer was gone, I cheered. My bott
was permanently imprinted with a wicker pattern, and I
to stand up slowly so I wouldn't rip off skin that
molded itself to the seat. Meredith looked tired and hot,
excited, like a child with a special secret. I decided to
her tell me in her own time. Besides, her excitement
infectious, and I knew that by the time we reached the g
I'd feel lighter.

I offered to drive, but she suggested we take both c
so we wouldn't have to come back for one.

At one time in my life I was physically fit, sort of.
my teens I was a Tae Kwon Do enthusiast and had beg
to work toward earning a black belt. Then my first love
My brain cells went into a meltdown. My body went i
a harmonic convulsion…not to be confused with a h
monic convergence, although the two have been known
occur at the same time.

Meredith does aerobics because she loves it. I do them
cause I'm trying to get into shape, not cheerfully, but
th determination and a great deal of sweat. Meredith had
ned a new upscale health club, and this was supposed to
a real treat. It was going to be tough.

We were in a wide foyer with mirrors, plants, and
rome lit by light reflected from outside. Meredith was at
road counter negotiating with a muscular young man so
t I could come as a guest for a reduced rate. An unmis-
able scent of chlorine told me they had a pool. There
s a thump of feet to rousing music.

I peeked through the doorway into a large room with
re mirrors at the front and the back where at least thirty
men, clad in amazing crotch outfits, were leaping and
ging in unison with no sign of perspiration. "Lift it,
ve it!" shouted the amazon at the front.

I scurried back to Meredith, who was filling out a card
me.

"Do we have to jazzercise?"

"No, I'm just working on my upper body right now."
e beamed at the young man behind the counter and
ned to me. "You can come absolutely free this time as
introductory offer. Then, if you like it, all you have to
is pay a small monthly fee after you put down an ini-
tion fee. How's that?"

"Fine," I said. I now know better than to say "fine,"
t we all live and learn. I handed over my driver's license
a good faith deposit and got a key to a locker in the
men's dressing room, then followed Meredith down a
rridor that gradually smelled less like chlorine and more
e body sweat.

The women's locker room was carpeted in mauve, and
 walls were lined with mirrors.

"Don't you love it?" Meredith asked. "You can
everything that you need to work on."

By now I had walked past at least forty feet of mir
and was acutely aware of every extra ounce on my roun
hips, my softened bust line, and my thighs. I'd have sig
up right then to have a body transplant if that had be
available.

She turned to me, suddenly quite solemn.

"Jane," Meredith said, and then she glanced at my fa
"I mean Stella, how do you really *know* all this astrologi
stuff that you're writing?"

"What do you mean?"

"Well, I mean, I know you get those spells...."

"My spells aren't involved."

"Don't get touchy. I mean, are you going on your si
sense?"

"No! I don't have any sixth sense, or ESP. I'm just b
ing the columns on astrological charts and common se
and the same intuition that you and everybody else h
Nothing more."

"I don't believe that," she said, squinting into the m
rored wall.

"Why? Has something I predicted come true?"

"I'm concerned, that's all. You're taking on a lot
responsibility."

"You weren't concerned when I worked at the accou
ing firm and was handling accounts worth thousands th
might mean the difference between financial wealth a
financial ruin to my clients. I didn't hear a word of dou
from you then."

"That was just money."

"And this is...?"

"This is people's lives. You're making light of the i

ct you have, letting people know what's in store for
em."

"Meredith! I'm predicting love, romance, relationships,
d attitudes. I'm not predicting events...no one sees
ents! What's with you?" She was already out the door
 her way to the gym.

EREDITH SHOWED ME how each person had a file with
eir name and a card that detailed their personal muscle
sessment and their program for fitness.

"With me, it's my arms," she said, flexing her slim
ms. "I don't have much upper-body strength, so I'm on
program where I do a warm-up, a light general workout,
d then I do a complete upper-body shaping and strength-
ing." She beamed and flexed her left arm. "See, I've
eady firmed up my biceps."

"Yeah," I said, impressed. I was impressed with Mer-
ith's fervor more than the thread of muscle on her arm.

"So when will you be finished?"

"About an hour and a half."

Ninety minutes of hell and not a candy bar in sight.

Actually I was finished after thirty-five minutes. At that
int I was completely incapable of lifting my body weight
 the last innocuous-looking machine. I was gasping nois-
 when the gym trainer who had been benevolently watch-
g my progress stepped up and began quietly talking about
ess and the cost of physical sloth. In front of yet another
rror, I sighed.

The gym class restored Meredith's good humor entirely,
d she finished her hour and a half of exercise in a glow
 achievement. I was not only glowing, but drenched in
eat and exhausted.

We were back in the dressing room heading toward the

showers when I decided it was time to break the news
Meredith about my troubles.

"You know yesterday, Meredith, when I told yo
needed to talk to you?"

"Yeah, now I can't really tell you a whole lot yet."

"I've got some pretty big news to tell you."

"I'll tell you just as soon as I can, but he's asked
not to talk about it yet."

"Meredith, there's something wrong with this conv
sation." Shower water was streaming over my head a
down my back. I wiped water from my face and eyes a
looked toward Meredith under the next shower. "I—'
stopped. Meredith was lathering her hair so that it was pil
up on top of her head. Her back was to me.

"Meredith! What happened to you?" On the left of I
back were two ugly black-and-blue marks, and on the sh
of her ear a vivid purple spot.

She turned to me, puzzled. "Oh, that!" She laughed.
fell down those damn stairs at the shop this morning. I
nothing. Looks worse than it is."

"You should have it checked out."

"It's just a bruise."

SIXTEEN

DON'T LOOK AT ME like that. You've been down those
airs before. You know how steep they are. You even
hewed me out about them. So. What's all this you've been
ying to tell me?"

I talked while I toweled off, almost expecting Meredith
laugh at me, but she didn't. And when I told her about
he shredded teddy, she became very serious.

"You can't stay at your apartment anymore, it's not safe.
Come stay with me." Meredith has an apartment at the top
f an older East Capitol Hill house. I'd already thought
bout it, because I knew she'd offer and I wanted the com-
rt, but I'd decided I shouldn't accept. It wouldn't be safe
r her.

I shook my head. "Thanks, I might do that later. Right
ow I think I'm better off moving around."

"Don't you think you should tell Detective Stokowski?
mean, surely he wouldn't think you'd shred your own
eddy. Anyone who knows you would know that." She
imed the dryer at her hair.

"This is a man who wears the same teal tie for days in
row. He wouldn't know anything of the sort." I finished
ressing and was working on makeup—such as I wear,
vhich isn't much—when she finished with the dryer. We
ould both hear again.

"I told you we shouldn't have gone to Grace's house
hat afternoon."

"But, Meredith, the trouble started when the killer sa
me coming up the alley to the back door of the shop."

"If you'd have kept out of it, nothing would have ha
pened."

"But something did happen, Meredith. You seem to fo
get. Grace was murdered."

"I'm not forgetting. I'm dead worried about *you*. I don
want that to happen to you."

"Great choice of words." I watched her apply mascar
"You don't have to get all done up just for me."

"It isn't just for you." She grinned at me, her ey
alight. "I'm meeting Jay after dinner."

A lump of surly resentment formed in the front of m
brain.

"That makes every night since Saturday, doesn't it?"

"Actually, since Friday. He's really special."

"So, do I get to meet him tonight?"

For the first time, Meredith looked a little uncomfortabl
"Well, not tonight. He wants to take it easy getting to me
people; he's a little shy."

"My ass! You mean, he's a little married!"

I expected at least a murmur of protest. At least, to hea
that wasn't it. But she made a production of dropping he
comb and fishing for it on the floor under the counter.

"Meredith, he's not married, is he?" I know it sounde
like I whined. "You always said you'd never go out wit
anyone still married. You know what a mess that is."

"Look, he's almost not married. He's living on his ow
in an apartment. It's a terrible marriage, nothing's goin
right, and the divorce is almost final."

"So have you talked to the former Mrs. Whoever?"

"God, why would I do that?"

"I just thought you might want to know something about s guy."

"I know a lot about him."

"Where did you meet him?"

"Will you cut it out? You sound like you're jealous!"

I looked at her. "Maybe I am. You're so wrapped up in n you can't find time for your best friend. And he won't et me. It's like I'm some kind of leftover at the bottom the fridge."

Meredith laughed. "It's not that bad. You'll like him. st give me some time. Now c'mon, let's go eat."

Dinner was part of the fitness routine, I discovered. We nt to a salad bar, and Meredith nibbled the kernels off a ni-ear of corn, while I ate everything that wasn't nailed wn. It's a challenge to find three thousand calories at a ad bar, but the prize is there for those who persevere.

"Are you trying to lose weight?"

"Jay likes me slender."

"He could take out a skeleton."

"Be nice."

I tried, but even dinner didn't quite do it. Meredith was l of Jay this and Jay that. I asked what Jay's last name s, but I was in my car on the way back to the motor tel before I realized she hadn't told me. I was more dis-bed than furious. Meredith had never, *never*, evaded my sy questions before. This was an ominous turning point our relationship. It was so ominous that I considered lowing her to find out where she was going, but I was cked at a stoplight by a turning bus and she was too far ay by the time I got around it.

It was only eight-thirty, and I had several choices. I could turn to the motel, I could go back by the newspaper office d check my mail, I could return to Adoree's and see who

else had come to express condolences, or I could go ba
and talk to Grace's neighbor and see if she remember
ever seeing Guy at Grace's house…at night. I couldn't
cide.

I decided to drive by Adoree and Nathanial's home…
see whom I could see without going in. I pulled up acro
the street and wished I had binoculars. Light from the str
lamps and the reflected city light, as well as from the ma
windows of Adoree and Nathanial's home, made a kind
gala evening twilight. There was an impression of be
able to see well without it actually being light. A num
of guests lingered in the rooms on the first floor, mostly
the dining room around the buffet table. I saw someo
who looked like Jason munching celery.

After a few minutes I decided there would be more
see if I were to stroll to the back gardens. I was j
crossing the street when the front door opened to let
some well-wishers. I scooted behind a shrub at the corr
of the house, ducking along the side until I was at the ba
corner, out of range of being seen.

The perfume of the hyacinths still lingered in the air
I tromped through the yard trying to look as though t
were a normal routine. I drifted forward until somewhe
along about the daffodil bed. From there I looked throu
the windows into the study where I saw Nathanial talki
to a slender, dark-haired woman. Nathanial seemed to
trying to escape her earnest chatter. The next wind
framed Adoree, who had found two broad-shouldered m
to console her in her hour of sorrow. I should be so luck
At least this time she looked a little solemn.

I stole closer to hear the conversation. It wasn't ea
through a closed window. The shorter man turned. His pr
file was chillingly familiar. It was Detective Stokowski

ctically hugged the house. The sound of their voices was
ffled, but I could still make out the words.

'If you see her, would you let me know?''

My skin crawled. I knew who the *her* was.

'Well, of course. I'd be glad to get in touch with you.''

Had I imagined the slightest emphasis on the word
"uch''?

Had I imagined that I heard footsteps? I looked wildly
und. There were bushes just twenty feet away. Lilacs.
a child I'd spent an entire afternoon hiding in a clump
lilacs and never was found. I ran for it.

was almost there when I felt a hand clamp down on
arm. I shook it off and ran harder.

'Stella!'' I spun around. Jason materialized out of the
dows. He motioned for me to be quiet, and we ran to-
her to the other side of the lilac clump.

'Stokowski is in there, looking for you. What have you
e?''

'What did you tell him?''

'I just shrugged and played dumb. Why's he looking for
? What have you done to yourself? Your clothes are
..different.''

was having trouble catching my breath. I shook my
d. "Why are you here?''

'I was checking on Nathanial and Adoree for you. Why
you sneaking around out here?''

'I think I'm being framed.''

'For Grace's murder?''

nodded.

'No shit.''

He looked just like Caesar when his tennis ball had been
en away...puzzled that anyone would do such a thing
curious about what would happen next. Maybe, just

maybe, he'd wag, you'll throw the ball to me. Only I did‡
have the ball.

"TELL ME WHAT Stokowski said." We were sitting a▪
corner table in Governor's Park bar on 7th Avenue an▪
was on my second club soda with lime. Jason was drinki▪
Molson. I was hoping he would pay for it.

"I'll tell you about Stokowski if you'll tell me what ‡
hell you're up to."

"I'm just trying to find out who killed Grace, only ev▪
thing I do lands me in more trouble. Now, what were y▪
doing at the Fosters'? Surely you weren't there just to co▪
fort the delicious Adoree." I would have been amused ‡
see the tops of Jason's ears pink up, but I couldn't get aw▪
from the feeling that someone was watching me ev▪
though I'd insisted on sitting in the most inconspicu▪
corner of the bar and had plastered my back to the wa▪
had this sense of impending doom.

Jason leaned against the back of his chair. "Well, I w▪
just trying to help you out. Remember? You wanted me‡
get info on the Fosters."

I took a slow sip of my soda. It was a kind of cat-a▪
mouse game. Only I was more skilled than Jason, althou▪
he was getting better by the day.

I almost confided in him, then something held me ba▪
It wasn't just that he knew Guy too well and was way ▪
trusting. God only knew who and what he'd tell, thinki▪
the world was a nice place, full of nice people.

"Stokowski's an okay guy, Stel, you should trust hi▪

"Real soon, Jason. And don't call me Stel. When w▪
you talking to him?"

"At Nathanial and Adoree's. He's really just worr▪
about you. Afraid something will happen to you."

Yes, indeed. Just like I was. "Jason, you are hopelessly ting. What did he say?"

'He said, 'Do you know where I can reach Miss ith?'''

'And you said...."

'I said, 'No. I haven't seen her since this afternoon when was leaving the paper office as I was coming in.'''

'Jason, I wasn't in the paper office this afternoon."

He grinned. "I know. I just said that to get you. I told that I hadn't seen you since the day before, and that I worried about you, that I thought you might get hurt."

'Did you really?"

'Yeah. And I meant it. You're in over your head."

'What do you know about it?"

'Nothing." His gaze swiveled around the room.

didn't believe him. "You're lying."

'I'm not. I'm just concerned."

That was the second time I'd heard that phrase tonight, it rang bells, big and loud. Meredith had said the same g. Her lover's name, was Jay, or did she mean the letter I thought about how little I really knew about Jason.

'Are you upset again?" he asked. He was looking in-ly at me, slightly flushed in the cheeks. Maybe it was beer.

'Are you married? Have you been?"

'No!"

He still could be Meredith's Jay. She'd met him Friday en she was there for the opening of the letter.

'The letter..." I'd almost forgotten about that first oking for Lochinvar letter. I knew that Grace had written Lochinvar letters, and now the killer had searched and nd them in my apartment, then slashed my pretty teddy care me. My skin got cold, and the club soda tasted flat.

So how had the killer found out about the letters? Unl
Grace had told him, or...

Jason, Meredith, and I were there that Friday. And G
I tried to remember how much attention he'd paid to
letter. My recollection was that he'd left the office be
the spell. Jason had been there, though.

I looked at Jason from a different perspective...that
hunted person. Where did he fit into this thing? He wa
friend of Guy's. Where was Guy?

"Jason, was Guy there when you were at Adoree's?"

"Guy? No. I haven't seen him since noon. I think h
working on a story."

"Oh?" The *Denver Daily Orion* wasn't known as a f
breaking news story kind of paper.

"Yeah, he's out a whole lot."

"You couldn't find out about that, could you? Ma
follow him like you did me? Just once?"

"Sure, I suppose."

The waitress came to the table. I said I couldn't possi
hold another soda and we'd take the check. She wrot
out and left it on the table between the two of us. I
relieved when he finally fumbled in his pocket for his w
let.

I wasn't sure what to do next. I didn't want Jason
know what kind of car I was driving or where I was stayi
I was convinced that out of naivete he might betray
I'd avoided telling Meredith as well, but that was beca
she'd never told me Jay's last name. Now he was going
take me back either to my car or to my apartment....

"Stel, I gotta tell you something." He looked like
was going to confess that he chopped down a cherry t
and his gaze swept the bar as though he expected to

meone. "Stella, uh I— Oh God! Stokowski's here. Go
the can. I'll stall him."

He sounded like something out of an old film, but I
abbed my purse and headed sedately, but fast, toward the
st room. At the last minute, instead of going to the rest
om, I turned, scooted around the end of the bar, down
short hall to the kitchen, out the kitchen door into the
ey, and took off.

I ran as fast as I could.

I had on a stuffy-looking suit with serviceable shoes that
re never meant to run in. I hiked the skirt up to free my
s and pumped those thighs. My bladder was sloshing,
etched, and screaming. It had to wait. I was a good
enty blocks from the car and not sure that they hadn't
otted it. How had they found me?

It was hard to catch my breath. My heart was pounding.
y footsteps sounded loud in the nearly empty
eets...Wednesday night not being one of Denver's late
hts out.

I zigzagged through the alley to the street, then down the
ck and on to the next shadowy alley. With every step I
nked the city fathers who laid out the city of Denver
th an alley in every block. Possibly they were prescient
d knew that I'd need to hide in them. In any event, the
eets are well lit to discourage crime, but the alleys remain
adowed and make ideal escape routes...or mugging
ces, depending on your inclination.

A car drove slowly across the mouth of the alley, and I
d behind the next Dumpster. I was gasping for breath,
d my chest felt as though it was in the grip of a slowly
sing vice. Headlights flashed into the alley.

I crawled farther behind the Dumpster and tried to quiet
breathing. The sound of the car motor grew louder. I

drew in a deep breath and let it out very slowly, willi
myself not to make noise. The tires crunched on the loc
gravel. The car was directly opposite me. It kept going, h
very slowly.

A growl split the silence.

My heart stood still. It sounded as though it was ri
beside me. The growl grew to a moan. Then the
screamed, a deafening, terrible scream. A second one joi
in. My hair stood exactly on end. I nearly burst from behi
the Dumpster and jumped into the car.

The car speeded up. I heard the crunch of loose pebb
and bits of broken glass growing more distant. The ca
screams fell, then rose again. I crept out. The noise of
movement interrupted the cats, and they hushed.

I ran. Faster than I've ever run in my life.

By the time I neared the place where I'd left my ca
was sore and limping. In the last six hours I'd done m
physical activity, burned more calories, than I'd done in
last three months. I promised myself brownies and stic
buns for breakfast. Or maybe pizza. With anchovies a
double cheese. Never mind that I'd have to swallow eit
an entire jar of Metamucil or a couple handfuls of sa
afterwards just to move it out.

My hearing had sharpened to the point of canine vi
lance, and I'd automatically begun to visually scan the ar
I've always had excellent peripheral vision, and now
found myself turning my head back and forth with ea
step, my gaze sweeping my surroundings, alert for any su
den movement.

Everything pointed to the fact that Jason was responsi
for Stokowski knowing where I was. Why he had warn
me at the last minute I didn't know, but something, may

guilty conscience, had made him give me just enough of an edge.

Or...he had underestimated me. And he'd only warned me to look innocent but had overplayed his hand. But when had he called Stokowski?

There was also no explanation for why Jason was outside the Fosters' at the same time as I was. I tried to think whether he had been following me. I didn't think so. How could he have known I was going to the gym with Meredith?

...Unless he was "Jay."

In that case, he would know I was meeting Meredith and that we were going out to supper, and he could easily have followed us from the gym. And that meant he knew what car I was driving. And where I'd parked it. But why would he care? What possible connection could he have to Grace? I knew there was a logical explanation. I just couldn't find it.

I slowed my step as I drew near where I'd parked my car. It had to be midnight, and the streets were quiet. Too quiet.

I stood in the deepest shadow I could find and just observed the car. Since I must have been spotted and followed, either at the gym or at the Fosters', I couldn't believe the car wasn't staked out, too. Only a few cars were parked on the street. In this neighborhood, I remembered, a few were too many.

A dog barked inside one of the houses. I thought I'd jump out of my skin.

I was getting stiff in the cold. I was ready to make a move when someone else did. A dark round blob, a head, lifted in the front seat of the car parked on the cross street. That did it.

It wasn't fun, but I walked all the way back to the mote[l] hotel. I stuck to the inner streets until the cross section [of] the Cherry Creek Shopping Center. I ran across to the sho[p]ping center, then over to the Creek itself.

I went along the grassy side path until I reached Col[o]rado Boulevard. From there I was home. Three huge bli[s]ters later.

Fluffy had been worried. I could tell. He'd moved to [a] different branch and was a very worried brown color. [I] knew he'd been frantic because he refused to eat his wa[x] worm.

SEVENTEEN

ow I WAS SAFE, but without a car, and I couldn't really
ford to rent another. On the other hand, another rental car
as cheaper than a defense attorney.

I was exhausted, but Stokowski was closing in and I
dn't have a lot of time left before he caught up with me.
gathered up my luggage and called a cab. I could live out
the car for a while, and when I couldn't stand it anymore,
en I'd check into a no-tell motel at the last possible mo-
ent but in time to shower so I wouldn't be smelly when
was arraigned.

So, with Fluffy in hand I went back to the airport...to a
fferent car rental agency.

I was getting good at this. I answered all the questions,
d just in case the police inquired, I dropped subtle hints
at I planned to go to the mountains. That should throw
em off my track. The only drawback I faced was that I
uldn't apply the expense to my frequent flyer account.
though I tried.

I think fear was keeping me going. I didn't know whether
was more afraid of Stokowski or the killer; either way I
od to lose big. Everything I'd done so far could only
ve made me seem more guilty in Stokowski's eyes. As
r as the killer was concerned, I probably looked more
reatening to him, too.

My plan, such as it was, was simple. One, stay alive.
wo, find the killer. Three, prove he'd done it. In forty-
ght hours or less. That's about as much time as I thought

I had before Stokowski found me and locked me away b
hind bars. I looked at Fluffy for sympathy. From behi
the bars of his portable cage he blinked. For him it was
outpouring of emotion.

I drove to the parking lot of the giant twenty-four-ho
grocery store. It's one of the few places where you c
spend time in a parked car and be perfectly normal. Pl
if I got a real terror attack, I was close to food.

I decided to make a little problem list. As I saw it, Li
was still my prime suspect, although dropping in the r
ings. She stood to get the shop, get rid of a partner w
was fiddling with her husband, and...and that was it. S
was mean, jealous, and passionate. The problem was, S
kowski would have looked into that. If Lilly had no ali
then she would have been his prime suspect, too. He w
no dummy, after all. So, she must have an ironclad ali
Damn.

That left Guy. He was mean, a wifebeater, so I'd like
nail him, and he might have killed Grace to keep her fr
telling Lilly. Except, if he wanted money he'd have had
from Grace, so why would he care? Except for that glit
he was a very viable suspect.

The only other suspects were long shots. Adoree a
Nathanial Foster, sister and brother-in-law. Adoree possib
stood to inherit, but she had oodles of dollars of her o
and all of Nathanial's besides. And Nathanial? W
frankly, he was a man defeated. And he was pining o
Adoree.

I considered Mandy, but discarded her right away
could see no motive at all for her.

I went back to Nathanial. Maybe I'd thrown that o
away too soon. Suppose Nathanial—jealous, discourag
with Adoree—decided to have a fling. Then suppose he h

is fling with Grace, but she took him seriously and wanted
im to leave Adoree. Then suppose when she threatened to
il Adoree, he panicked and killed her.

Something didn't fit right. I think it was the words I'd
verheard, "Did you think I'd never find out?" and the
iswering apology, "I didn't mean for it to happen."

Whenever I remembered that morning, I always pictured
illy as the one who asked the questions. So suppose it
as. Suppose Lilly and Grace fought, argued, and suppose
illy left. That might explain why Lilly was so defensive
id uptight. Suppose Grace mismanaged something in the
iop. Suppose that whole argument was over something
itirely different. I hated to give up a suspect, but this was
real possible explanation for Lilly's behavior. They'd
:en having serious trouble for at least two years, and
ey'd argued the day Meredith and I were in there, just a
:ek before Grace was killed.

I looked at Fluffy. His eyes were closed. He was thinking
:ry hard.

Suppose, then, that Lilly had left just as I had. Who knew
race sewed on Saturday morning? Everyone who knew
:r. Conceivably, then, someone could have come in after
at argument and argued with her over something else,
en killed her and removed her body to the car. The only
oblem the killer had was that I returned to the shop before
: drove away.

Who would benefit from Grace's death? Adoree presum-
ly would inherit. Lilly would presumably get the shop.
uy, the lover, would lose Grace and thus his threat of
posure.

I needed to find out about Grace's will. I didn't have a
ue how to do that. It wouldn't even have been read yet.

I flashed on Mandy and her remark about Grace being ju
about Lilly's last friend. Mandy must know something.

It was one-thirty at night. I decided to drive by Mandy
house, just on the off chance that she was still up. She live
about ten blocks away from Lilly. Not too surprising
guess, when you realize that if she worked in the shop, sh
probably lived fairly close. After all it wasn't the kind
job you'd travel miles for, or you'd use up your payche
on transportation.

Just for the hell of it I drove past Lilly and Guy's hous
Guy's car wasn't there, but Lilly's was. And she was si
houetted in the front window, looking out as I drove by.
made me feel sad, and a little angry. I don't know wheth
I was more angry at Guy for being a batterer or Lilly f
putting up with it.

Mandy's home was a tiny clapboard house south of th
Valley Highway. It was set at the back of a long narro
lot. In spite of the dark, I could see that the yard was tri
with irises lining the long sidewalk up to the front door.
light shone inside at the back of the house.

I've never understood why anyone would build a hou
so close to an alley, since anyone driving through it wou
be sure to wake up the homeowners with the noise. But
suppose that made the home less expensive, so maybe th
was why Mandy owned it. I was growing more tired by th
minute.

I circled the block, scouting the area. Then I travel
down the alley again, slowly but without stopping. I didr
see anyone through the windows, but that didn't mean an
thing because the blinds were set so I couldn't see in.
flickering light in the back room led me to believe that sh
was in there watching television. I wondered how uncou
it would be to call on her at one-thirty in the morning.

Very uncouth. But these were extreme times, so I decided to knock at her door. What was the worst that could happen? I parked in front of her house, put Fluffy on the floor of the front seat, cracked the window, and locked up the car.

It was very quiet. This was a neighborhood asleep. I walked up the narrow sidewalk that led to her front door and felt each of the blisters on my feet in spite of having changed to more comfortable shoes earlier before I left the motor hotel.

I double-checked the address and knocked on the door, two, then three times. Nobody answered. That seemed odd. I walked around the side of the house and tried to peek in the window, but I couldn't see anything except the ceiling because she'd tilted the miniblinds up. Now I could hear the sound from the television. I wondered if she'd gone to sleep with the set on. I knocked on the back door, then again louder. I tried the doorknob. It was open.

I knew then what I would find. I only hoped there was still time.

As soon as I stepped through the back doorway into the kitchen, I took two steps across the room and looked into the living room. Mandy was sprawled across the floor, a knife embedded in her chest, a surprised look on her face. I knelt beside her and felt her neck for a carotid artery pulse. I didn't find one. Her skin was a trifle cool. I called her name, but there was no flicker of recognition.

The phone hung on the wall with a cord that could reach to any room in the little house. I pressed in 911 and told the dispatcher to send an ambulance, the emergency squad, and the police.

Then I lost my head and decided to flee the place. I wiped the receiver of the phone and the back doorknob, went out the back door, and started around the side of the house.

"Hold it, I got a gun." A male voice boomed out of the next-door yard.

I stopped.

An elderly man with a nasty-looking revolver stepped out of the shadows. "I don't know what you're doing, lady, but don't move. I already called the cops."

The emergency truck from the fire department arrived first, followed closely by a squad car. The ambulance came then left along with the emergency truck. There was nothing they could do for her; she needed the coroner's wagon. The police took over from the man with the gun, from whom they took a lengthy statement. I tried to give them my version of the truth, but they repeatedly asked me to wait. More squad cars arrived.

It seemed as though it was hours, but it probably wasn't more than an hour and a half before Stokowski arrived. Things went faster then. He took me downtown. I asked if I was being arrested. He said, "Not yet. I just need to ask you a few questions."

"Don't you ever sleep?" I asked. I thought about Fluffy, but he'd be better off in the car than in jail. I could either collect him myself, if I were so lucky as to be free tomorrow, or I could get Mother to retrieve him in the morning, after I called her from jail.

Stokowski is not a man given to humor in the middle of the night, maybe not even during the daytime. It must take a lot out of your sense of fun to have to deal with murderers and thieves all day long. Look what it was doing to me. I'd begun to critically notice the color schemes at headquarters, mostly gray and concrete. I pointed out to Stokowski that criminals would feel much more at home and

mfortable if they'd create a warmer atmosphere, maybe
se pink in the color scheme. It might be conducive to
nfessions. As I said, he had no sense of humor.

He put me in the same stale interrogation room I'd been
before. It may have been my imagination, but in spite
the ordinance it stank of cigarette smoke mixed with
veat. I asked for a fresher room, but he just glared at me.

Stokowski wanted to hear all about what I'd been doing,
I told him, starting with the time I'd left this room. I
ld him about the shredded teddy. He looked disgusted
hen I told him that I'd instructed the building manager
t to let in anyone, especially anyone pretending to be a
lice officer.

"Why did you think I'd be coming to your apartment?"

"I wasn't sure it would be you, but I figured you'd want
search my place, since you've decided I'm a prime sus-
ct. Everything I've done has led me into more trouble,
d when I look at it all, if I were you I'd put me in the
ammer—"

"Slammer?"

"You know, jail. And then I figured you'd remember
at I had blood on my hand at Grace's and then you'd
zure that there might be blood on my jeans and you'd
ant those jeans for forensic examination and even though
would be my blood type, you wouldn't know that, and
nce I've got an ordinary blood type, it would probably be
ose enough to Grace's to put me behind bars. Because
u've got to find a killer before another day or the odds
e that you'll never find him."

"Really." He looked at me speculatively. "I got the
ans anyway."

"He let you in?"

"He had to. I had a warrant."

Stokowski wanted to know how I knew Mandy and wha my connection to her was. I explained all that and how I' decided to call on her that night.

"Didn't you think it was a little late to be calling o people, especially people you don't know?"

"Of course. It's absolutely uncouth, but between you an the killer I don't have much time to waste. And a light wa on in the back, so I figured she might be up."

"So she answered the door and you talked your way ir argued, and stabbed her."

"No. No one answered the door. I knocked at the fron and then at the back, two or three times, and then I trie the knob and the door opened. So I went in."

"You always walk in when the doors are unlocked?"

"Just like Goldilocks. Look," I said. "Things haven been going well for me. I find a door unlocked, I know it' bad news. But I couldn't leave without trying to find out she's still alive. Could I?"

"So why did you wipe off the telephone?"

"It doesn't look good, does it?"

He shook his head.

"Well, see, I figure I've done all I can there for Mand and once you guys get there, I'll be detained, maybe fc life, and so if I can just slip back out, I'll be on my way. I just knew he wouldn't like it.

"Slip back out?" He rubbed a hand over his face. I wa glad he was tired, too. Misery loves company, as Grann used to say.

"Look, Stokowski, this is the way I see it. If you fin out who inherits from Grace, you'll find the killer. Follo the money trail, as someone once said. 'Follow that mone trail' and you'll find him."

Stokowski looked at me, his eyes narrow, hard, and fla

et me tell you how I see it,'' he said. He didn't move
lips much when he talked, like his face was frozen with
gue. Fluffy has the same kind of stiff upper lip.

'You kill Grace, dump her body, park the car in the
cery store lot, for God's sake, and then hike back to the
p and call the police. You've got this bizarre story about
ing the body and a kind of cute act that you figure will
ke us dumb cops ooze sympathy. But you don't count
Mandy. You remember that Mandy used to work at the
p and she knows something that will identify you as the
er. You track her down, talk to her at the Fosters', and
lize she can put you away. So you go to her place at
ht and stick her.''

'That's ridiculous! What about the slashed teddy?''

'You slashed it. Part of your cutesy act.''

'That's not true. I'd never slash Grace's teddy, or any-
ng she made. It was too nice, dammit!'' I'm ashamed to
, my eyes leaked at this point. "Just find out who in-
ited, that'll be your murderer.''

'That's what you figure, huh?'' he said. He stood and
tioned to someone outside the room.

jumped to my feet. Stokowski shook his head and
nted at my chair.

EIGHTEEN

I'D HEARD OF black holes and black moments. This wa
black moment. It was nearly seven in the morning. T
room I'd been grilled in was the black hole. The only thi
that made me feel better was that Stokowski looked eve
bit as tired as I felt. Even his usually crisp hair was wilt
and his eyelids had lowered to half-mast. We'd been
gether so long that I'd memorized every one of the thir
five gray hairs on his head. My bet is that he'd have doub
that number before the case was over.

He finally finished and pointed me to a waiting roo
told me to wait, and said something about papers to sig
I was too tired to protest, even though I knew I didn't ha
to sign them.

Rooms without windows always feel airless and confi
ing, and bars scare the willies out of me. I think that's w
I've never been fond of vertical blinds. I was cold a
having trouble getting my breath.

A big, rawboned woman sat to my right, patiently hu
ming and doing something with her hands in her lap.
decided not to look. My eyes had been closed a millisecol
when she called out to me.

"You'll get use'ta it soon. Breathe slow. Gets better."

She went on back to humming. I forced myself to breat
slowly, especially on the exhale. It seemed to get better.

"Whatcha in for?"

"Short stay."

"Aren't we all." She laughed, a harsh, throaty soun

belonged at the other end of a cigarette sitting at a bar
a neat whisky. "You don't get to come talk to them
just for pissing in the streets. I'm here on murder one,
e it'll plea down though." There was a curious mixture
orrow, pride, and acceptance in her voice.

he hairs on my arm rose up in a chill. I raised one
id and looked at her. "I'm innocent."

Yeah, you pro'bly are." She held out two white car-
ons to me. "Here." She thrust them at me. I got up and
them. They were paper, made from toilet tissue.

They're pretty," I said. They actually were. I was
hed by her simple gesture of kindness. I hadn't had one
a while. And the way things were going, I might not
one for a while in the future, either. "Thanks." I
d feel my eyes welling with tears, and my vision grew
tle blurred, so I had to blink a lot to clear it.

Yeah, I make them to keep my hands busy."

Must use up a lot of toilet paper."

I've made them since I was a little girl," she said, her
e trailing off. I figured that was a lifetime ago for her.
as almost asleep when she spoke again. "The fucker
comin' down on my little girl."

took a minute for it to sink in, then I gagged.

he told me her name was Cleota Banks, and she made
ozen more carnations before they came and told me I
ld leave.

Bye," she called. "Nice talkin' to you."

expected to see Mother waiting for me, ready to fuss
r me, take me home, and feed me. Instead, I found Ja-
a crooked grin on his face, and Zelda.

Where's Mother?"

She called the paper to tell me you wouldn't be in,"

Zelda said. "I told her we'd take care of you. Jason
me."

"Gee, thanks."

Jason lumbered over and looked for a moment as i
wanted to put an arm around me, then thought better
when I stared at him. He patted my arm instead.

"This must've cost a bundle," I said.

"My first big story. It's worth it."

"Great." I looked at Zelda.

She grinned. "It's kinda exciting. Nothing like this
ever happened at the paper before."

"I believe it. What did Mr. Gerster say?" I figured
fire me as soon as I set foot inside the building.

"We didn't tell him. He doesn't do well with real new

"You guys realize that I'm in really big trouble r
don't you?"

"Yeah," they said. They tried hard not to look exci

As I was leaving, I passed Stokowski in the hal
couldn't resist asking, "Will you miss me?" Instead
frowning, he just looked tired and his eyes were linee
made me sorry I'd said that. "This isn't a game. You'r
big trouble, lady."

"What about Cleota Banks? She really kill a guy?"

"She tried," he said. "He's still clinging to a threa
Denver General. You just don't leave it alone, do you'

"You put me in there on purpose, didn't you?"

"Maybe you can learn something from her."

"Maybe I can, Stokowski, but so can you. Reality co
in different shapes."

"Who's Cleota Banks?" Jason was practically pluck
at my sleeve.

I shook his hand off my arm and walked out of the bu

, The first thing I wanted to do was pick up Fluffy and
wer. Then I needed to do something about my cars,
ral. And somewhere in there I had to find a killer.

"Who's Cleota Banks? What's it about?" Jason asked.

"Cleota's a woman I met in jail. She found a guy mo-
ing her daughter and she cut him up. She thinks she
ed him, but Stokowski said he's clinging to life at D.G."

"God, *all* the news happens where you are. Look, you
s, I'll meet you back at the paper, okay? Oh, here's the
s." He tossed car keys to Zelda and took off. Straight
k into the police building.

t took nearly the whole morning just to straighten ev-
thing out, get Fluffy back, sort out the car situation, and
ke a decision about where to be.

thought about Mandy. She'd let someone inside her
ise at night. It must've been someone she knew. I'd seen
ly at the window before I went to Mandy's but that
n't mean a thing. Mandy was killed earlier. Lilly had
e to kill her and get home again. As far as that went,
y wasn't there at all. He could've been out slaughtering
men the whole time.

really liked the idea that Guy was guilty. He made a
: suspect. There had to be a damn good reason why
kowski didn't pick on him. I asked Zelda to work on it
me. She was thrilled to do it. "I just love his tight
ghs," she said. I knew she meant Stokowski.

At the newspaper office I sat at my desk, stroking the
wers when no one was looking. I wasn't sure how long
be working at this job I loved, writing this column.

I hadn't answered mail for so long that the stack on my
:ktop and in my purse was huge. I was going through
ne of it when Mr. Gerster wandered over to me.

"How's it going?" he asked, eyeing the mail. His
tie was absolutely straight.

"Great. It's been very exciting so far."

"Really, that's nice. I don't think of this place as exa
exciting, you know. Nothing much happens here. We
report events that are...events."

"Yeah," I said. All the news you wish had happene

"I'm surprised to see how many letters you get,"
said. He picked one up and read it. A dull, hot flush
on his neck. I wondered if the damp heat would wilt
bow tie.

"Goodness, this woman sounds very disturbed."

I took the letter. It was from a Libra woman who'd b
having dreams about being a sensual grasshopper and
wanted to know what I thought.

"Well," I said. "She's not threatening to kill hersel
anyone else."

"What a lot of unhappy people there are in this wo
I never thought about it before."

"That's true." I was working hard to find something
say. "It's a deep thought." I wondered if he was work
up to telling me that I was fired.

He nodded, seemingly to himself. "Well, Stella, I he
that you've been working very hard."

"I try."

"Well, now this is very difficult for me to say, but I
I need to." He was truly distressed, I knew, because
Adam's apple was bobbing, which made his bow tie ju

"Okay." I knew it was coming. I sneaked another
of the desk.

"Stella, it just isn't ladylike to...wear such clothing.

"Clothing?!" I looked down at my outfit. My jeans w
torn a little at the knee, my shirt was wrinkled, but it was

I, all things considered. And I had showered and changed ce my stint in the jail.

'We have standards here," he said, straightening his t-sleeve cuffs.

'Mr. Gerster, you're right. These are ordinary clothes, I stargazers aren't supposed to look ordinary. I'll do my t from now on to dress accordingly. Thank you for your p. I'd better be on my way to work on the letters now. inks again. You won't be sorry." I swept all the letters stuffed them into my purse, and hurried out. The whole rld had gone mad. And Mr. Gerster was leading the pa- e.

L THINGS CONSIDERED, the motor hotel seemed safer than apartment, but I was woefully short of clothes. And ce the police had already found me they wouldn't be ising me. So, I decided to go home. I figured I'd be safe long as I didn't open the door to anyone I knew.

in the bedroom I discovered the teddy still on my bed. th tears of sorrow and exhaustion filming my eyes and ighing down my heart, I found a classy bag from Need- s Markups and put all the ragged pieces in it, then set bag in the corner by itself. It made a little shrine to dless losses. And I cried.

Fluffy was happy to be home, though; I could tell be- ise he climbed up on his twig and sunned himself. He s looking a little pale, though, and I was worried that night in the car had been too traumatic. I offered him vax worm, but he closed his eyes. He had an unusually scaly look about his head that I didn't like.

I needed to settle down, to spend more time with my il, in case I had less time than I planned. I sat on the or where I could keep an eye on him and sorted out all

the letters. There were a surprising number of them.
first one I opened was from a man who identified him
as a Scorpion. I thought at first that he meant a Scor
but after finishing the letter, I guessed he meant what I
said.

Dear Stella,
I'm a Scorpion and I'll bet you'll never print this let
ter. I've been married for seventeen years and I'v
been unfaithful every possible day of each of them
My wife looks like a hog, so I say it's justified. M
brother says I'm a sack of dog＿＿it. What do you say
Envelope enclosed.
    Jordan, the Scorpion

I scrawled across the bottom "You're right the first t
and your brother is a wise man. Listen to him." I ho
this wasn't the first of a series.
The next letter that stood out read:

Dear Stella,
What would you say to a woman who's lived with a
abusive man for nineteen years? I'm a Leo and my
husband is a Sagittarius. I was told years ago that Leo
and Sagittarius is a poor combination, what do you
think? I've been trying to make this marriage go fo
the sake of the children, but it's getting harder and
harder. He used to be much nicer, but lately it's so
bad. I try not to make him mad. I try to be a good
wife. Nothing seems to help. Do you think the star
could?
    I worry that something serious will happen. Still,
don't want to give up on my marriage if I can do

something to save it.
    Please help,
    Anguished.

I decided this one would definitely be printed, with a
able response. I might even send a copy anonymously
Lilly. I scrawled across the bottom of the letter. "Some-
ng serious is already happening...." I'd finish the re-
onse later.

Most of the rest of the letters were appealing in different
ays, and I looked forward to replying to each one. The
st one was different. As soon as I touched it, I had another
those spells.

I tasted old metal in my mouth, my vision grew dimmer,
elt faint. I was already sitting on the floor, so I just waited
out. Gradually I saw a dim form before me. It was the
ape of a body on the floor, again. I began to shake. I
uldn't see whose body it was, but it looked a lot like
ine. Whatever else was going to happen, I wasn't out of
e woods yet.

As soon as the vision cleared and I felt better, I ripped
en the letter. It was dated last Friday night.

Dear Stella,
How can I be so sure and so unsure? So sure of my
feelings and still unable to believe he could love me.
All these years...
    He says he loves me, but does he? Can he? I have
no confidence, except in my love for him. Yes, Stella,
I found my love to die for.
    I never knew love could make me so strong and so
weak at the same time. Pray for me and my happiness.
    Looking for Lochinvar

This clinched it. I didn't know her handwriting v
enough to identify it, but I recognized the stationery. 7
first night I'd gone to Grace's house to feed Saunci I'd s
some of this same unusual, fine notepaper with little t
lavender flowers traced along the edges. This letter and
others from Looking for Lochinvar were written by Gra
She found her Lochinvar, she found her love, and she d
for it. I returned the letter to the envelope and put it in
freezer. That's where I put most of the things I need
keep. All the rest I stacked carefully, banded, labeled, a
put on my little desk.

I called Meredith next. I knew she'd want to know abc
all of this, and I wanted to touch base with her. I had
uneasy feeling every time I thought about her, and I was
sure why.

She answered on the third ring. Her voice was a lit
more subdued than I remembered from the last few tim
I'd talked to her. She denied anything was wrong. Whe
told her about finding Mandy, she was horrified, even mc
so when I told her about jail. But when I told her abc
Guy being my best suspect, she laughed.

"I can see Guy doing lots of things," she said. "E
honestly, I don't think he'd kill anybody."

"He beats his wife. Now that's a fact. Anyone who'd
that has to be rotten."

She was silent for a minute, then said, "I think it's rea
hard to know what is going on between two people. Y
don't really know, unless you've been there."

"I *was* there and I *saw* it. I don't know why she sta
with him."

"I still say, it's hard to know the whole situation. May
she loves him." But she sounded doubtful. I was sure I
convinced her.

"Do you want to go out tonight?" If I had company I'd
el safer.

"I'm meeting Jay tonight."

"And every night?"

"No. Actually, I may break it off with him."

"Really! Why?"

"Talk to you about it later. I have a customer." She was
ing about the customer. She just didn't want to tell me
t. But she would, eventually. I was glad in my heart that
e was breaking off with him. I didn't have a good feeling
out that relationship. I think it was because it had
anged her so.

PROMISED MYSELF that I'd stay in the apartment. I'd be
fer there. I could pretend I was on vacation, but by one-
irty I was going nuts. Worse than cabin fever, it was
artment panic.

My innate good sense told me to stay in the apartment
r safety. The police, hard at work, would persevere until
ey had the killer. Then I'd think, what if they charge me?

I prowled every square foot of my apartment. Then I
illed out all the mail order catalogs I'd stashed beneath
e couch and placed telephone orders until I ordered my-
elf into a credit crisis. That soaked up a mere hour and a
alf. I couldn't take it any longer. I called Zelda to talk,
it she had to put the phone down after only forty-five
inutes.

Innate good sense had lost the argument. All I could
ink was that the police were happy with me as their prime
ispect. They weren't hauling Guy in for questioning. Lilly
adn't been asked to come down. So far as I could find
it, no one so much as gave a thought to Nathanial or

Adoree. If anything was going to get done to find the kill
I was going to have to do it.

It was four o'clock. I dug into my closet. At four-fifte
I emerged from my apartment building a new woman. I
found an old Halloween costume wig in red and a pair
butterfly-wing eyeglasses, minus the lenses, and put the
on. Now, who would guess that it was me?

Since any action at all seemed better than none, I decide
to stake out the Fosters'. With luck I'd learn somethi
telling about them. With even more luck they both mig
leave and then I could talk to the maid. It was four-thirt
I parked across and down the street where I could see bo
the front door and the pathway to the garage in the bac
Instead of an attached garage, they had an Italianate arb
with sprouting grapevines that led from the back porch
the garage.

I'd been there about fifteen minutes when Adoree cam
swinging out of the house in a splendid outfit. She we
into the garage, then drove out in her little red Miata. Sh
was a very fast driver. I followed her as she sped throug
homebound traffic going generally east. Finally, sh
slowed, found a parking place, and pulled in. She went int
a little neighborhood bar. Ten minutes passed, and I wa
about to saunter in after her when she trotted out on th
arm of none other than Guy Madison.

They drove separately to an apartment building east o
Monaco, almost in Aurora. As soon as I was sure they we
inside, I dashed to the door and read all the nameplate
There wasn't a Guy Madison, but there was a G. J. Mack
lin.

So Adoree was having a fling. My feelings churned whe
I thought about their sordid little affair. The memories o
Lilly waiting at the window for Guy and of Nathanial gaz

ıg lovingly at the album with the pictures of Adoree were
:ill vivid. Reluctantly, I lowered Guy on the list of possible
ɔvers of Grace. That left Nathanial, a long shot.

What I really had was a lot of suspicions, half-truths, and
∍mifacts. What I needed were more actual facts.

It occurred to me that this wasn't very safe. Less than
n hour ago I'd been cowering in my apartment, then I was
ı disguise, and now I was planning to walk straight into
ıe lair of one of the suspects. Then I thought about Cleota
₃anks, slab beds in cells, and bars on the windows. I
ʰucked the wig and the glasses and tossed them into the
ʲackseat.

Since Adoree would be busy for a while, I drove back
ɔ the Fosters' intending to talk to the maid, but when I
ang the bell Nathanial answered the door. The maid must
ʲave been busy. He asked me in, and I followed him into
ʰe great hall where he had a brandy snifter and crystal
ʲecanter set up on a tray. Incredibly civilized. I refused the
•ffer of a drink.

"I didn't expect to see you," he said.

"It's an unusual visit," I said, not quite sure how to
ʲaunch into this. "I thought it would be best to talk to you
ılone, though." I congratulated myself on a clever way to
ısk if he was really alone.

"I see." His eyelids lowered. He looked guarded.

I decided to shake him up. "How long had you been
∍eeing Grace?"

He startled minutely, then tried to cover it up. "What
makes you think I was seeing Grace?"

"Her letters. She wrote me a letter and mailed it on Sat-
ırday morning. I still have that letter."

"That letter?" He set his snifter down on the table next
ɔ his chair and rose. He paced to the fireplace. Turned,

and then looked at it again. There were fire tools there. Th
poker. The veritable blunt instrument. He stared at it for
long moment, picked it up, jabbed at a smoldering log i
the fireplace, then turned to me.

"What letter are you talking about?"

At that moment, it dawned on me that the maid ha
probably gone home and I was truly alone in a monster
sized house with a man who was very likely a murder sus
pect.

I wished I had done it all differently.

His expression was carefully blank, but his left hand wa
doubled in a fist at his side. All these things confirmed m
theory. He was Grace's lover.

"What are you talking about? And what makes you thin
I was Grace's lover?"

"The letter is clear." I lied. Now for the *coup de grace*
"And it says she kept all your letters, too. In a 'specia
place.' I'll bet you can think where that is." This was th
hook I hoped to set. If he were her lover, he'd go for thos
letters.

He took a step toward me. "You don't know what you'r
into...." His fingers gripped the poker so tight his knuckle
were white.

I back-stepped to the door, unable to take my eyes of
his enraged face. "Did you burn the other letters, too?"

He continued toward me, slowly, his brows drawn to
gether in a terrible glower. "I don't know what you're talk
ing about."

I back-stepped faster until I crashed into the front door
The doorknob was cold in my hand as I turned and yanke
on it. The door was heavy and didn't open. "Stokowsk
knows I'm here!" I yanked again on the door.

Nathanial kept coming.

NINETEEN

NATHANIAL WASN'T A man to be rushed into action. He waited a solid fifteen minutes before he came out of the house, into the garage, then out again in his maroon Mercedes. It occurred to me that he and Adoree hadn't coordinated the colors of their cars, but then they hadn't coordinated their lives all that well, either. So maybe it was a sign.

Nathanial drove straight to Grace's house. He parked in front, got out, looked about, then strode quickly up the walk. He pulled a key from his pocket and unlocked the front door. Five minutes later he came out. His blazer looked a little bulky in the region of his breast pocket.

Confirmed. He was Grace's lover. Now, to prove he was the killer.

I went back to my apartment. I have to admit I was disappointed. I wanted Guy to be the killer. Nathanial wasn't a very satisfactory villain. I knew Grace had loved him, and I hated to think how betrayed she had been. But thinking how he'd betrayed her made me furious enough to almost hate him.

I called Stokowski and told him this latest and said that if he hurried he might get to the Fosters' before Nathanial burned her saved love letters. Stokowski at his door sill could put the screws to Nathanial. Stokowski didn't even thank me.

"Butt out, for God's sake," he said. I thought he sounded friendlier.

THE LAST STEP of my plan, to prove Nathanial was th
killer, was to lure him out using myself and the last lett
as bait. If I knew he was coming, I could protect mysel
record the event, and vindicate myself.

I put a call in to Nathanial. I wanted to reach him befo
Stokowski got to him. He answered on the fourth or fif
ring.

"Nathanial, this is who you think it is. I've got the la
Lochinvar letter here. If you want it, you have to negotia
here, tonight, with me." It seemed to me that any kill
worth his salt would assume this was a blackmail attemp

"Go to hell."

I was sure Nathanial would be driven to get the lette
With this pressure, he'd be at my door before midnigh
And I'd have my proof. Now, I had to get prepared fo
him. I didn't want to end up dead.

I uncovered an old tape recorder and tapes and put ther
in the living room. I planned to tape the whole attack. The
I got the hair spray can from the bathroom and put tha
near the door. It would be just as good as mace. I know
I've accidentally sprayed myself in the face before.

There was a window weight that I'd bid on by acciden
at an auction and had used as a doorstop, and I hauled th
into the living room as well.

The tape recorder I set up behind the big easy chair, an
the microphone I pulled through and stuck just under th
throw rug. It made a sort of wrinkle. I put a pillow on th
floor, along with a couple magazines, to look like I'd bee
lying on the floor reading. Though I'd claim I had a ba
back.

I tucked the window weight in the crevice of the couc
where I could grab it at any time. And lastly, I pulled m

ir up onto my head and pinned it with a barrette. Then I
ck an antique hat pin in the whole thing.

Armed to the teeth.

Scared to death.

The letters wouldn't be enough for Stokowski to hold
thanial, so I was positive that Nathanial would come
re. It was seven o'clock. I sat down to wait.

At seven-thirty I got bored. At eight o'clock I was very
xious. I grazed through the fridge, but there wasn't any-
ng worth eating. I checked Fluffy. He'd moved off his
ig and was sitting on the floor of his cage. The scaly skin
the top of his head was cracked. He was sloughing.
hat a time to moult! I moved his cage into the bedroom.
moulting lizard is a vulnerable, miserable creature. I
ned on my radio to a classical station and hoped they'd
y Mozart. Fluffy is especially fond of Mozart.

I settled down again and tried to meditate. I could not
: the picture of yet another body out of my mind. It had
ked like me, which made me very nervous, in a hyper-
ive sort of way.

The idea of luring Nathanial here to confess began to
pear ridiculous and amateurish. I thought of calling Sto-
wski. Then I thought about what he'd say and decided
t to. I paced. Then I checked on Fluffy. He was eating
skin. It was nauseating.

My front door buzzer rang. I broke out in a cold sweat.
He'd come. He'd actually come.

I answered through the lobby phone. "Who is it?"

"Hey! Stella. It's me, Jason. Can I come up?"

Jason. What was Jason doing here? It was all wrong. It
uld ruin my plan. I had to get him out of there.

"Jason, go away."

"Hey, Stella. Let me come up. I've gotta see you."

"No. I'm busy. You can't see me tonight. Go away."

"Stel, it's really important."

"Jason, don't whine. I'll see you in the morning."

"Morning is too late. I've got to talk to you now."

"So talk, then leave."

"Dammit Stella, let me come up. I can't shout about here in the lobby."

"Yes you can. What is it?"

"Stella," he shouted. "I'm pregnant and you're the ther."

I rang the buzzer and let him in.

Then I thought about it. What if Jason was the killer?

No one would suspect that puppy dog. He could sm and drool on your knee all day. He was too good to true. Maybe that's how he got into Mandy's house. She have met him at the Fosters'. No, she couldn't. He wasn there then.

Then I remembered that he was there when I was hidi in the lilac bush. And how he must've called Stokows and told him I was at the bar.

He'd sprung me from jail. Maybe he did it so he cou kill me.

Then I remembered the broad-shouldered man with face in Adoree's well-endowed front. It could have be Jason. It probably was Jason. And he could have seen from the window when I was outside talking to Mane He'd see me, he'd know I talked to her, he'd go....

I heard his footsteps in the hall. My hands started shake. I got hungry. That must be why the condemned one last meal.

The chain lock was off! Oh my God, I'd forgotten to on the chain lock. I grabbed it and tried to slip it in t

de, but my fingers were stiff. It wasn't supposed to be
is way.

Not Jason! I'd trusted him. The doorknob turned. The
ad bolt was thrown. He still couldn't get in.

He knocked. "Stella, let me in."

The killer had a key. That's how the killer got in to shred
y teddy. I began to hyperventilate.

I backed up to the couch, reaching for the window
eight.

"Stella, open the door, it's me, Jason. For God's sake,
nat's the matter with you?" He rattled the door. I stared
the dead bolt, waiting for it to turn. I knew he had a key.
The killer has a key" kept going through my mind. I
oved around behind the chair and punched the tape re-
rder.

He shook the door again. "Stella, are you all right?" His
ice was raised. I thought I heard alarm in it. "Stella! Is
meone in there hurting you?" I dropped the window
eight and went for the hair spray.

I wondered when one of my neighbors would call the
lice. Then I wondered why I didn't call the police. I ran
the phone.

"Stella, I'm going to kick the door, stand back."

"Don't!" I shouted too late. The dead bolt was worth-
.s. The door popped open, and Jason blew into the living
om, red in the face and angry.

"What the hell are you doing?"

"Don't move." I held the can of hair spray aimed at
n.

"Stel, cut it out." He reached for his pocket. I knew if
vaited one more minute, I was dead meat. I sprayed him.
an straight at him. Sprayed him in the face, grabbed my
rse by the door, and flew down the hall to the stairs.

I heard him howling as I fled.

I had hit the ground floor and was out the back do
before he could possibly recover. There was a siren in ▮
distance, but all that told me was that I'd have been de
and cold and he'd have gotten away before they ever ▮
there.

My car was parked around the corner. This was plan
If you can't catch the killer, flee before you're dead. T
car keys were in my jeans pocket, and I wrenched the
free as I ran. I heard footsteps pounding after me.

I got to the car, unlocked it, got in, and locked the do▮
Then I tried to fit the key into the ignition. At first ▮
wouldn't go, but finally it slipped in, and the engine turn▮
over. Catch, please catch.

I looked up. Jason was running toward me. He had ▮
window weight in his hand.

"Wait!" he shouted.

Wait? Like hell! I gunned the motor and tore away fr▮
the curb. He ran after me, waving his arms and shouting
ran straight through the stop sign, swerved around the c▮
ner, and I was out of there.

I drove like a cat on fire. I wanted the police to find ▮
arrest me, take me back to jail. Maybe Cleota would sh▮
me how to make toilet tissue carnations. Maybe they'd f▮
me a room with rubber walls. Where were the police wh▮
I needed them?

I drove for a while to calm down; then when I co▮
think, and my hands weren't shaking so badly, I drove
Meredith's apartment. I didn't care if I surprised her w▮
her honey. It was time to meet the guy.

I pulled up in front of her apartment house, parked ▮
car, and put my head on the steering wheel. I needed
moment just to think before I had to deal with anyone el▮

heart had slowed to within normal limits, so I knew I
uldn't explode inside. My hands had stopped shaking
 were icy cold and clammy, and my respiration rate was
east life-sustaining.

 savored the cool rim of the steering wheel against my
ehead and managed to pull the ragged edges of myself
ter together. I hadn't suspected Jason was the killer, but
re were some very convincing reasons why he might be.

Meredith lives in the top of an old East Capitol Hill
ise that's been converted to apartments. The windows
re dark. She wasn't there, but I have an emergency key
Meredith's place, so I could let myself in. If I had a
ce to wait, to think things through, I'd feel so much
ter. I couldn't stay in the car much longer. I was already
ling as though someone was watching me.

 dashed for the house and ran up the stairs. My legs felt
 lead weights, my feet seemed to trip on the stairs. I
 so out of breath I could barely get there.

 pushed my key, her key, into the lock, twisted it, and
it in.

Meredith had lived here for several years, and her apart-
nt was as familiar to me as it was to her. I didn't have
turn the lights on to find my way through it. Besides,
light from outside lit the living roon.. The scent of or-
e candles and orange blossom was all through her apart-
nt. She loved the smell. I'd grown tired of it long ago,
 what can you say?

Then I saw that the cushions from her couch were on
 floor.

For a moment I thought perhaps she'd just had a wild
ht; then I became alarmed. Her place was messy. She
 a very tidy person. It looked like someone had thrown
f around.

She said she was going to break off with him. Him.

"Meredith!" I ran to her bedroom, reached for the lig
almost sobbing. "Meredith?"

Her bed was unmade. It looked like it had been pull
down, not slept in, but like the covers had been yank
down to expose the white bottom sheet. In the center of 1
bed lay a single red rose with a kitchen knife sticking
the mattress. Sick!

I turned off the light and staggered back into the livi
room. Where was Meredith? Who was this creep?

She'd called him Jay.

What if Jason was Meredith's guy? He was alwa
around.

I backed out of the apartment, pulling the door shut af
me. Down the stairs, three flights I ran, stumbling on
next to the last step. I had to get to her shop. She must s
be there.

The drive took maybe ten minutes. By that time I wa
mess, but a cool mess. Somewhere in all the panic I'd l
come angry, and anger is a great organizer. By the tim
got to her shop, The Candlewick, I thought I knew wl
I'd find.

The front door was glass, and it wasn't broken. Tl
much was good. I drove to the back, through the alley. F
car was gone. I checked the back door. It was locked.

Something was wrong. I could feel it.

I leaned against the back door of the shop, closed
eyes, and willed myself to see something. Nothing came
tried again. Nothing. I was furious. I knew something b
had happened to Meredith both in the shop and in her apa
ment.

I got in my car and drove to an all-night gas-a

oceries place and got change for a five dollar bill in quar-
rs. I started calling emergency rooms.

I found her at Denver General.

SEEMED LIKE a year since I'd been there on Sunday night
r a tetanus shot. It was only Thursday.

She was in one of the side rooms waiting for the surgeon
stitch her up. The nurse said she'd be all right in a day
two and led me to where she was.

I wasn't sure that a day or two would really do it. She
as bruised and had a blackened eye and a cut on her head
at had bled profusely, as head cuts do. It made her look
ke she'd taken a bath in blood. She didn't grin when I
me in. She looked like she was happy to see me, but
ars ran all down her face. She reached out for me. I put
y arms around her. I was so glad she was alive. I really
dn't care about anything else at that moment.

The surgeon came in and stitched her up before I could
gin to ask her what had happened. I had a pretty good
ea, though.

"Jay did this, didn't he?"

She couldn't move her head right then, but she squeezed
y hand. I waited until the doctor had finished, then I got
ght to it.

"He did this when you told him you were breaking it
f, didn't he?" She nodded ever so slightly.

The doctor tried to tell me to keep it down.

"Meredith, what happened?"

"Too hard...to talk. Wait?" Give her her due, she was
umbling through swollen lips.

"But it's so damn painful to see you. I just want to do
mething about it. Like, cut the bastard up. Was it Jason?"
She frowned. Her eyelids seemed to flutter shut.

"I've given her something to make her sleep, miss." Th nurse had her hand on my arm. "She needs rest. We' going to move her upstairs now."

"I'm coming with her."

"I'm afraid that won't be possible. Visiting hours ar nearly over."

"I'm coming with her. He might come back. I'm fam ily."

The nurse looked like she was ready to take me on, b a doctor, or maybe an orderly—I didn't know which, I ju know he wore green scrubs and had a stethoscope drape around his neck—came in and said something to her an she acquiesced.

We were rolling out of the emergency room and dow a hall when I heard a commotion behind us. I turned brief to see what it was. I was still so jumpy, I imagined ever noise to be some wild-eyed attacker.

"Stella!"

It was Jason.

"Oh, my God. It's him!"

The nurse looked at me, aghast.

Jason was jogging down the corridor toward us.

"Quick! He's the madman who did this!" I started run, pushing the gurney with Meredith on it. The nurse ra too. I yelled for help. She screamed. I glanced over m shoulder. He was gaining on us.

"Go, take her," I said, shoving the gurney ahead. "An don't leave her alone."

I turned and braced myself. And yelled. Just like in m old Tae Kwon Do classes.

And I almost got him where it hurt him most.

TWENTY

IT WAS VERY HARD to explain to the police and to Jason why I'd behaved the way I had. Actually, the police were the easiest to deal with, and by and large they were able to understand that I'd be upset after Jason kicked in my door. Jason had to spend some time with them convincing them that he wasn't the author of Meredith's injuries, but after an hour of interrogation and a brief time with Meredith, they were convinced. I wasn't, but they were.

But once they were convinced that Jason wasn't responsible for Meredith's injuries and that I wasn't going to press charges for the door, they disappeared to other urgent needs.

Jason was a larger piece of work. If I'd trusted him completely, it would have been much easier, but I didn't, so I couldn't completely explain why I'd first let him in, and then had refused to open the door to him, and finally why I'd attacked him and fled.

Meredith was sleeping in her room upstairs, and we were sitting in the nighttime cafeteria over coffee. Jason was still angry and hurt from our skirmishes. There was no way in hell he was going to look puzzled and drool faithfully at my feet like Caesar did after I'd punished him for eating the minister's wife's favorite rag rug.

"What in hell do I have to do to prove to you that I'm not a killer?"

"Why were you following me?"

"I wasn't following you."

"How did you know I was at the Fosters' that night?"

"I guessed."

"You did not. You followed me."

Jason buried his nose in his coffee cup, slurping the black, vile juices. Stalling, I could tell. He set the cup cautiously in the saucer, then skillfully cleared the table of crockery and the salt and pepper shakers. I recognized this as preparatory to giving me bad news. I clutched tightly the cup in my hands.

"Can I take your cup for you?" he asked.

"No."

"That's too bad." He pushed his chair back from the table, not too far, then rearranged his legs. It looked to me like he was preparing to bolt. I felt my eyelids get low and suspicious.

"Stella, have you ever tried to do something nice for someone so that you can find out some piece of information?" He looked hopefully at me. I shook my head. "No."

"Well, have you ever agreed to do something without thinking about the effect it might have on others?"

"Of course not." I lied.

He looked at me, skeptically. "Well, I did. What I actually did was agree to keep a piece of information to myself that I thought was harmless."

"And so?"

His feet shuffled as though he wanted to run away right then. "And so when I found out who Meredith was dating, I didn't tell anyone. I didn't think it was right, but I didn't know it was dangerous."

"Who is the man she's been dating?"

"She'll have to tell you."

"She broke off with him tonight. At least she said she was going to."

"I hope so." He leaned back in the chair but remained
gilant toward me. "Some women stay in those terrible
lationships even though they are beaten time and again.
just don't understand it."

"I think I do. But I hate it."

His big, awkward frame rested uneasily on the impos-
bly small hard cafeteria chair. I weighed the possibility,
w seeming small, that he was a dangerous man who had
lled two people. It seemed a very remote chance.

"Jason, everywhere I've been lately, you've turned up.
ow is it that you're always there?"

"Is that why you're so scared of me?" He ran a hand
rough his hair. "Because I'm around?"

"You're always there."

"And you don't buy the possibility that I just want to
: there where the news is happening?"

"That most of all. If you wanted to be where the news
as happening, you'd have gone where the real news is,
t to little nonevents like Adoree's at-home. You'd have
ne your own work on the background I asked you to get.
stead, you just asked Zelda for what she knew, which is
nsiderable I'll admit, but still, Jason, that isn't investi-
tive reporting."

"Shit." He flopped in his chair.

"You have to really get your teeth into a story. Pursue
and make something of it. You've been a dilettante, flit-
g from one cute item to the next, waiting for the news
happen to you. You have to go out and find the news.
nd then you have to put some of yourself into it." That
as far more than I'd planned to say to him. It made me
el like his great-grandmother giving him a lecture like
at.

"I'm going upstairs to see Meredith; maybe she'll tell

me who she was seeing." He came with me, and we wer
a silent pair that walked into her room. I had assured th
nurse that we were both family so we could stay.

Meredith didn't have family in Colorado, so in a sens
I was family for her. When we settled in next to the bee
she opened her eyes and tried to talk. I gave her water t
moisten her mouth, and she tried again to say somethin;
We could hear her better this time.

I found it was hard to reply to her; my voice was a
choked up in my throat. Jason patted her hand.

"Meredith, did you break up with him?" I had to hea
her say that she was through with him. The thought th
she could end up like Lilly, caught in a marriage trap wit
an abuser, was too terrible to think of.

"Yeah," she said. "That set him off."

"He didn't want to let you go?"

"He said nobody leaves him."

"Who is it?"

She dropped her gaze to the covers, unable to look m
in the eye. "Guy."

"Guy! You were going out with Guy? Don't you kno
he's married? He's a batterer, Meredith." Jason put a war
ing hand on my arm. I shook it off. "Meredith, he cou
even be a…a killer! How could you?" I jumped up.

Jason stood up and pulled on my shoulder, trying t
move me away from the bed. I whirled to face him, furiou
and ready to scream at him.

"Stella. Go easy."

Of course that wasn't the most effective thing he cou
have said, but in the end, it worked. Or else his sincerit
did. Something pricked my balloon of rage, and I collapse
back onto the chair before doing any more damage.

"Jane," Meredith said. "It wasn't your fault. And

wasn't mine. He told me he was divorcing. He has an apartment...."

"I know. I followed him there. I know about his place. He's such a slimeball. You're going to file charges, aren't you?"

"I told the police I wasn't going to. But I am."

MEREDITH MERCIFULLY fell asleep again, but neither Jason nor I could seem to settle down as easily.

"You never explained why you wouldn't answer the door after you let me in the building tonight. What was going on?"

"I was expecting someone else earlier. You came right in the middle of it, so I told you to go away. Then you insisted on coming up, making that scene and all, so I let you in. Before you got there, I remembered how you were always everywhere that I was, and so I began to think you were the killer."

"The killer? Grace's killer? You thought I was the killer?"

I nodded. "Well, actually, I thought Lilly was at first. Because she gets so jealous. But then I thought maybe Guy was because I know that Grace was in love with someone. You remember the letter from Looking for Lochinvar?"

"The one about wanting to find a 'love to die for'? Yeah."

"Grace wrote that, and several others. But, when Stobowski said that Lilly and Guy had alibis..." I saw the flash of pain on Jason's face. "Were you Guy's alibi?"

"No, but..." he looked at Meredith.

"Oh. I figured someone had given him an airtight cover. Well anyway, it's hard for me to think of you as the killer."

"Hey! I have no alibi. You're right to be suspicious. But

I didn't do it. Honest to God. I didn't.'' He sighed. ''Bu
I broke your lock. You're not safe there anymore.''

''I wasn't before. The killer got in, stole Grace's letter
and slashed a teddy...the one I bought to celebrate my ne
job.''

''What'll you do now?''

''Do what I was going to do before you stepped in. Tra
Nathanial.''

''Nathanial? He's your suspect?''

''The best I've got.''

''How're you going to do this?''

''Something will come to mind.''

IT WAS NEXT MORNING, and still nothing had come to mind
Meredith was well enough to go home, so between Jaso
and me, we got Meredith and her car back to her place an
Meredith ensconced in her bed. I called a locksmith an
arranged to replace my locks and to change hers.

She confirmed that her key to my place was missing an
had been for a week, maybe two. She didn't know whe
she might have mislaid it. One more point against Guy. Sh
was adamant that during the time that Grace and the
Mandy had been murdered Guy had been with her. Th
whole time.

I finally had to look in the mirror and tell myself I wa
being a stubborn person and it was time I faced it. If Gu
and Lilly had alibis, then I needed to stop trying to mak
them the murderers, no matter how convenient it would b
for me.

The other thing I had to do was to remind myself tha
the murderer was out there and still trying to kill me.
was looking very certain that Nathanial was the killer. Th
sobering thought led me to the conclusion that I neede

other identity. Which logically led me to borrow Mere-
th's, since she'd be in bed for a day or so. I decided not
bother her with the details.

Jason stuck to my side, saying I needed protection. By
on the only thing I could think of was to get Jason out
my hair by bewailing the cruel fate of Cleota Banks. He
early was reluctant to leave, but I assured him that all I
as going to do was visit my mother. I *did* visit Mother,
ng enough to have tuna sandwiches and tomato soup,
ased down with dark cherry gelatin with bananas floating
it.

"You know, you have an arrest record now. Things like
at discourage suitors. And there's nothing you can do to
t rid of it. But there's no reason to get depressed. Just
cause that poor woman was murdered after she talked to
u."

"Mom, Meredith could really use some tuna sandwiches
d tomato soup. And the gelatin. In fact, I'll leave some
this for her." I returned my mammoth scoop of gelatin
the dish.

"I've got plenty, eat up." She put the gelatin back on
y plate. "I'll take some fresh to Meredith. Now, Jane,
u have to keep two things in mind. One, appearances are
portant, and two, you have to be careful what you say
people, sometimes they believe you. And now and again
ey die."

"Mandy died because of what she knew but didn't tell
e."

"How could she tell you if she was dead?"

"Exactly."

"She could leave a diary."

"Or a letter...letters...Lochinvar..." I'd forgotten the
ters, the Lochinvar file. The killer had broken in to steal

it, and thought there was something that would give hi
away. Then I remembered the fire in Nathanial's fireplac
There was a good chance Nathanial had burnt it. Everythi
pointed to Nathanial.

He was Grace's lover. Her last letter had hinted of di
ficulties in the romance. He had killed her to keep her fro
telling Adoree. He wanted Adoree's money. Why, the
didn't he kill her? Maybe he loved her. But maybe the
was a clause in her will that he wouldn't get the inheritan
if she died. It would take days to find out.

I jumped up, dropped my napkin over the remaining hea
of softening Jell-O, and hugged my mother.

"Thanks. I'll call you."

Somewhere between Mother's house and my apartme
the hazy outlines of a plan began to form in my head.

TWENTY-ONE

THE MANAGER OF my apartment building was cranky about the door being kicked in, but I pointed out that the lock had been so inadequate there was barely any damage. When I told him that I'd arranged for the installation and would pay the cost of the dead bolt, installed securely this time, he was positively cheerful. I arranged for the lock company to leave the key with the manager when they'd finished. The catch was, this was Friday, and they couldn't do the work until Saturday. I'd need to stay somewhere else until the locks were installed.

With the manager as protection I went to my apartment and found Fluffy in his new skin, rejuvenated. He blinked hello, swallowed the wax worm in two chomps of his jaws, and breathed happily at me. He always feels more energetic in a new skin. Sort of like me in a new outfit.

Watching Fluffy I naturally thought of Stokowski and gave him a ring. He answered the phone with a grunt, as though his mouth was full of sandwich. I gave the thumbs-up to Fluffy. They had to be soul mates.

"Does the Foster maid live in the house, or does she come days only?"

"You are supposed to butt out of this. You are a suspect."

"If you tell me, then I won't have to go there. Did you get that packet of love letters from Nathanial?"

He swallowed. "And being in love with Grace, he'd naturally want to kill her."

"Maybe, if she threatened to tell his wife, and that wo[u]
mean Adoree would leave him." He hadn't denied it, so
me that meant he had the letters. "Did your lab find fi[n]
gerprints on the chair, Grace's chair? In the alley?"

"No. Now—"

"Is Grace's will already open?"

"Found a copy in her house. You must have missed
when you were searching it."

"I *never* searched her house. Did Mandy leave a diar[y]
Any hints?"

"You tell me. And stay away from the Fosters. If y[ou]
harass them anymore I'll charge you with that, too."

"Did you hear that Guy beat up my friend, Meredit[h]
You know he's a batterer."

"With an ironclad alibi. Sorry about your friend."

On the outside Stokowski played tough, but on the insi[de]
he was a cream puff.

I PACKED A SMALL overnight case again, put a few w[ax]
worms in a box, and explained to Fluffy that we had [to]
leave again but that it wouldn't be for long this time. [He]
blinked, sorrowfully. I sympathized. I missed my apa[rt]
ment, too.

I set the lights and a radio on a variable timer and p[ut]
Fluffy into his travel cage. I went down the back stairs a[nd]
took the mail from my mailbox while I was there. A qui[ck]
shuffle through it revealed nothing exciting. I shoved [all]
the envelopes with windows back in the box and put [all]
the grand-prize-winning envelopes and catalogs into m[y]
overnighter. The grand prize winners are a kind of reti[re]
ment plan.

My car was parked in the loading only zone at the ba[ck]
of the building so that I could slip out easily with minim[um]

osure. The manager agreed to check it before I went
. He was very cooperative. He seemed to think that a
e-crazed young man was out there stalking me. It prob-
y helped that I hadn't yet explained that Jason meant no
m the other night.

I had given considerable thought to whether I should rent
ar again so that the killer wouldn't recognize me, and
ugh I hadn't been able to make up my mind, I had at
st decided on a hotel, the Skyliner, opposite the airport.
was close to the car rental places, and if I panicked, I
ald always jump on an airplane. I'd seen a course ad-
tised in a mail order university...*Career Opportunities
El Salvador.*

The selling advantage of the Skyliner hotel was its un-
ground parking. I felt as though someone was watching
, but no one followed me that I could see, even after
eral quite clever evasive actions. I figured that if I
ked out of sight, the killer wouldn't be able to locate
very easily.

Then to make sure I was safe, I used Meredith's name
I identification to register. And her credit card to pay. I
In't discussed this with her beforehand, but I was sure
'd understand my rationale. I would straighten it all out
er. But if by some chance I didn't live through it, at least
vould have eased Meredith's sorrow by her anger at my
arges. Perfect all the way around.

Except when the clerk looked at Meredith's picture ID
I then at me. "Boy, most people's driver's license pic-
es are terrible. Yours is great. Especially your hair." She
utinized the little photo, her cheeks puffing thoughtfully
and out. "This doesn't look a bit like you."

"That was before my chemotherapy."

"Here's your key."

My room faced the east and smelled like wet ceme
Other than that it was okay. Fluffy looked chilly, so I turn
the air conditioner nearly off and put the wax worms
the vent in the trickle of cold air to keep them sleepy a
quiet. Otherwise they wear themselves out wiggling, a
Fluffy won't eat them.

I had to find evidence that proved Nathanial was
killer. I needed to verify where he'd been Saturday. Al
Stokowski had seized my jeans to test for blood type. E
idently he thought the killer would likely have blood on
clothing. Short of sidling up to Adoree and asking, "I
your husband have your sister's blood on his clothes af
he killed her last Saturday?" I figured I had to talk to th
maid.

I picked up the telephone and punched in the numb
for the Foster residence.

"Good afternoon," I said in my best plastic, electro
voice, a scrap of cloth over the mouthpiece of the te
phone. "I'm a representative of Eagle Crest Films, and I
looking for a person who has skills as a maid, who
photogenic, and who would be willing to help out in c
project. We understand that there is an excellent pers
employed there at the Fosters' and I was wondering i
could speak to her briefly?"

"I'm the only maid, Miss Anna Hand."

"Wonderful! That's perrrrfect. I think you're the ve
person I'm looking for. What hours do you work at
Fosters'?"

"Seven to five."

"Wonderful! And do you live in at the Fosters'?"

She was slow to answer, and her voice sounded sligh
suspicious. "Nnno."

'You have a wonderful voice quality. It's perfect. Did
one ever comment on it?''

'Oh, no.''

'And if this film project were to come to Denver, would
 be interested in work at, say, fourteen dollars an hour,
 benefits of course, as well as a small part in the film?
k about both because of course some people are hesitant
be in a film. And we would need both, if the film is
de here.''

'How much does the movie part pay?''

'We pay standard Screen Actors Guild rates, plus roy-
es.''

'How much is that?''

She was a real greedy guts. "Two hundred an hour. Min-
m forty hours.'' I prayed she wasn't a resting actress.
 think I heard her adding on her fingers. "Sure, I guess

'How should we reach you? I'm assuming you'd rather
 call you at home so that confidentiality is maintained.
hate to cause any trouble with your current employers,
o might not like us hiring you away.''

'You can call me at home at night.'' She gave me a
ne number.

'And may I have your mailing address? As soon as the
ject start-up date is confirmed, I'd like to be able to mail
 some information about it.''

She reeled off her address so fast I could barely get it
wn. She didn't live in the Fosters' home, but her address
s so close, she had to live in the garage apartment.

Anna Hand wouldn't be securely at home in the garage
il six at least, and it was only four-thirty at this point.
at gave me time to work on my plan.

I CAN ONLY SAY that the times were traumatic and I had
slept for several nights. On top of that, I was still angry
Jason. Not only had he not told anyone that Guy was see
Meredith, he'd even followed Meredith for Guy that ni
she and I went to the health club. That was how he'd kno
I was at the Fosters'. Then, he'd told Stokowski wher
was. Given all that, I wasn't thinking very clearly. In
event, I wasn't as cautious as I should have been whe
went to Anna Hand's house that evening.

I drove slowly and arrived about quarter to eight. It v
still light out, and a handful of children were playing soc
across lawns that were so big the kids didn't have to
into the street. Two teenaged girls sat on the steps of
of the porches, checking for boys in the cars that went pa
One of them started to wave at me, then dropped her ha
in her lap. The other laughed.

My hair was pulled severely away from my face a
piled on top of my head, and I'd pulled a cap low over
forehead. I wore a dark turtleneck shirt with a denim sk
I think it was the cap that drew her attention. I was nerv
enough that my hands were cold and sweaty. They slipp
slightly on the steering wheel, and I wiped them on
skirt as soon as I parked.

Anna lived in the apartment over the garage, and
door was up a flight of wooden stairs off the alley. The
was a wooden flower box right at the top of the stairs, a
she had already planted it with blooming pink geraniun
I strolled down the alley to her gate. There was a bell
the gate. I pressed it.

I held a tablet and pen obviously in my left hand a
wore what I thought looked like an earnest reporter's
pression on my face. I heard the raw jangle of Anna's be
then the gate lock buzzed and I pushed it open and start

the steps. I was glad I'd padded both the shirt and skirt
h a sweat suit that I'd cut to fit the hems so that I'd
e a different profile if either Nathanial or Adoree hap-
ed to look out. My hands were still sweating, so I wiped
m down again on the skirt.

Anna opened the door at my knock and looked curiously
ne.

'Don't I recognize you?''

So much for the disguise. "I do more than just the as-
ogy-for-the-lovelorn column. In my spare time I work
the Eagle Crest Film Company setting up stories for
ir projects. In the film business you have to do sort of
ilot to show the company, so that they get the idea. I'm
e you know all this. So, this story on the profession of
cutive housekeeper is perfect. I'm positive it will lead
film project that'll sell like you wouldn't believe.'' She
s still listening, so I plunged onward.

'When I was here the other day and saw the major en-
eering job you did, putting on that at-home along with
your other duties, I realized that you were the perfect
son for this project. You can give me exactly the per-
ctive I need for it. Tonight I'd like to get the...the *milieu*
the thing.'' *Milieu* has a great ring to it. She let me in.

'How much will you pay me?''

'What I need to start is an idea of a day in your life.
last Saturday.''

'How much will you pay me?''

'If you were to start with the minute you arrive on duty,
, how do you know who's here for breakfast. Like last
urday, was Mr. Foster as well as Mrs. Foster there at
akfast?''

'Neither one. Missus went for a hair appointment and
ster went to golf. How much does this pay?''

"She gets her hair done every Saturday at the Hair ▮ by Mr. Clyde?"

"Mr. Zeno at— How much does this pay?"

"I don't have a budget. I can't pay." Her face darker▮

I sensed the end of the interview. "The money co▮ through when they buy it. It's like an investment. A li▮ of your time could blossom into wonderful returns. ▮ looked at her sternly. "The film company pays well, ▮ this project is only a lead-in. My friend said you were ▮ fect and I think so, too, but if you can't help with this, ▮ hate to tell my friend that you aren't so perfect after ▮ Mrs. Foster goes to which salon?"

Greed struggled with ambition. It was awesome to wat▮

"The Curl Up and Dye Salon."

"So if they're both out last Saturday morning, when ▮ they each come home?"

"She got home at eight-thirty. I thought you wanted ▮ know about me."

"I do. I thought that when they come home you m▮ have to do special things for them."

"Yeah. Like laundry. He changes his clothes totally. Y▮ know how much laundry that makes? Two, maybe th▮ changes of clothes a day? Lots. And *her!* She changes ▮ clothes three, four times a day. And never picks a thing ▮ I have to know how to do all the laundry, where everyth▮ goes and just how to put it, just so. Time was when peo▮ were glad to have their house swept and dusted, but now ▮ have to be able to run the whole thing."

"Were his clothes dirty Saturday morning when he ▮ home at...?"

"Don't remember. Seems like there was something. M▮ I guess, or grease. He threw them away."

"Could it have been blood?"

"Blood? I don't think so. He didn't cut himself that I ow. He played golf."

"Maybe he got cut when he played...a rough game, golf. s that at the Creekside Country Club?"

"Yeah. The Fosters are fine folks, couldn't work for bet-. Generous and don't make much fuss, just like to change ir clothes a lot. That and all the linens makes a lot of ndry."

I didn't get much more than the laundry story out of her, t I praised her ability to articulate and said I'd be glad tell my friend that she was very photogenic, with good ong cheekbones. Actually, the cheekbones part was true. Nathanial had messed up his clothes and then thrown m away. That seemed like an indictment. I could check golf story at the pro shop the next morning.

It was Friday night, so chances were that the hair salon s still open. I ran down the steps and out the gate, con-tulating myself on success. Just as I turned to close the te I caught sight of a movement out of the corner of my e.

I ducked.

The side of my head exploded in a burst of stars and in. If I hadn't put my hair up, been wearing the cap, and dn't ducked, I'd have been very dead, no doubt.

I didn't lose consciousness. I fell like a rock to the und and curled to protect myself from another blow. ere would have been more, too, I'm sure, but a car turned o the alley and its headlights played over us. There was atter of feet running away and the crunch of tires on the mac.

My head hurt so bad I couldn't move. Fortunately, the ver of the car saw me, braked, jumped out of the car, d came over.

He helped me up, offered to drive me to the hospit[al], and looked totally relieved when I refused all of the abo[ve]. I asked him if he'd walk with me to my car. He agreed b[ut] complained all the way about the tone of the neighborho[od] becoming lower and more common. "Muggers at ev[ery] street corner these days."

I felt the weight of someone's gaze all the way to [the] car.

Once I was safely inside the car, I locked the door, [put] the key in the ignition, turned it on, and tried to convin[ce] myself that I'd be far better off to stay awake.

The Curl Up and Dye Salon was just down the str[eet] from Little Nothings and before the BonBon Bakery [I] rolled to a stop and glanced in the rearview mirror. T[he] white pasty face was mine. So was the enormous goose e[gg] on the side of my head. I thanked my peripheral visi[on] once again. It was the only reason I was still breathing m[ore] or less regularly.

My leg was half out of the open car door when a c[ar] roared into the parking lot coming toward me. I fell ba[ck] onto the car seat. The sudden change in position made [me] dizzy and nauseated. The car stopped abruptly. I pulled [my] leg back into the car, slammed and locked the door, a[nd] started the engine. I shifted gears, backed up, and floor[ed] the gas pedal. I almost hit a parked car.

I'd like to think someone was after me then, that [my] panic was justified by a madman who was trying to k[ill] me. But when I glanced over my shoulder as I roared o[ut] of the parking lot, I saw a little old lady stepping daint[ily] toward the bright lights of the salon. I don't doubt th[at] Nathanial tried to kill me in the alley, but there in the sho[p] pette, I think it truly was a harmless old dear on her w[ay] to a marcel wave.

Just this side of terror, I drove through a myriad of back
reets at a speed I should never have tried. Pure good for-
ne allowed me to get back to the hotel without running
wn half the citizenry of Denver. At least, I was reason-
ly sure no one was following me.

I spent the rest of the night with an ice pack on my head
atching old films on television. The emergency room
rse at Denver General recommended over the telephone
at I come in for an examination even after I told her I
as penniless and had no insurance. She finally told me
e symptoms to watch for. I fell asleep somewhere around
00 a.m. from sheer exhaustion.

My alarm clock went off at nine o'clock, and I woke
ith a headache the size of Kansas. I ordered coffee, juice,
d a roll from room service and stepped into the shower.
he blow hadn't broken my scalp, but the goose egg was
ill gigantic and mushy. The shower felt like rocks pelting
y head when I washed my hair. Coffee helped, and so
d several aspirin.

I called my friend who was checking on Lilly's financial
alth. It wasn't great, but he confirmed that by his second-
and information, she stood to inherit very handsomely
om an elderly relative. Oh, it was hard to give up a good
spect.

Next, I telephoned the manager at my apartment build-
g. He was excited and shouted that he'd called the police
hen my mad lover had come by to see me. I hoped he
eant Jason. The police had told him to go away. I felt a
ang of guilt and called Detective Stokowski.

It was Saturday, but he answered the phone on the sec-
nd ring.

"I was mugged last night."

"Someone had some sense, then."

"It wasn't funny. I've got a huge goose egg on my hea Could have killed me."

"Where were you?"

"In the alley behind the Fosters'."

"Now why were you there? Collecting aluminum ca to recycle?"

"Evidence. Collecting evidence. Since you won't, I ha to."

"There isn't an alley in this city that is safe for peop to cruise, whatever their profession. You know that. Y ought to stay at home."

"And wait for you to clear me? In your spare time? don't think I'll live long enough. Did you check to see Nathanial Foster played golf last Saturday morning?"

"Yes. He did."

"The whole time?" I didn't believe him. It was the litt pause before he said yes that gave it away. I was sure hadn't thought of the possibility that Nathanial had left an then returned.

"Did you know he threw away the clothes he wore th morning because he got something on them that he thoug ruined them?"

There was a long silence.

"Say thank you."

He didn't, but I didn't expect that he would. He doesn like to expose his sensitive side.

Next I called the hair salon. Good hair salons know tha maintaining confidentiality is the key to good customer r lations, so I knew I couldn't just ask out right if Mrs. Fost had been there last Saturday morning and for what and ho long. They wouldn't tell me.

The phone rang in my ear. I scrunched my face up lik Adoree and thought about honey.

"Hello, is this the salon?" It was a fair imitation. Adoree as easier than some people because she affected a distinctly semi-Southern drawn. "Is Adoree Foster there?"

"Why no, ma'am, she isn't."

"Oh! Did I say is she there? I meant to say this *is* Adoree Foster here. Oh, dear. I'm so upset. I need you to help me. This is awful. I just have to fix this damn bank account before Nathanial sees it. And you *have* to help."

"I don't know...."

"You *have* to. Now it's simple. Just tell me if I marked my charges down right. I'll read them to you, you confirm. Last Saturday, ninety-eight dollars for shampoo, color, style, set, and brush out."

"Uh, no. It says here you paid thirty-seven dollars for shampoo, trim, and set."

"Wonderful! That helps a lot. Now for today. What did I give you today?"

"You didn't come in today."

"I didn't? *That's* what I forgot. Oh, thank you. You've been a great help." I put the phone down. "Fluffy, they're really nice people. I didn't meant to tell such a big lie. You're my witness. My lips made me do it."

Next I called the pro shop at the Creekside Country Club.

"Hello, this is Mr. Foster's secretary, and he asked me check out some details for him. I know he has a regular tee time with his foursome. Can you tell me if he teed off last Saturday morning on time, and exactly what time that was?"

"He's scheduled for six-fifty-five but it looks like there was one who didn't show. They went off as a three-some at day."

"Can you tell me who didn't show?"

"Can't read it. Sorry." He hung up.

A HUNDRED TO ONE it was Nathanial who failed to sho
I called the pro shop back. A different person answered th
time. I explained again and asked if they could read to r
who went off. This one couldn't read it either, but he r
membered that all four had gone off, but five minutes la
He distinctly remembered Nathanial Foster was late. A
he remembered that Nathanial came in, too, after a tou
eighteen holes.

Still, after teeing off, he could have jumped in the ca
had his partner drive him to the parking lot, and left. The
he could have come back after he killed Grace and caug
up with the others at the third hole. It was possible. An
the perfect alibi. It was now ten-fifteen. Nathanial had bee
on the course for a little over three hours. If I hurried
could see him finish. I wanted to see what he was wearin

I parked and placed myself where I could see him com
in. I pulled a golf visor that I'd bought in the pro shop ove
my goose egg and slumped down in the chair behind m
sunglasses and a magazine. I figured I was safe while I wa
in such a public place.

My plan was to see what Nathanial wore to golf in. I
was my theory that being a creature of habit, he'd wear th
same kind of clothes each time he played. Then I'd cal
him, say I'd found his trousers with Grace's blood on them
and tell him to come get them. Then I'd somehow get Sto
kowski there as well and do a grand denouement.

Nathanial and his golfing friends dropped their ball
neatly on the green, then equally neatly into the cup. I trie
to detect a tremor in his game, but it wasn't there. Or a
least it didn't affect his score. They clattered my way o
their cleated shoes.

Nathanial stopped right opposite me.

"Surprised to see me?" I asked. He seemed surprised. I ondered if he thought he'd disabled me last night.

"Thinking of taking up the game?"

"It's an idea." My palms broke out in a nasty sweat. I as counting on the presence of all these others to keep m from attacking me. I hoped I was right.

"Let me introduce my partners in golf." He was trying sound amiable. But his voice sounded forced, like he as covering up a secret rage. The other men with him epped forward. "We play every Saturday, right?" He rned to the others, who obediently nodded their heads.

"And last Saturday, did he play the whole eighteen en?"

"Yeah, he was here," said the one closest to him. They oked vaguely puzzled.

"He didn't forget something and have to go back to get ?"

The shorter one laughed. "What he did was spill red ine on his pants on the nineteenth. I'll bet Adoree gave u hell for that!" He punched Nathanial in the arm, then ft for the bar. "Gotta make par on the nineteenth!"

The others followed him, but Nathanial stepped closer d leaned down. "Stay away. Get out of my life. Or else."

"Or else what? You'll kill me, too?"

His face turned ugly.

HERE WAS NOTHING else to do at the course, so I swung Meredith's to see how she was doing. She was de-essed. She wanted to back out of filing charges. I started rant at her, saying "If I never live to do another thing..." hen I realized that I might not live to do much else, so I doubled my efforts. While her bruises were vivid, I agged her to the police station and stayed with her while

she filed the complaint and the photographer took col
photos. I made sure they used a color strip. I wanted t
judge and jury to be able to gauge the real color of all tho
marks and make sure the bruises could be dated.

Stokowski came by, talked briefly to Meredith, and na
rowed his eyes with suspicion when I insisted he notice n
goose egg. I don't think he believed me until I did that.

Meredith was surprised to discover that I had her ide
tification, but I explained afterward that I'd used it to che
into the hotel. I also told her about the charges, but sl
shrugged them off. That's how I knew she was *very* d
pressed. I took her to Mother's. I didn't think she shou
stay alone.

TWENTY-TWO

ᴛ THIS POINT, there was no doubt in my mind that Na-
anial had killed Grace to keep her from telling Adoree
out their affair. I felt as deeply betrayed and angry about
is as if it had happened to me. But the reason I continued
try to prove his guilt was because if I didn't, I was certain
would go on trial for her murder. The charges against me
eighed very heavily, not only because I was innocent but
cause I had been so fond of Grace.

After they'd questioned me on Thursday night, Jason's
e piece of helpful information was that Stokowski
anned to meet with the district attorney the next day.
ey would decide early next week whether to move
ainst me now or build the case even further. I had to
ove Nathanial was the killer as soon as possible.

I'd considered breaking into Mandy's house to search for
letter or diary that she might have kept that would finger
athanial. But I calculated that both the killer and the po-
e would already have searched her place thoroughly. I
so remembered the neighbor with the gun. The chances
I find anything that would finger Nathanial were slim to
thing. I resolved to search the Fosters'. Anna had said
at Adoree shopped in the afternoons and that Nathanial
ually spent the whole day at the club, golf in the morning,
nnis in the afternoon. So, I only had to wait for Anna and
doree to leave.

I'd tried nearly everything except enlisting Adoree's aid.
wanted to try one last thing before I did that. Besides, I

wasn't sure how to go about getting Adoree to help me
needed to find out just how fond and adoring she really w
of Nathanial before I went very far out on a limb. Ju
because she went for a roll in the hay with Guy didn't me
she was ready to trade Nathanial in. He must know, I re
soned, that she wasn't faithful, but for reasons I couldn
fathom, they stuck together.

If I could get into their house, I might be able to find h
clothing, the Lochinvar file, the condition of their bank a
counts, whether Nathanial was in need of Adoree's esta
funds, or whether he had any letters or other evidence th
would point to him. I wasn't sure this would work, but m
bag of tricks was nearly empty.

I'd left Fluffy sleeping in at the hotel, digesting an
dreaming of flies. I was sitting in my car across and dow
from the Fosters' where I was reasonably sure that I cou
see them come and go without being much more obviou
than a boil on the end of my nose. I'd brought along som
basic sustenance…caramel corn, cookies, corn curls an
diet soda. And my letters. I couldn't spread them out, bu
I could read through them and make little notes on the
for later. If I lived long enough.

The lump on my head still ached.

As I've mentioned before, a grocery store parking lot
about the only place where you can sit and wait in a ca
and look perfectly normal. On a quiet residential street wit
a "tone," you're as normal as an elephant in the livin
room.

I had been sitting there for about an hour and a half. I'
read some of the letters and put the others aside until
could concentrate on them. My brain was remarkably de
void of inspiration. The only consistent thing in there wa
fear. And it left me chilled, disorganized, and shaky. Base

flight, fight, or feast, I'd hoped the food would counter-
t it. What I really needed was rage. If anger is an organiz-
, there's nothing like a little rage to get me going. I
orked on it.

Midway through a rage-increasing exercise in which I
viewed every insult that had ever come my way, a car
iven by an ageless woman stopped in front of the Fosters'
d honked. Anna Hand marched down the steps of her
artment and came around to the front of the house to the
r, where she got in. Because she was carrying a coat over
r arm and a large bag, I could assume she was out at
ast for the night. One down.

About half an hour later, Adoree left. I debated following
r. Something in the way she walked made me think she
as going to meet Guy. I shuddered.

Half the caramel corn and all the soda were gone. I felt
though I had gained forty pounds and the car had shrunk.
had to move soon or I'd be paralyzed.

I drove to the next block, parked, and locked the car.
en I went around the corner and up through the alley to
e back of the Fosters' house. At the point where I'd been
t the night before I stopped to take in a little extra oxygen.
still made me shaky to think what a close call that had
en. I looked for some indication that someone had waited
ere for me, like crushed cigarette butts or flattened weeds.
othing was there. Of course, Nathanial wasn't a smoker,
ther, so that didn't really tell me anything.

The fence around the Fosters' yard was actually a six-
ot high brick wall with a little iron picket railing at the
p. Not an easy thing for me to scale. I dragged the neigh-
r's garbage can over to the far corner of the Fosters' yard,
hich I remembered as having several sheltering shrubs in
From the top of the can I climbed up and dropped over

into the yard. Then I crept along from shrub to shrub un
I reached the garage, and from there up to the back of t
house.

Then the lock turned in the back door. I held my breat

Nathanial! He emerged, carrying several string shoppi
bags and a scrap of paper in one hand, a ring of keys
the other. Grocery shopping! He was supposed to be at t
club! He locked the door and went to the garage, hummi
to himself.

That changed my whole schedule. I calculated how mu
time it took to drive to the supermarket, about twenty-fi
minutes there, park, and back. Another half-hour, may
forty minutes in the store. It *was* Saturday afternoon, so t
trip could take a lot longer. But, I couldn't count on a ni
two-hour search. Instead, he would probably be back in
hour. I didn't have much time.

As soon as his car disappeared down the alley, I went
work. The ground floor was surprisingly secure, and t
basement windows had grills on them. I tried them to s
if maybe they were loose, but they weren't.

That left the second story. There was no convenient tre
lis. There were several shrubs and a big tree and, if I cou
find a way up to it, a little open porch off what I suppose
was the back bedroom. I could see an old-fashioned scree
door.

I'm not a cat burglar; I didn't think I could scale t
water pipe up to the porch roof. I went to the garage. N
thanial had locked this too, but there was a glass pane
the door, so I smashed it, reached in, and opened the doo
A six-foot aluminum stepladder stood against the far wal
I hauled it to the back porch, spread its legs, and climbe
up...to the next-to-the-top step. The only way I could po

bly reach the porch was to step onto the top of the ladder, reach the railing, and swing my legs up.

Some people can do this easily. Some can do it gracefully. I just managed to do it, but it was very hard. Especially after drinking three cans of soda pop.

I knew that if I left the ladder there, as soon as Nathanial came home he'd see it and know his security had been breached. He'd press breaking-and-entering charges against me. Stokowski would not be amused. I shoved the ladder over, tipping it toward the shrubs that grew by the back wall of the house. It fell where I'd aimed. It wasn't truly hidden, but unless someone was looking for it, they couldn't see it right off.

I figured I had half an hour to get what I needed.

The screen door was locked, but the screening was old and tore easily. I unlatched the lock. The back door was locked by an old-fashioned door key, left invitingly in the lock. I tried the knob, just on a chance. It was open.

I stepped into a little back bedroom daintily done up in white eyelet and pink roses. It looked like it was used primarily for storage. The closets were full of Adoree's last year's fashions. I went straight out and into the upper hallway and downstairs. I was going for Nathanial's library, where I figured he'd keep his records.

I pulled on a pair of latex gloves that I'd liberated from Denver General the night I was there with Meredith. I remembered Jason's surprised expression, but I'd just murmured the words "sterile technique" and stuffed them in my purse.

I used the back stairs to get down to the first floor and found myself in the kitchen. I raced through to the front hall.

And froze.

A shadow fell across the sheer curtains that screened t[h]
big glass front door. Someone carrying bags! An ar[m]
reached to the door. I couldn't breathe, paralyzed with fea[r].
Nathanial.

I looked right and left in a frenzy. Where was the co[at]
closet? I could at least hide there.

The shadow was standing in the door now. Any minu[te]
the key would be in the lock and the doorknob would tur[n].
I had to move. He'd see me as soon as he stepped insi[de].
I could feel his fingers choking me. I couldn't seem ev[en]
to breathe.

A metallic flap. The slop of letters on the vestibule floo[r].
The breath whooshed out of me. The mailman. I stagger[ed]
into the living room and fell into a chair.

It took precious minutes for my legs to firm up and m[y]
heart to return to normal, or at least something approachi[ng]
that. I finally had the strength to notice where I was sittin[g].

I had flopped into one of the chairs in the seating a[r]-
rangement where I'd seen Adoree being consoled so a[r]-
dently. I could see straight out to the daffodil bed whe[re]
I'd talked to Mandy. It was clear to me that the killer ha[d]
seen me talking to Mandy that day and had decided s[he]
had to be silenced. The flowers had all finished bloomi[ng]
now, and their little withered heads were drooping, li[ke]
they'd all been hanged. There was a sudden burning se[n]-
sation around my neck. It was hard to swallow. I had [to]
hurry.

In the library I found the picture album still on Natha[n]-
ial's desk, open to the same page as before. He seem[ed]
particularly to love those early ones with both Adoree a[nd]
Grace. Maybe because those were purer, happier days wi[th]
Adoree. I leafed briefly through the pages. All the re[st]
showed small group pictures of Adoree with colle[ge]

riends, Adoree in formals, Adoree looking every bit the
beauty queen. Did I imagine it? There seemed even then to
be a hardness in her eyes that looked out at the world.
Calculating.

His drawers were surprisingly unlocked. The top one was
incredibly neat, the paper clips were lined up, all lying the
same way. The pens and pencils all lay pointing to the right.

And in the middle of the tray lay a long, pointed, and
very sharp letter opener with an ivory handle. I picked it
up and scrutinized the handle. A peculiar brown spot was
on the handle near the blade. Blood spatter, I thought. I
wrapped it in a tissue from the box on his desk and slipped
it into my back pocket.

The side drawer contained envelopes ranked in order of
their size, stationery in order of its size, two rulers, a sharp
compass, and a pair of scissors with bright orange handles.
They were exactly like the kind Grace had at home in her
sewing room and at the shop.

All that neatness looked to me like the sign of a very
disturbed personality. The hairs on my arms stood up in a
chill.

A beautiful lateral file cabinet was against the wall, also
unlocked. Also boringly full of household documents. It
would take days to go through them all and understand
what they meant.

I scanned for a file with bank statements. It was filed
under *B* for bank in the front of the drawer.

At first glance I saw that he and Adoree had sufficient
funds to last. In joint accounts. Then I looked at the dates.
Then I started checking the balances against the dates. The
balances all looked fine. There was one single statement
from a personal account of Nathanial's. It held $135 and
hadn't had any activity in the last quarter. I returned the

papers and closed the drawer. All this had taken twelve minutes.

Something didn't sit right. I'd spent enough time in the world of accounting. Something was fishy here. Adoree had her accounts. Adoree and Nathanial had joint accounts. Where was Nathanial's real personal account? And why was this stuff unlocked? So that Adoree could see it? And not think about another account, a hidden account?

If I was going to syphon the accounts, where would I hide the statements? If I were Nathanial, I'd leave all the public stuff available to Adoree. I'd hide the others where she wouldn't find them. I decided to start in the basement and work my way up.

It was fairly daunting, but only because of the house's size. The basement was tidy and clean, largely spiderless. I searched the laundry room first, looking for those soiled trousers. Even checked the laundry chute, but there were no men's clothes with blood. Then I went for the main room. Nathanial had a hideout down there. A regular lair where he could hang out.

In an alcove in the main basement room he'd fashioned a very snug room, a kind of nest, with a soft worn couch, a television, several trophies from his high school wrestling team, and some remarkably bad art on the walls, including a large open-mouthed stuffed fish. He was also fond of watercolor scenes of mountains and streams with shadows that fell the wrong way.

The really spectacular exhibit was a sword and dagger collection on the far wall, which gleamed against the wood paneling and was arranged in a herringbone pattern. Not a single blade out of place. I was certain I'd find what I was looking for here.

I had already taken eighteen minutes.

Bookcases lined one wall. I tried the volumes of poetry
st, then went through all the larger volumes. Nothing.

Minute cobwebs were on the mountain scenes and in the
rners of the walls, but that fish glistened. I lifted it down.
I stopped, fish held high. Had a car door slammed? I
tened. Nothing. I peered into the fish's mouth.

There was a creak overhead. This time I was certain. I
ld my breath to hear better. Nothing. I shook myself. Old
mes, even well-built homes, creak, I told myself. I
ecked the time. Twenty minutes gone. I had to hurry, my
rves were giving out.

I peered inside the fish again. Sure enough, there was a
ender sheaf of papers. Bank statements. Adoree's bank
lance was steadily going down. Money was leaking out
her account and their joint account. I wondered where it
as going. Then I saw Nathanial's personal account. With
gular deposits.

What a slimebucket!

I folded the papers and shoved them into my hip pocket
d replaced the fish. The fourth finger of my glove caught
d ripped on a splinter at the edge of the mounting board.
had visions of Stokowski dusting it for fingerprints. He'd
d mine and know I'd been here. I dragged my finger
ong the edge to smudge the print. Then I ran an elbow
ross the board for good measure. Twenty-five minutes
ere gone.

I flicked off the light and started up the stairs. I needed
get out of the house. Then that night, with Stokowski
ere for safety, I'd have a nice little confrontation with
doree and Nathanial. That would ring a confession from
athanial. Just like the detectives in the literature. Great.

I was on the fourth step and moving fast when I heard
e proverbial groan of floorboards. I froze.

This time there were footsteps…in the hallway. Comi toward me. I held my breath. The steps went on past basement stairs, into the living room.

I raced silently up the stairs. They ended in the back ha and I took the steps up the back stairway two at a tin thankful for the thick carpeting.

At the top I turned and raced back to the pink and eye bedroom, out the door to the porch. Breathless, I thre myself forward over the porch railing. And remembered t ladder was gone.

I dangled, half over the railing, for at least sevente lifetimes before I could draw myself back onto the por and return to the bedroom.

I threw myself to the floor and slid beneath the bed. T dust ruffle, white eyelet, came down an inch from the ca peting. From there I could watch for feet coming my wa

My nose tickled; dust was rampant. I buried my face my sleeve to stop the sneezes.

Downstairs I could hear cupboards opening and closin He was putting away groceries. I remembered the compu sively neat desk. I began to shake. His fastidiousness cou be a sign of a very sick man.

What if he knew I was here? He'd know Ador wouldn't be back for hours. He'd know Anna Hand w out for the rest of the weekend. I'd be a decomposi corpse before Monday morning!

It was hard to get enough air. Then I realized I w breathing hard enough to suck up all the air in the room one breath, like a giant wind tunnel. Pretty soon he'd drawn in, too.

I forced myself to get a grip.

In the whole house, what was the least likely room f him to enter?

Aside from the laundry room...which is where I should ave gone.

Adoree's bathroom.

The footsteps downstairs were slow, heavy. In my imagation I saw those feet attached to a frenzied, drooling ller carrying one of the sharp swords from the collection the basement wall. I shook my head. And peeked out om underneath the bed. I could see straight down the hall.

Several rooms were on either side of the broad hall. I essed that Adoree would have a suite at the front of the ouse. If I could just get there.

Downstairs there was a thud, a heavy dull thud that unded like a...a sack of flour hitting the floor.

Flour takes a while to clean up. I knew that from expeence. I crawled from beneath the bed.

I tiptoed out of the bedroom and down the hall toward e front of the house. I could hear the sounds of cleaning the kitchen. He was grunting and sneezing. I reached the ont bedroom.

Adoree had decorated that room with pillows in purple. here were flounces over ruffles, pillows on top of pillows. I had to I could just throw myself on top of the bed and buried in pillows and no one would ever see me. And e whole thing smelled like there had been a perfume fight at morning. It was awesome, and very comforting. And ttered with clothes.

I sped to her bathroom. Opened the door. Flung myself .

And came face to face with Adoree.

TWENTY-THREE

SHE WASN'T VERY happy with me. I could tell. She was smiling, and she didn't look as though she was going She had a towel wrapped around herself and cold crea slathered on her face.

"When did you get back?" I asked.

"How did you get in here?" she asked. She look frightened and backed away from me.

"Please, don't worry. I won't hurt you." I tried to lo as innocent as possible, but it's hard when you know th you just broke into someone's house. I tried to think of way to explain that I thought her husband was a killer. I a tough topic to bring up under the best of circumstance

"You can't imagine...." I said.

"Try me," she said.

"I was so frightened. But now that you're here, it's right." I watched suspicion flash across Adoree's face; h eyebrows rose, her eyelids lowered.

"But why *are* you here?" She began swiping at the co cream on her cheeks and brow. She was watching me wat her in the mirror.

"I, uh, came to talk to you." It was more than a litt awkward. I didn't really want to say outright that I'd brok into their house.

"I didn't hear a bell."

"No, I don't suppose you did. I came in just ahead Nathanial."

"So he knows you're here."

"Well…"

"I see." She threw a wad of smeared tissues into the [w]astebasket and ran some warm water onto a facecloth. She [p]ut the cloth over her cheeks, careful to leave her eyes [un]covered. It made her look like one of the those big-eyed [ch]ildren that were so popular as paintings once. I felt ter[ri]ble about what I had to talk to her about. It was hard to [th]ink of a good way to begin.

"Adoree, have you been concerned about who killed [G]race?"

"Of course. But the police seem to think you did it." [S]he stepped back again, putting the most distance possible [b]etween us.

"Trust me." I tried to sound very soothing. "The police [ar]e wrong. I wouldn't ever hurt Grace. I loved Grace. I [m]ean, I liked her. She loved someone else. And that—"

"Really?" She looked even more alarmed.

"Don't shout. Let's keep this to ourselves. I need to talk [to] you about who killed Grace." I couldn't believe how [m]uch trouble I had saying this. My tongue seemed to be [f]umbling all over my teeth.

"If you didn't kill Grace and Mandy, then who did?" [sh]e asked.

I noticed that Adoree had dropped that silly fake South[er]n accent.

"Adoree, did you know that Grace was having an af[fa]ir?"

She looked at me, her eyes narrow slits of suspicion. [B]uffy has that same expression sometimes when he's stalk[in]g a fly.

"I don't want to shock you or anything, but I think Grace [w]as…" The only thing that moved in her face was her eyelids. She blinked twice. "I have reason to believe tha your husband was... The two of them..."

"Were screwing?"

"Yes."

She clutched the towel tighter around herself an marched past me into her bedroom. Then she threw it the floor and stomped to her closet where she drew o panties, trousers, and a shirt. She faced me.

"Have you told anyone?"

"Well, uh, no."

"Have you told Nathanial?"

"Well, that's what I wanted to talk to you about. Yo see, I think Nathanial still loves *you*. I know he does."

"How do you know?"

"I saw him looking at that album. I could see it in hi face."

"That album!"

"I think he was afraid you'd find out about Grace an leave him and so that's why..."

She stared at me, her mouth making a curious little roun *O*.

"Adoree, sit down. I can see you're in shock. You see I think Nathanial killed Grace because she was going tell you. Grace wanted Nathanial to marry her. But I figu he didn't want to leave you, just somehow got involved...."

Adoree was making little mewing noises.

"Now don't be too upset. But Nathanial—"

"You think Nathanial—"

"I talked to Mandy here at the at-home for Grace an he would have seen me then and that's why he killed he too."

"Have you told anyone?"

"I told Stokowski, but he thinks I did it. So you have —" I heard a footstep on the stairs. I couldn't go on.

Adoree stared at me. I stared back.

"Then, he doesn't know you're here?"

I shook my head.

"Quick! In here." She shoved me toward her closet, and jumped in. I stepped on a shoe and my ankle twisted. Pain shot up my leg. I saw her bedroom door begin to open. At that minute she shut the closet door.

Fortunately for my claustrophobia, the upper half of the closet doors were louvered. I could still see out through the down-slanted louvres, although I could see only the floor. My ankle hurt so badly that tears formed in my eyes and I did all I could do to keep from moaning.

I heard her greet Nathanial, heard him ask her if she'd used the ladder. Very sly, I thought. Trying to trap even her.

She said something I couldn't hear, then asked him for a drink.

"You're certainly looking casual tonight, dear," he said. I thought I could hear the implied question, "Why are you dressed like that?"

"Let's get that drink, dahling."

They left together. I could see his feet. He left the bedroom door open.

As soon as I dared, I stepped out of the closet and hobbled to the bed. I flung myself into the pillows, holding my ankle high overhead in hopes the swelling would go down or at least hurt less.

I felt guilty letting Adoree face that monster by herself. I wondered how she'd manage through the night, asking him questions, talking to him, laughing at his jokes, know-

ing all the time that he killed her very own sister. I'd ha▼
found it impossible.

The pain in my ankle continued. I got up, hopped to th
bathroom, and rummaged through the bathroom drawers f◖
aspirin. I picked up a nail file and started to pocket it. The
I felt the sharp little letter opener in my back pocket.
replaced the file. Adoree had a veritable cosmetic count◖
right in her own bathroom. There was an impressive arr▲
of items, any one of which would preserve the female f◖
posterity, if anything could.

No aspirin, not even a varietal.

I looked in the wall cabinet. There I found aspirin. An
hair spray. It worked on Jason, it might work again. I trie
to stuff it into my pocket, but the can was too big. Then
saw the travel spray cologne and pocketed that.

I tried to put weight on my ankle and found I coul◣
hobble a little. My toes moved easily, as easily as toe
move, so the ankle wasn't broken at least. Probabl
sprained. I limped to the bedroom door and listened to th
soft murmur of conversation from downstairs. It was a ma▸
vel to me that Adoree could talk to him.

I sat gingerly on the edge of the bed and thought. The
I pulled open the drawer in the bedside stand. Tissues, mo◣
nail files, books, pens. I picked up the top book, a myster
entitled *13th Floor*, by Kay Bergstrom, and opened it. ◢
slip of paper fell out and floated to the floor. I reached f◖
it. My fingers tingled as I drew it toward me.

I unfolded it and read.

Dearest Nathanial,
Thank you for last night. If I were to die right now,
I'd still be the happiest woman in the world. I can't
wait until we're together forever. I couldn't sleep for

all this happiness so I got up and wrote to Stella and then this note to you. Just to think of you is to be happy.

I told Addie. She wasn't angry at all. She said she understood. She wouldn't stand in our way. She accepted my offer of money, said she'd need it. It's a small price to pay for our happiness. I'm to meet her later this morning at the shop.

Until tonight my Lochinvar,
Grace

A love to die for. That's what she'd said she wanted. nd that's what she got. The letter slipped from my fingers, d I watched it float to the floor. Adoree had acted as ough she didn't know. She'd been, or acted as though, e was shocked.

The puzzle suddenly reframed. It wasn't only Nathanial ho saw me talking to Mandy, Adoree had also seen me. s she was being consoled by the gent with his nose in her eavage, she could have seen me talking to Mandy.

She could have gotten Mandy to open the door, maybe ore easily than Nathanial.

I pulled the sheaf of bank papers from my pocket. The oney was leaving Adoree's accounts and it was flowing to Nathanial's. I looked closer. The amounts and the dates dn't match. It could just as easily be that Adoree was ending her own money and Nathanial was saving his own oney.

I'd been looking at the wrong villain. It wasn't Nathanial ho had killed Grace. It was Adoree. It was her sister.

I refolded the papers and jammed them into my bra. aybe they'd slow a bullet down.

Footsteps sounded on the stairs. I hobbled to the door,

hid behind it. There was no murmur of voices. Where w[
Nathanial?

The door swung open and Adoree stepped in, looke[
blankly at the open closet door, then turned and saw m[
Her lips curled. Her eyes were cold, calculating.

"It's all right. I've talked to him. I think I've got it a[
solved." Her right arm was awkwardly behind her bac[
She started to come farther into the room.

I remembered the incriminating letter on the carpet at th
side of her bed. I had to distract her.

"Oh, great. That's wonderful. It's all settled then."
shrugged my shoulders, flapped my arms, and grinned un[
my lips pulled out of shape. "Well, let's go down." [
couldn't tell whether or not she saw the letter.

"My ankle's sprained," I said. I started toward her, sta[
gering, trying to block her view of the side of the bed. Sh[
didn't move. "You go ahead, it'll take me longer." [
waited for her to move toward the stairs. She started t[
then turned.

"You go ahead. I forgot something." She ducked bac[
into the room, and I heard her walk toward the bed. Sh[
returned. In her hand she held Grace's letter.

"He's waiting for us in the basement," she said, and sh[
glided down the stairs to the first floor. I hobbled after he[
the pain in my ankle no longer important. My palm[
sweaty, slipped and squeaked along the banister.

At the foot of the steps I hesitated as though I had n[
notion of where to go. I tried to head toward the front do[
to escape, but she called me back.

"This way!"

"I think we should call the police. They'll be wonderin[
where I am now. You know Stokowski, always likes [
keep close tabs on his suspects."

"Nathanial is waiting." There was no trace of the soft-
ing Southern accent in her voice now. It was cold as the
wn. She motioned to the kitchen and the basement stairs.
small, ugly little gun nestled in her hand.

A gun is a gun. I'm not knowledgeable about them. I
d once that small guns weren't accurate except at close
tances. We were about four feet apart. I thought that
alified as a close distance.

Unfortunately, not close enough to use the letter opener
ked in my back pocket or the spray perfume in my front
cket. An iron skillet sat on the stove. If I could stumble
it and smack her, knock her off guard, I might be able
get to the basement stairs, then the landing and the door
the outside.

"Move!" she ordered.

I stumbled, bumped into the wall, rolled and tripped,
rposely this time, into the kitchen, reaching for the pan.
e shoved me aside, and I fell, short of the stove. I shouted
the pain seared my ankle.

Adoree stood calmly, the gun still in her hand, the busi-
ss end of it still pointed at me.

I rubbed my ankle, the pain so intense that I felt giddy.
anted. "Always...was...clumsy." Pain was shooting up
 leg from my ankle so badly that my eyes stung and
ked a little. Adoree jerked open the basement door.

"Get down there."

I had this surreal sense that this was a dream sequence,
t really happening, as though I was floating in time and
ce. My feet, though, were solidly on the ground, my
kle aching relentlessly, a sickening dull pain.

The stairs to the basement are arranged in two flights,
th a landing halfway down and a door that leads outside.
ybe, I thought, I could catch her unawares at that point

and spray her eyes with the perfume, then fling mys
down the steps and into the laundry room. She looked
sort to be unfamiliar with that room, so it seemed the safe
I *really* didn't want to see Nathanial.

"I have to hop, my ankle…"

"Go."

"Just don't shoot…it'll leave blood spatter on ye
white wall." I took her silence for assent.

She prodded me in the back. It cleared my brain a
helped me to hop. Clumsily I made it to the top of
steps, then slowly thumped down each one. I drew out
slowness, hoping to lull her into security. My plan hing
on using my painful ankle to advantage. I would round
corner, put weight on my ankle, and throw myself to
wall, flattened, and spray her with the perfume. I'd hav
few precious minutes while her eyes were blinded whe
could get to the laundry room.

My hand was on the corner. I concentrated. Put weig
on the ankle. Howled and spun around, pulling the spr
out of my pocket. I flattened myself against the stairw
wall, right hand clutching the banister, left one at my si
ready to rise and spray.

It was a dumb plan.

She didn't flinch. The little round eye of the gun star
right into my face. I sagged to the step, the spray hidd
in my hand. I shoved my hand down as though rubbing
ankle and slipped the spray into my sock.

"Can't move."

"Move. Now!"

I kept the spray can hidden the best I could and scoot
down the last four steps. There wasn't a way in the wo
I could get away. On a good day I had trouble outrunni
my weight gain; how could I outrun a bullet? I lurched i

basement room where I knew Nathanial would be wait-

A small light was burning in the corner of Nathanial's leout, on the little table at the end of his worn, lumpy uch. The couch on which he was slumped, looking ter- ly gray about the lips. A small but spreading red stain is on his shirt. And a pillow with a hole in it in his lap. e must have muffled the shot with a pillow.

A telephone sat on the table next to him, but there wasn't ope in hell that he'd been able to dial out. The cord had in jerked from the wall. I saw the end trailing on the or. Nathanial's index finger twitched and his left eyelid ed as I limped into his nest. He was still alive.

"I'm so sorry, Nathanial." I was sure I saw his eyelid tter. Possibly a signal, I thought. When you have nothing, traw looks good.

I'd always thought that if I were ever in such a situation, be overcome with emotion. But I wasn't. I was just sad, th a deep, bottomless sorrow in the pit of my stomach. d a sense of loss.

My hands felt numb, my brain was numb, even my ankle emed to have subsided into a dull interminable ache. I de a great production out of any movement. To convince that I couldn't move if my life depended on it. Which, course, it did.

I hesitated, then swung around so that I could aim to flop o the couch next to Nathanial, on his left. Not too close, ittle forward. Just enough. I was facing Adoree. I turned t enough that she couldn't see as I reached behind to my ck pocket. I pulled the letter opener up so it stuck out of pocket enough to be seen. I prayed that Nathanial saw

"Sit over there!" She pointed to a chair.

"Can't...help it." I flopped onto the couch next to N
thanial. I felt him sag onto my back, his arm sliding acro
my back. I think that's when the complete futility of t
situation finally sank in. At that point I knew he and I we
basically dead meat. Goners. *Before my time* flash
through my mind.

I reached around and gently pushed Nathanial off of
and against the back of the couch, positioning his head
that if he could open an eye he would see Adoree. His fa
was still warm. The tiny vein at the corner of his eye puls
feebly. I scooted forward so she wouldn't see it.

"Why did you kill Grace?" Maybe if I stalled her
thought.

"Why? Because Nathanial is mine."

"But you've killed him. Now he's dead." *Please do
twitch, Nathanial.*

"*He* doesn't leave *me*. He's mine." Her voice rais
eerily and she waved the gun. I was afraid her trigger fing
would squeeze convulsively. "Get away from him. I sa
move over there!" She pointed at the chair with the gun
moved slowly, careful not to look at Nathanial.

"I've killed Nathanial, and now I'm going to make
look like you did it."

She was nuts. I forced myself to keep my eyes on h
but it was painful. Her face was a hateful twist, and all
beauty dissolved in mad vengeance. I inched toward
chair.

She laughed. "I'll just put this little love note next
him. And then, I'll heroically shoot you. It'll be the trage
of the century. And, I'll inherit from Grace and I'll ke
my Nathanial. Move!"

"The letter doesn't implicate *me*, and he'll be dead. Y
don't want that."

She held up two pieces of paper. "This one does impli-
te you." She leveled the gun at me. "If he's dead, he
n't leave me. Now sit."

It didn't make any sense to me, but it wasn't the right
ne to argue. I kept my right hand behind me as far as
ssible. I sidestepped toward the chair she'd indicated. It
ok all the strength I had to continue barely moving. If I
ent slow enough, she'd lose concentration and I could
nge at her. Maybe it would work.

"You're the one who slashed my teddy, aren't you?"
She frowned. "Move it."

"Why?"

Adoree grimaced. "I thought I could scare you. You're
goddam dumb."

"You got the key from Guy, right?" I felt my back
cket. My heart jumped. The ivory-handled letter opener
as gone. I took another side step. Each movement took
closer to her. It was a very difficult thing to do. I
uldn't take my eyes off of her.

She stepped back, surveying the scene. "Yeah, I got a
of things from Guy. Well, on to bigger things." She
pped forward holding the letter, then halted.

"Sit!" she ordered. She waited until I was in front of
chair and on my way down. I flopped into the chair,
unced forward, and sat with my left hand at my sock.

She stepped in front of Nathanial and leaned down, con-
ent that he was dead. I pulled the spray out of my sock.
sed forward in the chair.

She laid the letter on the table next to Nathanial. At that
oment she was focused only on that one thing, and her
n was pointed into the wall.

I pushed with my good foot, threw myself forward.
ought my right hand up and sprayed.

At that same moment, I saw the letter opener in Nath-
ial's hand. His arm jerked up, and the letter opener dis-
peared deep in Adoree's breast. It entered below her bre
bone, slanting up into her heart.

Her gun exploded. I fell to the floor. She crumpled
slow motion, an expression of surprise and outrage on
face. Her gun hand raised, she aimed again at Nathan
The whites of his eyes glistened in the light. I pulled mys
away, desperately trying to reach the shelter of the far s
of the chair.

I couldn't drag my gaze from her gun hand. The tend
on the back of her hand stood out. She squeezed the trigg
She was falling. The gun exploded. The bullet smacked i
the wooden paneling an inch to the side of Nathani
head. She missed. Then I saw the blood spurt from the s
of Nathanial's head, streaming down his cheek and o
his shirt.

The stench of gunpowder filled the air, a curiously a
pealing combination of sulphur and acrid smoke. The g
went off one more time.

I peeked out from under my arm after what seemed I
hours. Adoree lay on the floor, collapsed on her side,
gun still gripped in her hand. The letter opener sticking
of her chest. A trickle of blood spreading blackly onto
carpeting.

Nathanial was slumped on the couch. Grace's le
clutched in his fingers. His eyes were open, but he look
as dead as the grave.

I DIDN'T THINK Stokowski would ever get there. It was
least several lifetimes before he clumped down the sta
The guy in uniform had been there and had tried to talk
me. The ambulance had arrived and found a thread of I

ll in Nathanial, so they whipped him over to Denver General.

Stokowski looked like he'd lost his best friend, but maybe losing your favorite villain is almost as bad. I tried to console him, but it didn't work. He sat on the couch in Nathanial's living room and stared disconsolately at me for an hour, asking one quiet question after another.

The best part of the evening was when Jason strolled into the living room carrying a giant box of tissues, offered to mop my face, and told me that Lilly had filed assault charges, a restraining order, and divorce papers on Guy.

Later, after I had convinced Stokowski that I would absolutely, positively come down and see him again in the morning, just to keep his spirits up and explain it all again, I went with Jason to Denver General myself.

We found that Nathanial had been wheeled into emergency surgery, their third gunshot wound that night. They were getting good at saving gunshot wounds. We saw him in recovery. They said he'd be all right, eventually. I figured they could heal his broken body, but I wasn't sure they'd be able to do anything about his broken heart.

They X-rayed my ankle, confirming that it was only sprained. They put a splint on it, gave me an ice bag, crutches, and two pain killers, and told me to come back in the morning. I said fat chance and left.

Jason took me to the hotel where I collected Fluffy, introduced him to Jason, and checked out.

Jason was remarkably helpful, carrying my overnight case and most of the rest of my paraphernalia back to my apartment building.

In the lobby the manager raced out, waving his arms at Jason. "Get out of here. I called the police. They'll be here in a minute."

"It's okay." I tried to assure him. "It was a mistake
other night."

There was a siren in the distance.

"Really, it's all right. It was a mistake before."

He hesitated, clearly not convinced.

"Please. Call them back. Tell them they don't need
come. Then come up for a drink."

"Drink. Right. Okay." He ran for the telephone, and
heard him cancel the call for the police. The siren raced
by. It was a fire truck headed somewhere else, anyway.

Jason grinned his crooked little winning grin as we
to my apartment. "I called a few people while you w
in the ER. It's only ten o'clock."

Zelda arrived in minutes and brought me a gift. Saun
She said Stokowski told her I loved the dog. She h
sprung her from the kennel just for me. She jumped up
the couch next to me, snarled, and sat down.

Meredith came and brought a half-dozen copies of t
next day's daily paper, one of the ones that focuses on
news as it happens, as opposed to the *Daily Orion*, whi
prints all the news that we wish would happen. On the fr
page was a human interest story on Cleota Banks with
byline: Jason Paul.

Finally Mother and Dad joined us. Even Mr. Gers
came over with his wife, who brought me a crocheted
ghan. We even found a fly for Fluffy and watched him st
it. It was a great party until Stokowski called and said Gra
had left everything to me and asked if I wanted to ta
about following the money trail.

I'm going to miss Grace. Stokowski and his tight thig
are another matter.

THE CONCRETE PILLOW

RONALD TIERNEY

First Time in Paperback

A Deets Shanahan Mystery

Shanahan wasn't keen on working for an addict.

They couldn't be counted on for either their perceptions or their payment. But something about Luke Lindstrom made the Indiana private investigator take the case.

Perhaps because he remembered when Luke and his brothers were the local high school basketball superstars. Maybe because adulthood had only brought them failure—and untimely death. Mark took a fatal dive off a balcony. Matthew fell off a cliff. That left Luke...and John. Until John takes a deadly tumble.

Now Luke decides to find out who wants him dead—before the killer succeeds. And while Shanahan is all too aware of how tough family relations can be, he's discovering that in Luke's case, it's just plain murder....

"Shanahan is a terrific character, feisty, even noble."
—*Publishers Weekly*

Available in March at your favorite retail stores.

To order your copy, please send your name, address, zip or postal code along with a check or money order (please do not send cash) for $4.99 for each book ordered ($5.99 in Canada), plus 75¢ postage and handling ($1.00 in Canada), payable to Worldwide Mystery, to:

In the U.S.	In Canada
Worldwide Mystery	Worldwide Mystery
3010 Walden Avenue	P.O. Box 609
P.O. Box 1325	Fort Erie, Ontario
Buffalo, NY 14269-1325	L2A 5X3

Please specify book title with your order.
Canadian residents add applicable federal and provincial taxes.

WORLDWIDE LIBRARY®

PILL

HARLEQUIN®

I N T R I G U E®

THAT'S INTRIGUE—DYNAMIC ROMANCE AT ITS BEST!

Harlequin Intrigue is now bringing you more—more men and mystery, more desire and danger. If you've been looking for thrilling tales of contemporary passion and sensuous love stories with taut, edge-of-the-seat suspense—then you'll *love* Harlequin Intrigue!

Every month, you'll meet four new heroes who are guaranteed to make your spine tingle and your pulse pound. With them you'll enter into the exciting world of Harlequin Intrigue—where your life is on the line and so is your heart!

Harlequin Intrigue—we'll leave you breathless!

INT-GEN

DEADLY PRACTICE
CHRISTINE GREEN
A Kate Kinsella Mystery

First Time in Paperback

NURSING A GRUDGE

Kate Kinsella has fallen on hard times when her work both as a nurse and as a private medical investigator dries up. Until she gets a break—if one can call it that—with a murder.

Friend and landlord Hubert Humberstone—also the undertaker and local busybody—practically tosses her into the investigation of Jenny Martin, a nurse whose body is found in the trunk of her burned-out car. She had been beaten to death.

Kate not only gets Jenny's old job, but she's hired by the mother of the chief suspect, and starts probing the most convoluted—and most dangerous—case of her career.

"Impressive...fine writing and skillfully drawn players abound."   *—Publishers Weekly*

Available in March at your favorite retail stores.

To order your copy, please send your name, address, zip or postal code along with a check or money order (please do not send cash) for $4.99 for each book ordered, plus 75¢ postage and handling, payable to Worldwide Mystery, to:

> Worldwide Mystery
> 3010 Walden Avenue
> P.O. Box 1325
> Buffalo, NY 14269-1325

> Please specify book title with your order.
> This title not available in Canada.

WORLDWIDE LIBRARY®   DEAD

By the bestselling author of *FORBIDDEN FRUI.*

FORTUNE
ERICA SPINDLER

Be careful what you wish for...

Skye Dearborn knew exactly what to wish for. To
unlock the secrets of her past. To be reunited with her
mother. To force the man who betrayed her to pay.
To be loved.

One man could make it all happen. But will Skye's
new life prove to be all that she dreamed of...or a
nightmare she can't escape?

Be careful what you wish for...it may just come true.

Available in March 1997 at your favorite retail outlet.

MIRA The brightest star in women's fiction

Look us up on-line at: http://www.romance.net

ME

Dust Devils OF THE Purple Sage

Barbara Burnett Smith

A Jolie Wyatt Mystery

First Time In Paperback

BACK IN THE SADDLE AGAIN

With one solved murder behind her—a worthy credit for any fledgling mystery writer—Jolie Wyatt is now working as a newscaster for a local radio station. And the news is as hot as the blazing Texas sun: an escaped convict, a local boy named James Jorgenson, is believed to be heading straight for Purple Sage.

When a college kid is found dead, everyone thinks Jorgenson did it, even Jolie's teenage son, who vows to catch the killer of his longtime pal. But Jolie is riding a different trail that's leading her straight to a killer. She may even get a new way to experience the murder mystery—as a corpse.

"[Jolie] Wyatt is a charming, strong-minded contemporary character..."
—*Houston Chronicle*

Available in April at your favorite retail stores.

To order your copy, please send your name, address, zip or postal code along with a check or money order (please do not send cash) for $4.99 for each book ordered ($5.99 in Canada), plus 75¢ postage and handling ($1.00 in Canada), payable to Worldwide Mystery, to:

In the U.S.

Worldwide Mystery
3010 Walden Avenue
P.O. Box 1325
Buffalo, NY 14269-1325

In Canada

Worldwide Mystery
P.O. Box 609
Fort Erie, Ontario
L2A 5X3

Please specify book title with your order.
Canadian residents add applicable federal and provincial taxes.

WORLDWIDE LIBRARY®

DUST

Bestselling Author

Margot Dalton

explores every parent's worst fear...the
disappearance of a child.

First Impression

Three-year-old Michael Panesivic has vanished.

A witness steps forward—and his story is chilling.
But is he a credible witness or a suspect?

Detective Jackie Kaminsky has three choices:
1) dismiss the man as a nutcase,
2) arrest him as the only suspect,
   or
3) believe him.

But with a little boy's life at stake, she can't afford to
make the wrong choice.

Available in April 1997 at your favorite retail outlet.

MIRA **The brightest star in women's fiction**   MMD

Look us up on-line at:http://www.romance.net